THE TOKEN 2
ABSOLUTION

MARATA EROS

VIP LIST

To be the first to hear about newTo be the first to hear about new releases and bargains—from Tamara Rose Blodgett/Marata Eros—sign up below to be on my VIP List. (I promise not to spam or share your email with anyone!)

SIGN UP TO BE ON THE
♥TAMARA ROSE BLODGETT/Marata Eros♥
VIP LIST
HERE

MUSIC

Fuoco
by
Ludovico Einaudi

TOKEN THOUGHTS

*"Love sears the heart immortal -
The embers burnt down to the token which remains."*

CHAPTER 1

Tears cool on my face as Jay tries to move on the floor. The toes of Thorn's shoes fill my wavering vision.

A shaky inhale later, I take his hands. He hauls me up, and we face each other.

I jerk down my ruined dress.

"Well that sucked balls," he says.

A hysterical laugh bubbles from me. "Yeah..." I agree through a fresh wash of tears.

"Faren..." Thorn says in a warning tone. God, he's a tough bastard.

Onward and fucking upward.

"What?" I seethe, moving back a pace.

Thorn shrugs as Jay moves to his hands and knees, struggling to stand. But Thorn and I only have eyes for each other.

Orbital hate flows.

"You had to know that Mick might wonder where you were taking off to—wearing those outfits," he says.

Actually, I hadn't given his curiosity much thought.

Getting by day to day, paying my mom's debt, and ignoring my short time left had been my concerns.

They're still my concerns.

I sigh, popping my hands onto my hips, the left hand jumping. I let it fall and do its routine. I know from experience it'll be useless for minutes.

I shake my head and answer Thorn, half-sobbing. "No, I had more important things to worry about than Mick going into stalker mode."

He certainly won't be stalking me anymore.

I cry harder, his face etched into my memory. The betrayal, the misery, the hate.

Thorn puts a finger to his lips, swinging his eyeballs to Jay.

I turn and see the lap, his penis hanging like a pathetic sausage out of his torn fly. I try to feel sympathy for the beating he received at Mick's hands, but Jay used me. He went one step past what we agreed to.

I'm not feeling compassion right now; I'm not feeling much of anything.

"Who... the blue fuck was that?" he asks, wiping blood from his mouth.

Thorn's brows pop as he cocks his head to the right. "Lunatic ex-boyfriend."

Oh god. *I want to hide.*

"Well he messed me up pretty good." His only open eye slides to me, assessing my reaction.

I give a shaky laugh. "Yeah... I didn't know he knew where I was."

"I don't want to pay," Jay says in a flat voice. "That was a finale I didn't need."

My stomach falls.

Mick has let me go in the worst way. The lap that was supposed to be my last, the way to rid my mom of debt, got what he wanted. I hold the wrist of my left hand to stop its shaking.

"Listen, Jay," Thorn says in a soothing voice, his hands splayed away from his body, palms out, "it was the fluke of fucking flukes. You wanted the girl—she did her part."

Thorn's eyes flick over my dress, identifying the evidence easily.

My guts churn.

Jay crosses his arms, throws his jaw to the side, and spits out a mixture of saliva and blood.

"If I pay, I want something more. I deserve it after that beat down."

Thorn and I look at each other, his eyes saying it doesn't hurt to hear the lap out. After all, it's worth ten thousand dollars.

I look at the floor and try to breathe. My rage, loss, and frustration boil under my skin like a witch's cauldron.

"I want a date with Faren." Jay points his battered jaw up, all defiance. He's combative and determined.

I'm numb and emotionally bereft.

My chin sinks, and I look at my toes peeking out of my high-heeled stilettos.

"Faren." Thorn's justification whispers against my ear, tickling it. "We're getting off easy... you gotta know that."

I think a little better of him for not forcing me, though I know I have no real choice.

I think of Mick, his sense of betrayal moving through the cracks of my emotional fissure.

He won't want me no matter what.

My mom needs this.

If I go on this date, I still don't ever have to do another lap. I slowly release hope of being with Mick in lieu of saving my mom.

I take a deep breath and blow it out. Wisps of my undone hair float around my face as my gaze meets Jay's.

I can't help but gasp at the damage Mick's fists did, Jay's face chewed up by the punishment of knuckles against flesh.

"Okay," I whisper.

Jay puts his hands on his hips. "What?" He cups a hand around his ear. I stare at him, too empty to hate him.

But the part of me that's not dead—does.

"Yes," I hiss. My voice sounds like the crack of a whip.

"Good," Jay replies. He looks at Thorn. "Then we have a deal. One date with Faren, then I pay."

"I'm not going to sleep with you," I say. They need to know that even if I have to do four weeks of poles, I'm not actually a prostitute.

Apparently even I have limits; money isn't every damn thing. It's good to know. I had begun to question my own humanity.

"Only if you want to," Jay says.

I open my mouth, but Thorn's hand closes around my elbow, squeezing just shy of pain.

The sharp retort I plan becomes, "Okay."

Jay and Thorn smile. Mine is a grimace.

No one notices the difference.

* * *

THE REPAIRED security panel at my apartment building endures my three fumbling attempts to input my code.

Finally after the third attempt, the buzzer sounds and I step inside. The dumb Out of Order sign still hangs crookedly vigil from the elevator door. The edges of the torn sign seem to laugh at me as I begin the five-story trek to my apartment.

I keep moving, one foot after the next, and get to the large metal door at the fifth floor hallway. I thrust my good palm into the bar in the center, and it opens noiselessly.

I blink.

My duffle bag full of stripper clothes greets me at my door. I walk to it slowly, as if it contains a ticking bomb. My tears stain the canvas bag as I unzip the top.

I remember exactly how I put my stuff in there—without care. I just jammed all the crap inside willy nilly.

My fingers find each crease of the stacked outfits.

Mick took the time to go through each item, take it out... and return it perfectly.

I sit back on my ass, legs splayed in front of me, and dump my face into my hands. Somehow, this is the greatest battering of my fragile emotions. It shouldn't matter. I don't have enough *time* to care.

But I've been intellectualizing everything for weeks, and all that careful containment spills into my emotional cup until it overflows. I have no dam to stop the torrent. It pours out the edges of the barricades I've put up to protect myself from thinking.

From feeling.

I let my shaky hands fall to my damp dress, wet with my accumulated grief and begin to collect myself off the dirty floor of my apartment hallway.

I slide out my cell and text Kiki.

Please come.

I feel my pride break further with that simple request.

I've stupidly thought I could remain self-contained. That I could leave this blue marble on my own terms.

But it doesn't work that way. There's a force in play that I didn't consider.

I wait.

Then I decide to stop polishing the floor with my butt and haul the duffle inside my apartment.

The phone chime sounds.

I'm on my way.

Air leaves my body as I lean against my closed door. Moments tick by until I finally move toward my bathroom.

The dress I'm wearing joins the other.

My wastebasket is full with the discarded remains of dances done for men's lust.

For money.

Chunks of my soul gone forever in the name of profit.

I let the shower rinse my tears down the drain, but the despondency remains like a layer of grime.

CHAPTER 2

The tile is cool against my forehead as the hot water runs down my back. I can't get any cleaner.

I still feel dirty.

A pounding breaks through my reverie, and I lift my face, feeling my brows scrunch.

Kiki!

I jerk the faucet to the left, and the spray cuts off.

"Just a sec!" I hop out of the deep porcelain tub/shower combo.

I whip the towel from the hook buried in the cream subway tiles, jog to the door, and tear it open.

Kiki stands there in a deep gold, skintight breath of cloth that literally just covers her nipples. It moves down her torso to a tight, knotted twist at her belly button and flares at her hips, ending at the junction of her thighs and hoohah.

God, and I think my stuff is skimpy. My outfits don't hold a candle to what Kiki's outfit says.

In a word: *sex.*

Kiki breezes in, checks out my dripping self, and says, "Okay." She slaps her cell in her open palm.

"I know it's ground-shattering if you're asking for help."

I huff, giving her the look and closing the door. "I'm not that bad."

She stares at me hard enough to make me squirm. "You suck it up, Faren, it's what ya do. Remember when Ronnie did your hand... the rest of you?"

I remember perfectly.

Her words are harsh, her eyes expectant.

Yeah..." I tighten my towel with a shiver that's only partly from chill.

"I asked to help you then—begged. You said you didn't need anything. It was Faren going to the accelerated physical therapy school, Faren visiting her mom and going home—the whole circle of No Life again." Kiki makes a sarcastic twirl with her index finger.

"I got it," I say through clenched teeth.

I hate the truth... but the truth knows me.

Kiki sits on my couch, and I lower myself opposite her.

"What happened?" she asks in a hushed voice.

I tell her. Well, I attempt to tell her. I only break down once.

She runs around the coffee table.

"Oh my God, Faren!"

She crashes next to me and pulls me against her, stroking my wet head. "We'll get you through this."

I shake my head, pulling away. "No, we can't. Remember?"

Dark eyes look back at me. "How can I forget?"

My hands clamp together and wring into knots on my lap.

"What can I do?"

Kiki sighs explosively. "You *fight*, Faren."

My head rises, eyes locking with hers. "What? No—"

"Hell yes!" Kiki's eyes glitter with intent.

Absolution.

"I can't." I wipe my eyes with my hand. "I've blown it! I mean—*damn*—Mick came in with my naked ass in the air, covered in... ugh!"

She strokes my back.

"It's beyond disgusting," I wail.

"Hmmm... He's not the only guy who owns his own vault of cum, y'know."

I put my face in my hands. So not funny.

"Okay... it is pretty gross," she says. "But you were nailing it for your mom, right?"

I nod miserably.

She lifts my chin and I randomly notice her apricot glitter gloss. "He bothered to follow you—or have you followed." She looks at the ceiling momentarily, thinking. "There's strong emotion there."

"I only get the money if I date Jay."

Her eyes bulge. "A lap?!" Kiki squeaks.

I hold up my finger. "Just once."

"Once is too damn much."

"I know, but he was pissed because he'd gotten his ass kicked by Mick."

Kiki laughs, and I glare at her.

She bobs her head. "I know, it's not really funny, but somehow... it is."

She puts up a palm to stave off my scathing rebuttal. "You're working a lap, doing the nastiest extra I've ever heard of without actual..."—she moves her hips back and forth in a parody of humping—"and the guy you don't want to be your boyfriend does the most boyfriend thing of all and cleans the dude's clock."

Her brows rise. "I have to say, I like it."

"What are you saying? Because I think you just went down an *Alice in Wonderland* rabbit hole." I cross my arms and my towel slips, so I hike it back up.

"What I'm saying is, tick off the Bennies with Mick our man." She throws up her hand.

"He's rich."

Her eyebrows pop.

"Duh," I say.

Her brows go impossibly higher. "He's rich."

"You said that."

"Bears repeating, baby."

I roll my eyes, and she thwacks me with her palm.

"Hey!" I say.

Her eyes narrow. "He hired someone to clean your entire apartment when you were getting the tongue treatment." She sticks out her tongue to emphasize her point.

Oh god.

I shouldn't have said anything. But some things are just too amazing not to share.

"God, girl, are you embarrassed?"

I put both palms to my hot cheeks.

"Don't be—that's a precursor to the big one," she says.

I give her a sharp look.

"I'm not... I am not telling you how big Mick's dick is!"

Kiki laughs. "Feel better?"

I think about it. I give her a crooked smile. "Yes."

"Good."

Kiki leans forward. "Get dressed. We're gonna come up with a plan."

"No." I'm instantly back to fighting tears. "It's too humiliating."

Her gaze bores into me. "What is? Going after what you want for once? What you want from Mick?"

"I want him to be my first."

"And last...?"

I nod.

"I'm sorry. I know that's harsh, but you told me..."

"Months," I finish for her.

Kiki nods. "Yeah, so if he's going to be your one and only, and you've set your sights on him, why let him get away because of a misunderstanding?"

A misunderstanding.

"He punched Thorn."

She smiles. "That's okay. Thorn can take care of himself."

"There's that assault charge against Mick."

Kiki waves. "It's trumped up. He never even poked the kitty—tonguing doesn't count. And that dipshit Taggy, Taggert..."

I stifle a giggle. "Tagger."

"Tagger! That assclown should have been the one arrested since he interrupted what could have been an expert deflowering." Kiki looks thoughtful, and more than a giggle erupts from me. More like a guffaw.

She grins. "See? You just have to toss the pride and talk to Mick."

"He'll hate me."

How can he not? I kinda hate me.

She shakes her head. "I'm thinking he wants to fuck you *more*."

"Kiki—"

"Tell me I'm wrong."

I can't.

"What do you have to lose... except that pesky cherry! Maybe, just maybe, when you tell him the *entire* truth"—she lifts her shoulders, her eyes widening—, "he'll see the entire mess you're in and give you H.E.L.P."

My eyes slim down at her.

"In the form of what?" Even I hear the suspicion in my tone.

Kiki shrugs innocently, her eyes sliding away from mine. "I think... it could be more than a milestone hump."

"Kiki!"

"Okay, I know I'm a little ridiculous, but hear me out. After all, I know something about maneuvering."

I look at her, not a hair out of place, and have to agree. She's my rock because she is a rock.

Kiki is sharp, astute, and my true friend.

"I know you don't want to use him *use him*," she says. "But there comes a time when, and if, he knows the whole truth... that doing you might be only part of the fun."

"I don't want his money."

"Pfftt, I do!" Her eyes drill me. "Don't have a rack attack. Just be open to what he offers. It could be more."

"Live short, live deep?" I say.

Our eyes lock as Kiki takes my hands. I clamp my armpits on the top of my damp towel.

"It might mean something for Tannin's situation. Her long-term situation," she says.

I can't argue with that. But mooching off Mick is not my real agenda. Not to mention it would make me feel like shit.

She squeezes my knee. "Now about this lap..."

"Jay."

"What do you have to *do* with him?"

"I don't know, but I want to resolve this with Mick first. I need the money that Jay hasn't paid. I don't want to date him at all!"

"Gotcha. But ten K rides on this, right?"

I nod. "Yeah."

"Okay, contact Jay and get the lead out. Date his conniving ass—one time—then get over to Mick's. Text Jay now. Get it the fuck over with." Kiki tosses her hair behind her shoulder, her expectant expression on me like white on rice.

"Okay." I grab my cell from the coffee table and text Jay, asking when and where.

A minute later, his response comes in.

"Done."

My stomach rolls.

"See? Now there's no reason *not* to make arrangements to meet with Mick."

If he'll agree.

My hand hovers over my cell, and Kiki's hand closes over mine.

"No... I think he's probably a little raw," she says. "Go out with this dick lick, then reach out to Mick." Her eyes remain on mine.

"What are you gonna do?"

I outline it briefly.

"So you're back to poles and hoping Ronnie doesn't pull a repeat?"

"Yeah... I mean, I don't know why he'd compromise his freedom for revenge."

"Because he can. That sick perv is just pissed enough about things not going his way four years ago. He wants another shot."

"He almost killed my mom! He beat and stabbed me. I'm thinking that's plenty." I think about my trashed apartment, the mask he left at my job like a calling card. This is way too personal.

"Nah. Guys like him aren't happy unless they're forcing women beneath him." She shakes out her hair, and it slips forward to cover her ample cleavage. "He's not a pimp by accident. He's a deliberate douche." She snaps a big bubble, and it blows up, coating her cheeks.

"Damn, my makeup!" Kiki fumbles with the gum remnants.

"I'm going to bed." I'm so tired from this horrible night's events that I'm trying to fall asleep where I sit. Plus, a small part of me wants to lick my wounds in private.

Or a big part.

Kiki kisses my cheek. "You know how much I love you."

I hug her. "I know."

I can't breathe from her grip, as if she'll never let go. No matter what happens, I'm so grateful for Kiki's unconditional friendship.

"Get this guy gone and nail Mick," she says.

My smile turns into a yawn. "I think it's the other way around."

I expect her to smile, but her face is serious. "You might be dying, Faren, but don't stop living."

I have no answer for that.

CHAPTER 3

I watch him come out of the Millennium, and I shiver inside my trench coat. I've become a cliché. The stalkee has become the stalker. My tears mingle with the rain.

Mick doesn't break into my apartment anymore.

There are no texts.

No calls.

Nothing for days going on a week.

It's like he saw a ghost, blinked... and then I disappeared.

Not that I can blame him. Or forget him.

It's Seattle, and the rain sheets down. It's not big droplets like people who don't live here envision, but a fine soaking mist that drenches in minutes.

From a shadowed stoop across the street, I watch a lush, unflappable Mick stride out the entrance and down the red carpet, looking so much a part of the scene he appears to grow right out of the ground.

Like he's always belonged.

Where we shared so much... and not nearly enough.

Henry holds the door open with an umbrella between the open door and the plush interior of the limo.

My idea is such a risk, so unlike me, it just might work.

I'm counting on it.

Even with the umbrella sheltering him and the day as gray as living pewter, his hair glows like a low burning red flame. Embers cast to ash, I watch his head bend as he slides into the limo.

My eyes latch onto the disappearing slice of flesh at his nape and a soft sound escapes me. I have the sudden overpowering urge to touch him.

How could I ever have convinced myself that all I want from him is sex? When—*if*—he takes what I offer, he will take more than my innocence.

I won't have to suffer that long with the loss, as the clock of my life ticks.

I'm doing what Kiki says. Knowing my death is coming doesn't have to rob me of the life I still have left.

I wait as the long limo pulls away.

Looking both ways, I cross the street.

In a trench coat.

And nothing else.

* * *

"Yes, Miss..." the doorman begins.

I can tell by the way he looks me over that he recognizes me.

Of course he does.

I'm the tramp Mick slummed with and supposedly assaulted.

"Mitchell," I supply.

His eyes move over my scarlet lipstick, heavy mascara

that breaches the round sunglasses I'm using for concealment, and my long locks of almost strawberry blonde hair.

We both know it's bullshit.

"What may I do for you, Miss Mitchell?" he asks reluctantly.

"I..." This is where things get dicey. I have to play this just right and that's never been my best thing. "I wanted to save Mr. McKenna any embarrassment..."

He cocks his brow, a white gloved hand picking some lint off his immaculate uniform. "We do appreciate the courtesy."

He knows.

"I thought I'd stop by and pick up some of my things while Mr. McKenna wasn't at home."

Our eyes meet, and I can see him weigh his options. If he makes me wait until Mick returns, it might cause a media storm. The potential for negative press in their swank tower of million dollar plus condos is high.

However, Mick might be pissed if he finds out the doorman let me inside without his express knowledge.

Choices, choices.

The doorman scans the interior lobby. A chandelier anchors the ceiling in the center, casting golden amber diamonds across the ivory and mocha Travertine floor.

I do what works and flash a George Washington I can't spare. It disappears inside his pure white gloved palm.

Finally he appears to make a decision. "Fine, I'll key you through, but Miss Mitchell?

Make it snappy... I don't know when Mr. McKenna will return."

I do.

Thorn told me.

"How's Mick?" I asked, pressing my cell against my ear.

"How the fuck do you think he is? We sort of tag-teamed his ass.

You ripped off his dick, and I stabbed him in the back. Yeah, he's doing goddamned peachy."

I sighed.

"I have a plan."

After I told him my plan, he answered with a low hissing whistle. *"Holy fucking smokes, girl. It's your damn funeral."*

I envision him scrub his short hair with an agitated palm.

How close he is to the truth without knowing it.

"Will he hurt me?"

I won't lie, I was nervous as hell.

"Hell no, Mick's pissed but he's not a chick beater."

"Just a dude beater."

Thorn gave a low chuckle, "Yeah, he's damn fine at that."

"What about you two?"

"I'm not ready to share."

"Are you... guys okay?" I asked.

"No."

"Did he fire you from Black Rose?"

"It's more complicated than that."

"What did you tell him?"

Thorn doesn't answer right away. "He wasn't much interested in my bullshittery. It was all he could do not to kick my ass some more. But I think it's safe to say he thinks I coerced your lily white ass into doing laps."

He didn't. We both know it.

I said, "I think when I'm all through here... he'll see things differently."

"He'll see somethin'!"

"Faren?"

My heart beats faster when he calls my name. Two syllables said with an almost frantic intensity. "Yeah?"

"Be careful with Mick. He's not... as hard as you think."

He will be.

"Okay," I said, but not like I meant it. I had a plan and I was sticking to it.

Remembering our conversation reminds me why I'm here. The doorman and I ride the elevator to the level below the penthouse. The still-unfinished penthouse will eventually become Mick's domain.

We reach his floor, the nineteenth story, and I step out.

The doorman walks to Mick's half of the story and slides a card through a coded slot.

He pushes the door open, and I finally notice his nametag. It's jet black, and the name is just another texture in all that glossy darkness.

Tom.

"Thank you."

He steps away, hands to his chest. "I don't know how you got in, so don't thank me. Just... get your things and get out."

His brows jerk up as he waits for my response.

"Right. Yes," I confirm.

He nods and moves swiftly to the elevator.

I walk inside and latch the door, looking around.

I can't help that my ceaseless thoughts continue to churn through the machinery that is my mind.

I need to visit my mom.

I want to protect what's left of my life from Ronnie.

I'll have to date Jay one time to get that money.

I need Mick.

The wheat-colored trench coat swirls around my ankles as I move. My high heels offer a lick of bright red as I walk toward Mick's bedroom.

I walk in as though I own the place and stall out, suddenly uncertain.

One wall is solid glass. If there's a seam somewhere, I can't find it. His bed centers the room. It's orgy-sized, custom for sure. It takes up the entire wall and is surrounded by the same wood as the floor. The burnished walnut looks like mauled whiskey, with knots and pockmarks lending to its rustic elegance. The smooth lines of the built-in shelving counters the weathered wood, and they combine to look homey.

I can imagine myself in that bed.

Beneath Mick.

I don't want his last vision of me to be my naked body on top of another man.

A man I could never want the way I want him.

I turn around, absently moving to the built-in dresser that mimics the bed across from it.

Sparkling cufflinks are scattered around the top like discarded jewels.

I pick up the ones he wore the first time I saw him.

I close my good hand around them and the precious metal warms inside my palm. I set it down with a sigh that sounds like a sob.

I make the rounds to the closet. It's the size of my apartment and a laugh boils out of me.

I put my fist to my lips. The floor-to-ceiling closet is a sea of walnut with nooks, crannies, and rods. An island stands in the middle like some people have in their kitchens.

I'm so entranced, I miss my cue by a mile.

"Like what you see?"

I whirl, my hand automatically coming to my chest, where a bird the size of a house tries to escape.

Mick stands there with dewdrops of rain on top of that rich auburn hair.

He doesn't look angry. I expected anger.

What I see instead is so much worse.

Indifference.

I don't have to be wise to understand that hate is not the opposite of love.

I don't know if I'm brave enough.

"Get out, Faren," Mick says calmly, like repeating the local weather forecast.

I know I'm not brave enough.

But his dark eyes do hold heat.

Not desire, but anger. I guess that's better than the vacant lack of care that was there first.

I carefully undo the tie on the coat.

His eyes track my fingers.

I fling it off in one of the most graceful moves I've ever executed. No dance, no pole, nothing has ever mattered more than this moment.

I stand there perfectly nude, the crimson heels my only accessory.

The sun breaks through the clouds and cuts through the room like a golden promise.

Dust motes travel between us like floating specks of molten gauze.

Mick's deep brown gaze travels my hair that I know looks as though it is on fire and lingers where his mouth has been.

My face.

My sex.

Those burning eyes slow... then travel to my feet.

When they return to my face, his expression has changed.

Mick doesn't utter a word. With catlike grace, he crosses the room and stops abruptly in front of me, so close it would be easier to touch.

The tables have turned. I am the aggressor.

I grab his buttocks with both hands and jerk him against me.

Mick's face tightens, his body stiff and unyielding.

He groans, his forehead leaning down to rest against mine for a heartbeat. He locks his eyes on mine and picks me up. I lose my grip on his hard ass and cling to his shoulders.

He tosses me the six feet onto the bed.

I bounce when I land in an ungraceful pile, legs spread for his perusal.

Suddenly I'm looking into eyes that have all the lust I want... and something more.

Maybe hate.

My desire turns to something heady and more sinister.

Fear.

CHAPTER 4

"You want this?" Mick growls, grabbing the straining package at the crotch of his trousers.

I widen my legs in silent reply, the spikes of my heels digging into the plush coverlet. I kick up my chin in defiance and watch Mick struggle with a myriad of emotions.

I can tell he doesn't want to take me in anger; he wants to take me any way he can.

My stare locks onto the rigid outline of his cock as his hands remove clothes in angry quick movements.

His jacket cascades to the floor. Nimble fingers undo the buttons of his shirt one at a time, then in sudden impatience he tears it off.

Buttons scatter across the wood floor like plastic rain.

Mick unwraps himself like a sensuous, volatile package. The rose tat at his left shoulder bleeds into his chest as his muscles flex and dance. It has vines of ebony with a scarlet bloom, and I belatedly understand the symbolism.

I finally answer. "Yes."

His eyes are hard with anger, his body tense with lust.

"We're getting something straight."

I shake my head, and his hands clench into fists as the last scrap of reason leaves him.

I do the thing that will break him and bring him to me without words.

I stuff a pillow under my head and touch myself with my good hand. My bad hand cooperates for once and tweaks my nipple.

My breast shivers and jiggles with my attentions.

Mick makes a strangled sound, his eyes locked onto my tit like a warhead.

"My way, Faren."

His pants slide to the floor, and he climbs across the bed between my legs.

"My way," I whisper.

Mick's expression tells me no, but he keeps coming. His penis bobs as he nears me, and I sigh. I fling my arms behind me. He wraps his strong hands around my forearms and pins them there.

Then his hands slide down to my elbows as his mouth lands on my sex.

My hips buck, and he dives harder, his tongue boring into my wetness. I shout his name, knowing I can't lie anymore.

I've fallen so deeply that I drown in the moment. His tongue plugs me like a hot spear of heat while his hands hold me down.

I whimper and he lifts his head. "Keep your legs spread, Faren. No more lies... no more acting."

My eyes fly open. I haven't told him.

He doesn't really know.

Mick doesn't read my expression though, because his mouth is on me again. He uses the flat of his tongue to rub my clit faster and faster. One of his fingers enters me and misses my barrier, sliding against and inside me. He must mistake the tight fit for something other than what it is.

I stop thinking as he stabs back and forth with a single digit. His tongue's heat never lifts, never leaves my soft sex. A deep throb stabs through my core, and I know I'll blow.

I gaze down my body as his tongue works me, his left hand has circled my upper arm, as his mouth nails me.

The erotic sight fills me, and I can't escape—don't want to.

He releases my arm and uses his hands to spread my thighs. My knees flatten against the bed. He plows his tongue against me in a hard stroke, entrance to clit, and I shatter.

My hands rake through his hair as I shriek. The pressure of his mouth lifts, and my orgasm shivers at the chasm of more. The return of his soft lips and hot breath pushes me over that shining edge. The orgasm crashes back to me like a tidal wave coming to shore. My legs shake underneath his hands.

My arms fall to my sides, and I feel his tip at my opening.

It's the moment of truth.

I've forced his hand, used his feelings—anguish, anger, care, lust—in a deadly combination to further my ultimate goal.

We look at each other, and he shows a hesitation I won't allow. His hands are on my ass, my hips lifted slightly off the bed.

I watch him barely nudge inside of me. Before Mick can do anything, I shove my body against him, forcing him to the end of me.

I take my own virginity in a brutal plunge.

Mick's jaw goes slack, his head thrown back, as our bodies joined in a marriage of flesh and fresh agony.

My breath slides out of me in a hiss of pain. It hurts so much worse than I imagined. My pussy feels as if someone stabbed it with a hot poker. I'm so full of heat, pain, and lust that I can't decide which one I'm feeling more.

I feel torn, filled, divided... *alive.*

Mick's deeply inside me, his cock a throbbing mass of pain and pleasure. His strong hands cup my ass.

Neither of us move. When his eyes open, his face levels with mine. His eyes hold anguish; they hold awe.

"I didn't know."

His dulcet tones caress my wounds like salve.

Mick dips his head, covering me with his muscular body and our foreheads touch. His lips graze my cheek and his hips pull back, my walls grabbing at him.

I hold his naked ass, feeling my muscles clench and stop his escape.

"Don't," I command. *It hurts... I want more.*

"Faren," Mick says, "I don't know what kind of screwed up game you're playing..."

"Just fuck me, please. It's what I want."

He closes his eyes. "I don't know if I can stop once I start."

He rocks into me deeply, kissing my womb, pulls out, and drives deep again.

I writhe beneath him, catching him deeper inside me. I feel more alive from the raw burning pleasure he gives me than I have in weeks.

Mick stares into my eyes, swirling his hips and I gasp at the sensation. "I thought..."

"Shh... stop talking," I say.

I push my hips against him. The searing pain begins to take a backseat to the exquisite feel of him inside of me.

Mick sits up on his knees. One hand moves to my breast, the other to his mouth.

He licks his thumb and places it on my clit. He moves it with a slow, expert swirl, and my breath catches. I throw my face to the side, sinking into the sensation.

He thrusts into me and my sex meets his like a perfectly choreographed dance.

I turn my head just enough to see Mick's eyes watching me. Something I thought I'd never see again creeps into his warm brown gaze.

Tenderness.

A token of his former tenderness that I'd thought was lost comes back as his body moves against me, deeply, thoroughly—savagely perfect.

Mick mounds my breast, bending over me as he uses my body into a delicious friction of consumption. His mouth covers my breast and I slide against his body.

He pulls out, and I feel empty. The pain is only a shadow to the release that was building between my legs.

I must have it.

Him.

Mick flips me over, and I instinctively lift my ass. I feel him at my entrance, teasing my tight, slick heat, but he doesn't plunge in as I expected he would. His hand trails away from my face, pressed against the bed, up to the curve of my ass.

I shiver against the burning trail his fingertips make.

"Spread your legs, Faren."

I push my knees farther, completely vulnerable and open to him. I offer myself like a sacrifice.

His thumb slips inside me, and I moan. "Mick... yes, please yes..." I pant, my chest tight.

"Tell me you want this Faren."

His thumb slides in and out of me and I cry, tears of relief, agony and *want*.

"Tell me you want me to fuck you, Faren."

My carnal response is instinctive and immediate. "Fuck me, fuck me. Please fuck me." Need has roughened my voice into a harsh plea driven out of me.

His former tenderness is replaced by a need to brand my body. He shoves himself inside, conquering every inch of my virginity, stripping away what I wanted him to take.

I shove my hips backward as he drives into me.

My pussy is so swollen and heavy with him inside of me. I can't help the tears of need or the greedy whimpers that slip from my lips as he pounds me from behind.

His wet thumb rims the bud of my ass and I scream as his lubed digit enters me.

His thumb and penis fill me in dual ecstasy, and I come. I drive back against him, and it pushes everything more deeply.

I stop breathing, thinking... My internal circuitry blown.

I howl as Mick thrusts both bits inside the center of my body.

My soul.

I feel him infinitesimally harden inside me.

With a last deep thrust, his release fills me. Our bodies are locked together as I rise on my elbows. His hand moves to my hair, and he rides me like I've wanted since the minute his lips touched mine.

I want his ownership.

I am Mick's—body and soul.

I always was.

CHAPTER 5

We lay together, and tears roll out of me in an unbidden river of tumultuous emotion.

I did it—I reached the pinnacle.

Then I realize there's nowhere to go but down.

And I don't want to.

I want to stay in this ecstatic pocket of my life. If this is the wonderful finale before it all ends, I never want it to.

Mick spoons against me, his hand tracing my side. The tips of his fingers move down to the valley of my waist, back up to the curve of my shoulder, then around my neck.

My pulse lifts his fingers.

"You weren't acting." He breathes against my neck, warm and alive.

"No."

He wipes a tear from my cheek with the pad of his thumb.

"I hurt you." His voice is full of so much emotion.

I could mine for what's there, but I'm too full myself to dig.

I laugh instead, turning my head to smile at him.

"I think I hurt myself."

Mick grins, cups my chin, and kisses me so gently I smell his skin before he touches me. "You did... surprise me."

My brows lift. "I impaled you."

Mick nods, suppressing an evil smile. "All of you—on all of me. I couldn't ask for anything better." Then his face darkens.

"Had I known you were..." He rolls over onto his back and swipes my body on top of his as I squeal. "God... a virgin. I would have handled—hell, everything differently."

I shake my head. My hair falls forward, smothering him.

"It's all me. I wanted to."

He puts a finger under my chin, lifting my eyes to his.

"What?"

"I wanted it to be you."

"Thank Christ," he says with an abrupt laugh.

He cradles my face, and his lips pull on mine, sucking them into his kiss.

He grows hard underneath me and I want him again.

His eyes sink into mine. "God, Faren... what are you doing to me?"

"Making you hard," I say against his mouth.

He pulls away, and I love his easy smile.

I put it there.

"True," he answers. "But... I think you might need a little break. It'll make you too sore."

Mick jumps up, and I fall back into the mussed covers. For the first time, I'm unashamed of my nudity. With Mick, I'm naked by choice.

He stops in his tracks, his eyes roaming me. The brown of his irises warm like chocolate over heat.

"You're so beautiful Faren."

I can't help but notice the proof, his arousal underscoring his words.

What he says echoes in the chambers of my heart. I capture it, holding it tightly inside of me.

The memory of the way he cherishes me is something I know I'll never forget.

Mick steps up to the foot of the bed and wraps his hand around my ankle. "Stay right there. I'll take care of you."

I enjoy the naked view as he walks away.

I hear him in the kitchen, glasses clinking, something pouring. My ears prick when footsteps signal his return.

I sit up on my elbows, crossing my legs. I tingle and ache.

It's all so good I can hardly stand myself.

Mick enters the bedroom holding two glasses of red wine in one hand and a half-empty bottle.

His eyes gleam, and my lips part. He notices. His gaze lands on the parts of my body he's touched.

Which is everything.

He owns me, and I uncross my legs. Mick's chest heaves with an explosive exhale, and he sets the stemmed crystal on top of his nightstand. He disappears into the bathroom.

I frown when he walks away from the view of me I so proudly produced.

He reappears with a pure white washcloth. It steams with hot water.

"What-what are you doing?" I ask.

"Spread your legs for me." His voice is as soft as mine, but there's a demanding edge to it.

I shiver from his tone, moving my legs apart.

Pain edges into my euphoria and I wince a little.

Mick smiles gently and moves between my legs with the bottle of wine and the hot washcloth. He pours wine on the washcloth and moves it to my sex.

I catch his wrist and question him with my eyes.

"I'm cleaning you."

I can feel my frown. "Why?" *I can take a shower.*

"This is what a man does for a woman when she's given him what you gave me."

My hand slips from his wrist, and the tears come.

He shakes his head. "Don't cry. This is a good thing."

"What did I give you?"

The answer is obvious but he surprises me with it anyway.

"All of you, Faren."

Mick puts the warm cloth against me, and I sigh in relief. The wine and heat feels deliciously soothing. I close my eyes to enjoy the sensation of gentle, moist warmth.

The first swipe of his tongue undoes me. I'm hot, wet, and utterly relaxed.

"Mick?" My gaze moves to his mouth working on me, licking where he's just cleaned.

His hands slip underneath my ass and jerks me tighter against the seal of his mouth. I cry out.

He checks to make sure it's not a pain sound.

It's not.

Mick goes back to sucking me. My hips move against his mouth, and a flush covers my skin.

"Let me... let me... finish you," Mick says.

I think I'm too sore, too spent... too everything to deny what he wants.

With no fingers, just the heat of his lips and breath, he brings me.

My hoarse cries fill the room and come back to surround our panting.

Mick stands, using a sheet to wipe his mouth and falls on me, holding his body off me by inches.

I laugh and wind my arms around his neck.

He kisses me, and I taste myself on him. I groan, our tongues twining.

"Thank you," he says, and I laugh.

Thank you.

He looks at me for a moment longer, satisfied with what he sees on my face, and walks away. A minute later, I hear water filling the tub.

It's hard not to cry as Mick takes care of me.

For the first time, I hold back my tears.

I want to feel the joy without the sadness.

* * *

HE SLIDES me into the hot water, and my toes curl. It hurts; it feels wonderful.

Mick's only semi-hard. He catches me checking out his cock and grins, wagging a finger. "We will have plenty of each other. Right now, you rest. No arguments."

"Yes, sir," I say and give him a look that takes him from half-cocked to all the way in seconds.

"Look what you do to me." He swings a palm at himself. "Nice."

"Very nice," I reply with a wink.

He steps into the heated water and swims to me. The tub is the size of my bedroom. Mick's arms tuck me in tight against his front.

Lacing our fingers together, he nuzzles my neck, pushing my wet hair away.

I feel his hardness against my ass. "I thought you told me to rest."

"Mhmm..." He dives and pecks until my head falls back against his shoulder in surrender.

"I want to take you again and again. I don't want to hurt you."

I move my ass against his hard-on, and he groans, nipping my neck. A a small sound slips out of my mouth, and his arms tighten around me.

"Behave," he says.

I laugh, and his dick falls between the cheeks of my ass.

"Faren..." he warns in a growl.

I relent. Truthfully, I'm sore.

We're quiet for a minute. Mick lifts our hands and slides a finger over the scar in the middle of my palm.

"We have to talk about what happened."

I tense, and his lips fall on my shoulder.

"Why are you doing it?" he asks.

I knew this moment would come, but I didn't want it to. No matter what happens in my life, the world keeps spinning.

The world moves even when mine grinds to a halt.

"It's my mom. If I don't pay off the debt at the place where they care for her, she'll be moved to a state home." I tell the first truth. A whole piece of it. I thought it'd feel like surgery without anesthesia, but instead, it feels like closure.

Mick says nothing.

He hates me. He thinks I've set him up. Maybe this whole thing was a ploy to get something from him. But even if he tosses me out, I know I gave myself to him completely. I didn't hold back one part of me back—he got all of me.

The horrible threads of those spoiled musings unravel through my mind in seconds.

His voice rumbles against my wet back. "I said I would take care of you."

My breath hitches.

"I didn't want you to feel obligated; I don't want to... ask."

My voice grows smaller.

"Maybe I only want you to take care of parts of me."

"No," Mick answers.

"Oh." My heart is crushed. He doesn't want to take me, not with my stupid baggage.

He swivels me around to face him, and water slops over the rim of the tub.

"You misunderstand me."

Then tell me so I can live another moment in your arms, my heart shrieks.

His eyes nail me to the spot.

"I want *every* part of you."

My eyes widen and neither of us catch the tears that fall.

His lips show me how every part of him, wants to take care of every part of me.

I believe.

CHAPTER 6

"I want to watch you," Mick says. I stand, the cooling water running off me in rivulets that make small greedy noises as they fall into the tub.

He holds out his hand, and I slip mine into it as I get out of the water. Mick steadies me for a moment then wraps me in a huge fuzzy towel that covers me from armpit to shin.

People don't own towels like this, do they? It's like a blanket.

He tips my head back and kisses me, slow and peaceful. As though my clock isn't ticking. As though we don't have a ton of messy shit to discuss that waits in the shadows of our happiness.

His lips press and suck at my lower lip and finally come away.

"Come on," he says, leading me into the bedroom.

He's been busy while my fingertips became pruned and the water cooled. The bed had been stripped, and new linen graces it. It's a rich cream with a hint of mocha, a gazillion thread count I'm sure.

I drop the towel and swim into the sheets. The satiny

material caresses me like a lover, and Mick climbs in after me.

His strong arms wrap around me, and I straddle him, fitting against him perfectly. Every bit of what he just plunged into is spread against him again.

"Faren," he says, his hands cupping my breasts, "you make things so difficult."

"Or just hard," I say. My sly smile makes him laugh.

I fold against him, his erection between us.

"I don't know what to do with Ty," he admits softly.

"I call him Thorn," I say.

He nods.

"A thorn to protect the rose," Mick recites as though by rote.

I pull away to look down at him. He tucks a damp tendril of hair behind my ear.

"He told me, Mick."

His eyes close.

"She was young. Younger than you."

I don't interrupt.

"Rose told my parents that she had a scholarship to the university. But she didn't, she was stripping to pay her way."

His eyes open, the normal soothing brown churning to black with his remembered rage.

"Then one night, a client"—he spits the word out—"wanted more than a dance."

He covers his face with a forearm, hiding himself from me.

Mick's silent for almost a minute.

"I was supposed to pick her up. I had football practice and asked Thorn to do it."

He sighs and restlessly strokes my hair when I put my chin on his chest. "He was eighteen. My birthday was a couple of weeks later."

I wait. I know there's more.

"The bastard used her like no woman should ever be used. I don't know every fucked up thing, but Thorn came on the tail end of it. There were two of them."

Thorn told me he murdered Rose's killer.

He hugs me as if I'm the last solid thing in the world

"Thorn didn't know any better. He hit one of the fucker's over the head with his hockey stick, but the other guy had a knife..."

"He stabbed Thorn?"

Mick nodded. "Yes. Then he ran off. The cops came, and Thorn had Rose's blood all over him. His hockey stick was caked with blood and hair, and a dead guy had a bashed in head and leaking brains. They tossed Ty in prison."

Horrible image. "No... There were two?"

He nodded, gently fisting my hair and releasing and fisting again. "Thorn had a juvie record a mile long."

Things came together like a horrible puzzle.

"Tagger," I guessed. "He was the responding cop?"

"Fuck yeah."

"Oh god." *That's why he's such a prick.*

"I don't bother trying to reason with that dick anymore. He took one look at Thorn and there was no trial, just a ramrod with no lubricant."

I pause. "What about his folks?"

"They were users. Well, his mom was. He didn't know who his dad was. He had it rough," Mick says.

"So Tagger just thought where there's smoke, there's fire?"

"Yes, he was lead, and his word was golden. And here's the kicker. When I finally got the money from my invention and funded clearing Thorn's name?"

I nod.

"He was made a hero for taking out one of the killers and trying to save the helpless stripper." Mick gives a small shrug.

"But by then, it was too late. Thorn had a record, and my sister's secret was inadvertently told through her murder. It wrecked my parents, wrecked Thorn..."

"And wrecked you," I expound, including him in the net of condemnation.

My hands slip to his strong jaw, and I see the conviction in his eyes.

"I've been broken, not beaten," he says.

"At least Thorn got a chunk out of the second bastard."

My brows lift.

"Yeah, he got a swipe in with the asshole's own knife."

"Did Thorn see who he was?" I ask.

Mick shakes his head, dislodging me gently as he lifts up on an elbow.

"He just won't buy it. He's convinced Thorn's guilty and I bought him out of jail. There's only Thorn's word there was another assailant; *his* DNA was at the scene, not some secondary attacker."

"Where's the knife?" I ask.

"Good question."

Everything seems to point to evidence tampering from where I sit.

Mick's eyes burn with his hatred. "Like I'd ever let anyone get away with hurting someone I love."

He says those words, and I can't breathe. What he's implying is what I wish most to hear.

"How can he get away with it? You've got thousand-dollar-an-hour lawyers. They could pick the meat off his carcass."

"Oooh... so violent." Mick jerks me under him and covers my nipple with his hot tongue.

My hands twine through his hair, my legs fall open and he crawls more deeply between them.

"You presume to know how much legal team costs?" he asks around my moaning.

Mick brings his teeth together on my nipple in a gentle bite at the same time his fingers find me again and I groan.

He abruptly takes his hands off me.

"Do you?"

I shake my head, wanting him over me like flesh covered steel.

He puts a finger on my mouth.

"Tagger thinks I'm fucked in the head. That my best friend from high school raped and murdered my sister, and I hid it from him. He believes her death meant so little to me that I opened a string of successful strip clubs."

"The Black Rose," I say.

They're all for her.

Rose McKenna.

"Her death did mean that much."

His eyes fill with passion, and he squeezes my hips. "Her death is not going to be for nothing. Every stripper who works for me doesn't have to worry about their safety—that it might be their last dance."

Mick rolls onto his back, and I throw an arm over his torso. Our erotic mood is muddled by the heavy conversation.

"I can't forgive Thorn for doing the lap revolutions," he admits.

I don't look at him but answer, "You have to."

I hate Thorn, *I understand Thorn.*

Mick needs him; Thorn's a part of the fabric of who Mick is.

"Why?" The hand that had been stroking my back stills.

"Because he did it for you."

Mick's silent as we lay there, my head resting on his shoulder. "He killed one of your sister's murderer's."

I can't believe I'm defending Thorn.

"I'm aware, Faren."

"He went to jail for it."

Mick pulls away.

"Thorn put you on the laps of men who don't deserve you. He was running illicit shit behind my back."

"All true." My eyes peg him to the bed, my arms wrapped around his.

"But he did it for you. He wants to pay you back."

Mick groans and falls back.

"He doesn't need to."

I smack his arm.

"He thinks he does—don't you get that?"

Mick's eyes narrow. He grabs me, flips me over, and puts his knee against my naked sex. "I think what you don't get is that I'm done talking."

He flattens his lean body against me, and I feel him against me, ready to split me apart with his cock.

I groan, moving my legs farther apart.

"I thought I had to 'rest,'" I say with airquotes.

Mick captures my wrists and pins them above my head, a favorite position. He nods, kissing me so thoroughly I can't speak. Moisture pools.

"I'll go slow," he says.

When I don't object, he adds, "And Faren?"

"Yes?"

"If I ever see you with another man, I think Tagger will be able to jail me. Legitimately."

He kisses the tip of my nose.

"I can only understand so much. A man can only forgive so much."

His eyes search mine, and I nod within the cradle of his hands.

He punctuates his point by nudging me, the tip of him begging entrance.

I forget Thorn, debt, my illness... almost everything.

Except Mick.

CHAPTER 7

"Oh my god!" Kiki swoons back in her chair. "I don't know if god has anything to do with it," I say, but I'm smiling.

"You gave it up," Kiki swings her palm up and I slap it, a goofy grin riding my face like a permanent fixture.

"I did."

Her brows sweep up. "And you told him why you did the laps?"

I nod.

"What's that face for? Girl, you *had* to tell him."

"I know."

I bite my lip.

"Still doesn't feel solid?"

I shake my head. "I'm just so used to not having help, to trying to maintain a low profile."

"Well, suck up your g-string and say yes for goddamned once."

Kiki goes to her stove and pours hot tea into two cups. I gaze out her windows and see a slice of Puget Sound, churning and gray.

She sets a steaming cup in front of me.

"So?"

I take a sip and my brows hike. "So?"

"Don't be fucking coy. Deets, baby."

"He won't take no for an answer. He's taking over Tannin's monthlies."

"Thank whatever's holy!" Kiki slams her palm on the table, and a little of her tea joins the sodden bag on her saucer. Kiki squeals like a holy roller,

"I've been healed!"

I laugh, but sober quickly. "I feel bought and paid for," I say.

"Okay, whatever!" Kiki rolls her eyes. "Let's go over stud's good points—"

"Mick."

"Mick-shmick."

She ticks his assets off on her fingers.

"Money, hot-in-the-sheets, his give-a-shit meter still works."

She lifts her brows again, and I reluctantly nod—all true.

"Great sex."

"You said that," I point out.

"Does it bear repeating?" Kiki throws her hands out, waiting.

Hell yes. My cheeks heat.

"Yes."

"Now that's what I'm talking about! Buck up, Faren." Her chocolate eyes don't let go of my gray ones. "Don't dick this up. Live in the *now*."

Kiki realizes what she just said and her face falls.

"I'm sorry—"

"It's okay. I know what you meant. Technically, you're too right."

"He doesn't know about...?"

I shake my head. "I'm thinking one revelation at a time. You think he's up for the lap dancing, my mom's debt and my terminal punch card?"

Kiki puts her head in her hands, peeking at me through her fingers. "God, you're so harsh on yourself."

I shrug. I've spent weeks coming to terms with it. As much as anyone can.

"Actually, my short lifespan bothers me less and less."

Kiki is obviously surprised.

I dip my head. "Yeah, I've actually been worried about Ronnie reappearing and making it shorter. Or..." I look down at my hands and my foot jiggling underneath her table. "Not having ever been with Mick."

"It's about damn time! I was about to call in reinforcements."

I laugh. "You were, were you?"

Kiki gives me a serious look. "Ah, yeah. Legit. I thought you'd leave this blue marble without ever getting anything Faren Mitchell wanted but a tough hand."

She's right of course.

"So tell all."

I don't know where to start, but the burn of my embarrassment flares to life again on my face.

"Wow, look at you blush. It must be something." She scrunches her nose. "My first time hurt like hell."

"Yeah," I say softly. "And he didn't know."

"Oh my god, don't tell me he just rammed you with the beef fuel injection!" Surprise unhinges my jaw.

Tea spurts out of my mouth, making a wet mess on her glass top.

"Gross! Faren, ya pig—calm your tits!"

"I can't help it! Your description... And no, he didn't just impale me."

My head drops, my shoulders shaking with silent laughter.

"Well, later he did."

"Ha!" Kiki shrieks, jiggling her ass on the tall chair. "Knew it!"

She waggles her brows.

"So you got the whole tamale?"

"I think your verbiage is off base. He put it in *my* taco."

Her brows pull together. "Ah... are we talking Mexican food or anatomy?"

"It's all body parts."

Kiki leans forward. "I know the first time isn't that hot...."

"It hurt. Then it was hot."

We stare at each other like co-conspirator's. "The second time was amazing."

"Ooh!" Kiki squeals.

"Twice! Ya slut!" She cocks her head. "Weren't you sore?"

I nod.

"But somehow that didn't matter."

Kiki flops back against the chair, tea forgotten in front of her.

She fans her crotch.

"What are you doing?"

"Fanning my vagina. What does it look like?"

I bark out a laugh. "Huh... that's..."

"About where *that's* at. So Mick...?"

I fold my arms, putting my spent tea bag inside the empty cup. "We're not going to play house, I've got my house—he's got his."

"Stubborn."

I shake my head.

"It's not that. I don't want to overtake his life. And when I get sicker... Well"—I look down—"I think he's the kind of man who wouldn't make me leave but wouldn't want that burden."

"Shit! Faren!" Kiki yells.

A small squeak erupts from me.

"What?" My eyes jerk around her condo. Everything looks okay.

"What about protection?"

I groan.

Kiki chastises me, eyebrows to hairline, "You're such a prude. Still—"

"No, you're just so out there with it all."

"I'm not much for sugar-coating the turd, sweet thing."

"Uh-huh."

"Uh-huh, what?"

"I'm on the pill. The day after I met him, I rushed my butt to the clinic and got loaded up."

Her shoulders sag with relief. "Okay. When you were giving me the play-by-play, I missed the throwing-the-raincoat-on-the-umbrella part."

I laugh. "Huh?" *Oh.*

"Protecting the pecker?" she prompts.

"I gotcha!" I say, a tad grumpy. *I'm not a moron.*

She frowns, tapping a nail on the table. "Y'know, it's weird he didn't ask. Most guys live in terror of knocking someone up or having a surprise kid."

Her face lights up. "I got it! He's trying to trap you."

"No." I smile. "Mick McKenna has a boatload to lose if I get with child."

"With child? That tickles my ass hairs."

"You don't have any."

"Brazilian, baby. It's a wonderful thing."

I shudder, imagining the pain.

Kiki smirks.

"You'll stay at your place, he'll have his..."

My cell chimes.

Jay: *Hey, we still on for tonight?*

I gulp, and my palms sweat.

Me: *Yes. I have the time. Did you decide on the place?*

I wait for the response. When it comes, Kiki watches my face.

She hops up from the chair and circles the table, peering over my shoulder to read the text.

I tap out my answer.

Me: *see u then.*

"That sucks so bad."

She hugs me, and I wind my arms around her.

"It's such a joy-suck."

Yeah, that too.

"Just keep your eyes on the money, chickie."

"Don't I always?" I say.

Kiki strokes my hair as my tears dampen her shirt. She doesn't pull away or complain.

"Yeah, hun. Yeah, ya do."

* * *

THE SAME GLASS elevator encases me.

The view doesn't move me.

Nor does the ride.

The doors whisper open, and I glide out in heels that used to feel awkward but now feel as though they're an extension of my body.

The maitre'd escorts me to a table only one away from the one Mick and I used.

Jay stands, and somehow it's a little like seeing my teacher outside of school.

He's a handsome lap with healing bruises, and I realize he's a person.

THE TOKEN 2

Who needs to eat.

Who breathes, sleeps, has a life. Wants more.

That old shame nips at my heels, and I stomp it out.

Money.

Thorn has it, and he'll return it to Jay if I don't do this last thing.

Jay moves to my side of the table. My shoulders shiver when his hands brush over them, and he kisses the back of my neck.

Only Mick's lips have touched me there, and I feel so much like I'm cheating on him that my stomach clenches. I struggle not to pull away.

Jay mistakes my trembling for want.

"This is so much better. No irate playboys to break up our fun."

Playboy?

A cold lump settles in my gut. I can still feel Mick's weight between my thighs. It's a memory I never want to escape.

Jay watches my face. His dark hair glints blue in the candlelight, and his hazel eyes glitter back at mine.

I cast my gaze to the floor, but this is the Space Needle. The floor revolves, making my stomach turn harder.

I snap my eyes back to Jay's.

He moves back to his side of the table and sits.

His finger strokes the rim of his wine glass, over and over. The crystal sings with a bell-like ring. It's just short of making me wince.

"I know your boyfriend," he says like a question.

"He... Mick's my boyfriend."

I don't know if that's technically true, but it sounds right.

"Too bad." Jay leans back in his chair. "I was hoping you'd switch it up."

I feel my face stiffen. "Um... I thought this was about enjoying a night out with me, not discussing Mick."

"McKenna could get in a lot of trouble for beating the shit out of me, Faren Mitchell."

My heart thunders. *He knows my last name.* More importantly, he knows Mick's.

I don't bolt, even though every muscle begs me to.

"No," I say, reaching deep for bravery.

"Whatever this is"—I swing my index finger back and forth—"it's just one night."

My eyes don't release him.

"I'm not doing anything further."

A moment of silence engulfs the moment.

"I've been to the police. Got my handsome mug immortalized like a *Vogue* photo shoot."

I think of Tagger.

My bad hand trembles.

"Why can't this be over?" Despair drips from every word.

I don't really expect an answer.

His stare bores into me.

"Because I don't want it to be."

CHAPTER 8

*J*ay's not-so-subtle blackmail doesn't slow my step as I walk through the doors of my mom's medical clinic.

I compartmentalize the bullshit. I can only take one mess at a time.

Even so, I remember his parting words: *I'll be in touch.* They echo inside my mind, though I've put them on a shelf to gather dust.

I charge up to the glass partition, very much like the one that is where I work as a PA and silently slide the ten grand through the slot.

Her careful eyes look at mine.

Curious.

I don't waver. "Here's that final payment."

The girl smacks her gum and counts every dollar. Twice.

"Okay, all here." She clicks the bills on top of the counter to settle them into a cooperative stack.

She laboriously writes out a receipt.

Tears swim in my eyes as I see that word stamped on top of her loopy, round writing.

Paid.

It makes my soul lighter, weightless.

"Hey, ya okay?" she asks. *Heather*, her name tag reads.

"Yeah." My heart is full. I've eased one burden... only to have a dozen vie for position behind it.

But my smile is genuine. A perfect fit for a face that hasn't held one in a while.

* * *

I HAVE to see what happened between Mick and Thorn. More importantly, I've made up my mind.

Thorn's expression tells all. He's subdued—frazzled.

"So, what happened?" I ask tentatively.

His dark eyes rove my face. "You must have put a good word in for old Thorn." He gives a disheartened laugh.

"What?" I ask, leaning forward.

He rolls those huge shoulders into a shrug. A flash of me holding onto them while he explodes underneath me sears me and is gone.

God.

I swallow. *The sins of the past.*

"He said you guys *talked*."

He's straight-faced, and I sit on my hands to keep them still.

I nod.

"What'd you say? 'Cause we're not right, but it's better," he says.

"I told him how much it meant to you—to return what you'd been given."

Thorn crosses his arms across his chest, a tired wisdom permeating his gaze.

"You're quitting."

I take a deep breath.

"Yeah."

"I knew you weren't for this life Faren."

I look at my hands again. "Yeah, I was."

His dark brows lift. "How's that?"

"I'm not better than any of those girls. I did it for the same reasons they did. Money."

"Yeah." He scrubs his short hair. "But the difference is, the money wasn't the motivator. Your mom was.

So we cool?"

I lift a shoulder.

"Yeah. I mean," I look at him and give a nervous laugh. "I won't lie, you kinda scare me a little."

He doesn't smile. "I should."

I point at him. "See! You don't even try to make me feel safer."

"I'm not a good guy."

"That's not true."

It was hard for Thorn to show compassion toward me, but he had. Wasn't that worth something?

He looks away, leaning back in his chair, and I notice his biceps look almost as big as my waist.

He also has a rose in his tat sleeve I'd never noticed before.

The men who loved Rose McKenna.

His dark eyes pierce me, the whites so pure they're startling in his dark face. "Listen, I *know* this gism jockey, Jay."

My heart speeds, and my cheeks flush in embarrassment.

His eyes flick to me then away. "He's done some deals with Mick, but they've never met. He let me keep the money, so I know you had your date with him."

We look at each other.

Silence beats at us.

"Did you fuck him?" he asks.

Like a slap, my face is on fire.

I remember with perfect clarity what it felt like to have Mick's body invade every part of mine.

I could never be with anyone else.

"No."

My head dips.

"No," I repeat in a whisper.

"Faren."

I lift my head. "Don't fuck with me."

"What? I'm not." *What is he talking about?*

"I think Mick's gone on you," Thorn says. "I don't want you doing the stiletto tap dance on his soft little underbelly."

I stare at him.

"I don't want anyone else."

Thorn exhales in relief and stands.

"I'm glad we had this little chat."

I'm still reeling from Thorn's revelations and his normal bald delivery.

I don't tell him about Jay's insinuation that I'll see him again or he'll make trouble for Mick with the cops.

More press.

Tagger's full attention.

Ronnie seeing more and knowing more than I want.

"So this is your two weeks' notice?" he asks, slinging an arm around my shoulders.

I'm horrified. I'm done with laps!

Thorn sees my expression and chuckles.

"Just messin' with ya."

I smack him.

"Not funny."

He grabs my wrist, pinning it behind me.

My heart gallops.

He could easily hurt me.

"No hitting." His breath is warm on my face.

"Okay," I whisper. "I didn't mean anything by it."

He slowly drops my hand, and I fight not to rub where he held me.

"Nobody hits Thorn."

Mick did.

"Do you hit them?"

My question stuns us both.

He gives me a considering look.

"Sometimes."

I back away, and he grins, flashing white teeth.

Somehow, it reminds me of a shark.

"Everyone has a dark side," he says.

"Yeah," I answer, my hand on the knob.

"You've got nothin' to worry about."

That captures my interest. "Why?"

"'Cause you're Mick's bitch."

I scowl.

"Do you have to be so crude?"

He shakes his head. "I don't see it that way."

Don't ask.

"So how do you see it?" I'm so dumb.

"If I give enough of a shit to say a woman's mine, nothing in this planet is gettin' in the way. She's my property."

God, and I thought I could thaw toward Thorn... "So the poles come naturally—running them."

He nods. "Yeah."

He studies my face.

"I know what you think. I'm such a bastard."

He robs me of speech.

"But you ask that sweet piece-of-ass Kiki what she thinks of Thorn's follow-through skills."

"You are aware of how creepy it is that you talk about yourself in the third person," I say.

He shrugs.

"Now blow outta here before I change my mind about

you being Mick's. 'Cause I gotta say, you put the 'P' in the male protection quota."

"What the hell does that mean?" My good hand tightens on the door.

Thorn palms his chin, the rasp of his stubble a rough caress of noise.

"It means"—his eyes arrest my movement, so raw and sincere I can barely maintain eye contact—"that you're the kind of woman who makes every man want to take care of you."

I stare.

A long moment passes.

He breaks the silence by flinging his hand at the door.

"Now get outta here."

He turns his back on me.

I look at a broken man who is all right with not being fixed.

I'm almost envious.

* * *

I PUT on lipstick that Mick will kiss off the instant he sees me.

Rolling my lips together, I make kissing faces at the mirror. I can't wipe the happiness off my face.

Perfect.

I have such pale skin that the rich apricot looks amazing. It's Kiki's lip gloss, and it looks great on me for the same reason it looks great on her—contrast. I'll have to thank her for the lend.

I brush on one more stroke, framing my cupid's bow, and pucker at my reflection.

The doorbell chimes, and I stroll over to the door, sweeping it open with a smile.

"What... no trench coat?" he asks.

I stagger back from surprise, falling to the ground and twisting as Ronnie tackles me.

My heart lurches in my chest, adrenaline surging to my extremities in a sickening tingle of pins and needles. My elbows take the brunt of my fall.

Ronnie grips my shoulder and flips me over. My head smacks the wood floor, and pain slices through the back of my skull.

"Help!" I shriek.

He slaps me so hard my ears ring, cutting me off mid-scream.

His face fills my vision. Beady eyes, slight double chin. So ordinary.

So lethal.

"You little cunt, did you think I'd let you get away?"

No, sadly, *I didn't.*

My hand bats behind me, slapping air... then a cord. Ronnie's eyes follow my left hand as I jerk on whatever's attached to the cord.

My lamp sails forward and bashes the fucker in the mouth. My bad hand snaps the cord, checking it at the last critical moment, and the second strike is a bouncing smash against his nose.

Porcelain shatters, the shards scattering like jagged bullets.

"Argh!" he wails, blood spraying from the mess I've made of his face.

I glance at my hand, behaving perfectly when I need it to.

Amazing.

I scramble backward, and Ronnie falls on me.

I grunt as the breath leaves my body. I manage to knee him in the gut and crawl away.

I'm ten feet from him when I take in what he's wearing.

Gloves.

Mask.

Holy shit.

He's the one who helped kill Rose. It makes a terrible sense. I don't dwell on the revelation. I take off running for the open door and smack into Thorn.

I bounce off him, and he snags me.

His eyes move behind my shoulder.

"Move, Faren."

He sets me gently aside.

Mick follows him and I retreat a step, Ronnie's blood is a stripe across my dress. My beautiful lipstick is indeed smeared.

No longer amazing.

"Now this is the kind of hand job I love," Thorn states.

Mick's eyes move over me, assessing injury. When he sees I'm unharmed, his gaze moves to Ronnie.

Ronnie doesn't stand a chance. It's two against one, the kind of odds Rose never had.

My mom.

Me.

I watch them beat Ronnie Bunce into an unrecognizable pulp on my living room floor.

I silently shut the front door.

CHAPTER 9

"Stop!" I yell. Two pairs of primitive eyes meet mine. Maybe that's how males have always looked when they defend.

Thorn's a hot mess of blood and torn knuckles. Mick's tie is askew. Blood spatter like macabre pinpoint polka dots cover his creamy button-down.

His cufflinks twinkle in the moonlight.

I tear my eyes away from the surreal vision of the two gore-covered men.

"C-check his pulse," I stammer.

I want him dead so bad I can taste it, but I know that Tagger will come and at the very least, Thorn will get sent back to prison—or Mick.

I won't be responsible for that too.

I don't want the melody of my life to end on that discordant note.

"Fucker," Thorn says. His spit latches on to the front of Ronnie's torn clothing in a gleaming dollop of phlegm.

I shudder.

Mick tears off the ski mask, and Ronnie's head bangs against the wood floor.

I flinch.

He places his index and middle fingers on Ronnie's pulse point.

Three of my heartbeats pass. God knows how many of his—if any.

Mick's eyes meet mine. "He's alive."

"Don't kill him," I say.

Thorn's expression nails me. "This fucktard is the one who did that." He points at my trembling hand with the mangle of scar tissue in the center. "He's the lap, remember?"

Mick looks between Thorn and me. "What is going on?"

"We need to discuss this later," I say.

Sirens wail.

Thorn and Mick look at each other.

"Fuck me running."

Mick's face darkens, knowing there're more revelations to come.

Damn.

I look to Thorn.

"Why—how did you know?"

Mick exhales, putting his hands on his hips. "I have you under surveillance."

My mouth drops open. *Is he kidding?* "You're snooping on me?"

"No, Faren. This is the man we suspect wrecked your apartment. I'm seeing you. Why wouldn't I use the means at my disposal to secure your safety? And now Thorn says *he's* responsible for permanent damage to you?" His brown eyes don't let go of me.

It sounds so reasonable.

And true.

"So you and Thorn show up and beat this shitbag because

you don't have the resources to take care of him any other way?" I ask.

Mick takes me into his arms and cups my chin.

I feel so fragile in his arms. So safe.

"There are some things I don't wish to delegate," he says. "Don't emasculate me by robbing me of that option. I'm rich, but I'm still a man."

"You go, Mick," Thorn says blandly.

Mick gives him the finger.

We hear stomping on my stairwell. The damn elevator's not working.

I look at Ronnie lying on the floor.

I tremble in Mick's arms. "They're going to arrest you." My eyes move to Thorn. "Or Thorn."

"It was worth it," Mick says.

I shake my head. *So not worth it.*

"Police!" yells a voice I recognize.

"Well isn't this special."

We turn and face Tagger.

His weapon never drops. Two cops move into the room, flanking him. Their eyes go from Thorn to Mick to me—then to Ronnie Bunce.

"Who's the perp?" asks one of the cops.

It bears asking since there are three bloodied males.

"Alleged," Tagger corrects.

"Oh fucking please," Thorn spouts. "Look at this wardrobe, guys—classic black with a chaser of ski mask. Seems legit."

"You, shut up." Tagger lines the barrel of his gun up with Thorn's chest.

"Hands up!"

The other cops give each other uneasy looks.

"Listen," I say, "I know this guy. He's my stepfather—missing for four years now. The police will be happy to have him, believe me."

"He broke in here and beat on me." My voice stays level.

Tagger never looks at me.

"Tagger," one of the other cops, *Largent,* says. "Let's cuff the suspect and call the medics."

"We're doing this my way. I've had trouble with Mr. Simon here." Tagger smirks.

Thorn's face goes rigid.

"I paid my dues for something I didn't have anything to do with. So you can get off my dick."

Tagger steps forward and pistol whips Thorn across the face.

Blood flies, and Thorn stumbles backward into Mick.

It's so unexpected we all stand there in shock.

Mick's lips curl back in a baring of teeth that is so incongruous with his typical elegance. He steps into Tagger and swings, but the gun gets in the way.

It flies, the safety apparently off as a bullet embeds itself in my wall.

I scream and hit the floor as things slide down a horrible slippery slope I couldn't ever imagine.

Ronnie comes awake, groaning and looking pathetic for about two seconds.

His eyes roam the room, taking in Thorn's lacerated face while Tagger and Mick struggle and the other cops charge in to break them up.

Ronnie's gaze falls on me. We're a body length away from each other.

The gun lies between us.

We jump for it at the same time.

And that's when my hand decides to not cooperate. My fingers circle the grip of the fallen pistol, and Ronnie tears it out of my twitching grasp.

He turns it on me and grabs my ankle, jerking me in a hard pull beside him.

The scuffle stops.

"I'll litter the floor with her brains," he says with quiet resolve.

The circle of metal against my temple feels like an icy brand.

Death has found me too early.

The sudden silence is deafening.

All eyes go to me, a gun barrel against my head and Ronnie caressing a stocking encased ankle.

"Who's the perp now, dumbfuck?" Thorn asks, spitting bloody saliva on my wood floor.

Tagger looks as if he swallowed a dead mouse.

I feel as if I'm going to.

"Let's go, bitch. We've got some closure we need to work out."

"Faren..." Mick says.

Ronnie presses the muzzle deeper into my skin, and I can't stop the hiccuping sob that erupts.

"Stand up, slut," Ronnie says.

He jerks me up by my armpit.

Mick's and Thorn's hands are clenched in fists they can't use.

I bet they're both wishing I'd let them kill Ronnie.

I know I am.

Tagger steps forward. "Listen, Bunce, this isn't going to work."

I can't keep the shock off my face.

"What. The. Fuck," Thorn asks.

Largent and Duffin, the other cop, looked just as shocked as the rest of us.

Everyone is looking at Tagger.

With suspicion.

Except Mick. He watches the beaten but emboldened Ronnie who is slowly backing out the door with me.

"Stop," Tagger says.

"Nah, my days of informing for you are over. You've got your scapegoat, and you don't need me. Let me take care of my long overdue business with her."

I feel his hand like a band of steel on the back of my neck, slick with blood as he shakes me.

Mick's eyes tail me, and he gives a small swivel of his head.

Don't fight him.

"You can't put the drop on me without hurting the girl," Ronnie says. "Blame it on Tyson. That's what you want."

Thorn laughs, taking a shaky hand away from his split lip.

"Figures."

Mick steps forward. "This man's a criminal. He broke into my girlfriend's apartment."

"A second offense," Thorn interjects.

Mick nods. "We came to her defense, and you"—Mick points at Tagger—"allowed her into harm's way."

"Tyson's going down for this," Tagger says in a low voice, tearing out a small pistol from an ankle holster and raising it to Thorn's chest again.

Mick's outrage is comical, or it would be if Ronnie wasn't hauling me out the door.

Largent turns his pistol on Tagger.

His stays on Thorn.

"Tagger," Largent says, "you have the wrong perp."

Duffin's pistol is trained on Ronnie, and me by association.

"No, he's always been the right one," Tagger answers in a dreamy voice.

Thorn puts up his hands, Mick is watching Ronnie slide me completely out the door.

I hear the hammer click.

A gun goes off, and I see the flash before my eyes clench. The vision of Thorn's beautiful muscular rawness, dying in a pool of blood, fills my mind.

I open my eyes and see Tagger on the floor, bleeding.

Duffin's gun sinks to his side, a look of dumbfounded realization on his face.

I don't see much more because Ronnie drags me down the hall.

A second flash momentarily blinds as the crack of gunfire deafens me in the shallow corridor stairwell as he disables the door with a bullet.

We make our way down the stairs. My pretty high heels echo through the fog of my hearing.

How Ronnie is still alive and walking after what Thorn and Mick did to him numbs me.

He tears me out of my apartment building, and the last thing I see before he stuffs me into his car is the Out of Order sign on the shitty freight elevator.

They can't get to me in time. Fate's asserted itself neatly into the space reserved for my untimely death.

It doesn't seem fair. My chest is tight with destiny's inevitability.

Ronnie has nine lives, and I don't have even one to spare.

CHAPTER 10

Ronnie slows the car in front of my mom's care facility. The thick air of the car suffocates me. I'm going to barf right now. He's come to hurt my mom. Mick doesn't matter at this point.

I don't even matter at this point.

He'd planned it all. The car had been waiting, he'd driven straight to where it all began.

My whole miserable focus for the last few weeks has been on providing whatever bit of comfort I can for her.

"No," I say in a low voice. "Just kill me." Then I laugh.

I laugh until I'm hysterical.

I don't even feel the gun hit me. I slump against the window, hiccups stutter out of my mouth instead of the horrible laughter of the insane.

"Shut up, Faren."

I swing my head around. The pain is nothing, the realization everything.

"Kill me, kill me, kill me. I'm dead anyway."

"You'll die when I'm ready for you to die, and not a fucking minute before."

Something flows down and settles between the crevice of my breasts.

Ronnie watches the blood and licks his dry lips. He grabs my breast and squeezes painfully.

I don't respond.

I'm numb inside the shell of who I am.

"Tannin gets to listen to you beg for it. Then I'm going to do her—and splatter her vegetable brains all over the place."

I groan at the thought of my mom having to witness that.

They say coma patients can still hear something. That's why I am so faithful about visiting.

Ronnie puts the barrel of the gun against my mouth as his hand kneads my unwilling flesh. He flicks my lips open with the cold tip.

I open my mouth.

"Shoot me," I say around the barrel.

It comes out intelligible, but Ronnie's eyes narrow and his face tells me he knows what I said.

"You fucking crazy bitch!" He flinches back from me in shock, wheezing like a teapot out of his clearly broken nose.

I jerk my face back. "I'm fucking terminal, you dipshit! I've got months to live anyway."

"Kill me now or kill me later—*I'm still dying.*"

My words ring in the car. Ronnie has the honor of being the second person I've told.

We stare at each other.

I watch the wheels of his sadistic mind turn.

Ronnie smirks. "Then it's a mercy fuck and kill in one deal. Get your sweet ass out of the car."

I get out of the car, and so does Ronnie, training the gun on me.

People on the sidewalk move out of the way like the Dead Sea parting. One idiot takes video with his phone.

Can he call 911?

No.

"Fuck off," Ronnie says to the amateur cinematographer, swinging the gun his way.

The guy takes off in a jerky trot.

We walk up the steps to my mom's clinic. Ronnie tells me how to open the doors, where to walk, how far.

"Where's her room?" he asks.

"No."

He points the gun at my kneecap. "I can still fuck you with a shattered knee."

There's no physical therapy for that.

"I'll just keep taking chunks out of ya until there's only little bits of Faren left."

His eyes gleam manically. "And still, there'll be enough for me to play with. With Tannin as the perfect audience of one. Now speak, little puppy."

I tell him.

There's no helping my mom. He'll do what he says.

I know he will.

We make our way toward my mom.

Orderlies pass us. Some see the gun, most don't. They're not looking for it.

We get to my mom's door and he jerks his head toward it. Everything burns.

My eyes wishing for tears to relieve the pain.

My guts.

My head.

I push the door open. There she is, almost as white as the sheet she lies against.

I gasp and enter.

"I'm sorry, Mama," I whisper.

"She looks like shit," Ronnie says from behind me.

I hang my head as he pushes me in farther.

I look up and meet Doctor Forrester's troubled gaze.

"Hey, Doc," Ronnie says.

"What is the meaning of this, Faren?" Doctor Forrester asks, looking between me and Ronnie.

She can't see the gun.

"I..."

How do you explain the inexplicable?

She gives me a small smile but frowns at Ronnie. I can tell he's given her pause. He's crude and doesn't seem to make sense being with me.

If she only knew.

Then there's the blood and our obvious injuries. That would be enough to throw the dumbest person off base.

She looks confused, but she keeps trying to delve silently into what this is about.

"I've been trying to reach you," Forrester says.

"Your mother has... well..." She steps aside to fully reveal my mom.

Tannin Mitchell blinks at me.

My mom's awake.

THERE IS a moment of crystal realization.

My mom's eyes move to Ronnie behind me, then to mine.

She always was my own personal mind reader. That's still there, in her expression, in the body that holds her prisoner in deep atrophy.

Her eyes widen, telling me something.

I guess she's seen the gun.

I know the message. I get it loud and clear.

Fight.

Ronnie doesn't expect that Faren the little mouse, who took every beating he ever delivered, would fight back.

I don't either.

It's purely reactive, instinctual; I'm ruthlessly glad.

I know he can't pull the trigger as fast as I can bat the gun away at this distance.

There is more than just me to fight for.

I slap the barrel away. It flings his arm out to the side, and I step into Ronnie's body, ramming my elbow into his already bashed nose.

His reach is longer, so I don't give him anything to latch onto.

I don't think about anything but my mom.

A frantic buzzing pierces my consciousness, but I ignore it.

Emergency buzzer.

Ronnie staggers back, trying to turn the pistol on me again and I jab him in the throat with my knuckles. He drops the gun to grab his neck.

I know anatomy, and I use my knowledge as a weapon.

I stab my heel onto the top of his foot. He falls to the ground, hands slapping behind to brace his fall. Instead, he's too unbalanced and lands on his back.

The gun spins on the slick hospital tiles when I kick it away. I move forward with a vicious disregard for life.

I rear back and stab my heel into his throat until it meets the vertebrae of his C spine region.

I put my body weight into it. I feel the resistance of the flesh, tendon, and muscle as I spear it.

"Faren!"

Someone calls my name.

I hear it as though I'm underwater.

"Faren!"

The frantic voice doesn't deter my grisly goal.

I grind my heel, finally to the bone, and hear the gurgling of a life ending. My knowledge of anatomy is saving me. And killing Ronnie.

Strong arms jerk me from what I'm doing. I hear a sucking pop as my stiletto leaves Ronnie's trachea.

Mick swings me into his arms, squeezing me so tightly I can't breathe.

Or maybe it's the view over his shoulder that steals the air from my lungs.

Tears stream out of my mom's eyes.

Yeah, that could be it.

I WATCH the mop swish back and forth as I hold my mom's hand.

The bleach burns my nostrils.

The forensic crew has come and gone and Mick stands vigil beside me.

He has almost as many people in the room as the police.

My evening has been such a nightmare of corruption that the police concede to the presence of a publicist, two bodyguards, a lawyer, and a personal physician.

Doctor Forrester corroborates everything that happened. Duffin and Largent admit Tagger went off the deep end. Mick barks into his cell. I listen to him orchestrate everything.

My mom can't talk, but her face says plenty. I answer the questions I see there.

Telling my mom how long she has been sleeping is the hardest.

More tears fall.

I can't tell her about my diagnosis.

"Yes, Faren will need a full diagnostic," Mick says into his phone.

My face swings to Mick. "I'm fine."

Fear coils like a snake in my belly. He doesn't need to find out like this.

Mick cups the back of my head. "Let me take care of you, baby."

I melt at *baby*. My mouth quivers, and his thumb runs over my lip, his eyes meeting mine.

He says into his cell, "I want it now, whatever the cost."

Mick's eyes flick at two men who bleed out of the shadowed corners of the room. One moves to position himself to sight the door. The other settles into the corner that is closest to my mom.

The bodyguards in the room aren't for me.

They're for my mom.

Now it's a rainforest of tears.

I grip mom's hand and she gives the lightest squeeze back.

"I can't leave her," I choke out through a shuddering series of gulps.

Doctor Forrester puts a hand on my shoulder. "She needs to rest, Faren. Waking like she did—I've never seen that in a patient who has been in a coma this long."

She gives me steady eye contact. "The small movements Tannin made, we didn't *think* they were purposeful."

Apparently, they'd been a precursor of sorts to her waking.

She lifts her shoulders. "After this... horrible event, Tannin needs stability and calm."

"And you do too." Her eyes hold sympathy.

Forrester squeezes my hands. "Take care of Faren, and let me take care of Tannin."

Mom looks at me from eyes so much like my own.

It's such a gift to see them.

My vision shimmers with tears well.

I let Mick's personal physician take me for a checkup.

It's the hardest thing I've ever done.

I leave hope behind, grabbing onto the faith that it'll still be there when I return.

CHAPTER 11

"Don't move, Ms. Mitchell." His voice reverberates inside the sausage tube. That's my nickname for it.

The banging begins, and I grit my teeth. Mick wants to make sure I don't have any soft tissue damage from my altercation with Ronnie.

I don't have any broken bones, but bruises pepper my fair skin and my ribcage is sore when I breathe.

Mick's eyes were dark when he saw many of the marks were Ronnie's fingerprints. A reminder of how terrible it could have been.

Any of us could have died.

I close my eyes as the rhythm of the cat scan beats against me.

A clear memory of my stiletto being bagged fills my mind, the heel thick with Ronnie's shredded throat.

I open my eyes to the sudden silence. The machine whirs, and my body jerks as I slide out of the tight capsule.

Dr. Ludwig helps me off the platform, and I stand and sway, suddenly dizzy.

"Hey now." He steadies me. "You okay?"

No. Fainting, vertigo and loss of consciousness follow me everywhere I go.

I laugh at my own thoughts.

His brows pull together like conjoined caterpillars.

I belatedly realize how weird my reaction is.

I lace my hands, his palm circles my bare elbow. "Yeah, I'm fine... just a big day."

He clears his throat. "Yes, it would be a trauma for anyone. But in your case... fending off an attacker in collusion with your mother's miraculous recovery..."

Miraculous.

That word floats around in my head while Ludwig makes all the right noises. He guides me to the room where my blood will be drawn.

"Do I need all this?" I ask.

"Ms. Mitchell, Mr. McKenna insists."

"I just bet he does." My eyes narrow. "And you're his personal physician?"

He gives a sage nod. "He is my sole patient. Though I am called upon to treat... others from time to time."

Our gazes meet.

I think we understand each other.

Ludwig smiles and I notice his teeth are crooked and bleached a bright white. "Then you understand the tenor of our Mr. McKenna."

Mick gets what he wants. Gotcha.

I nod.

"Good girl." He sweeps his palm toward the door where the physician's assistant sits at nine o'clock at night. No one mutters discontent when Mick says they'll draw my blood—they just do it.

I turn away when my blood fills the tube. I've seen enough blood for a lifetime.

I walk out of the cloistered suite of offices. A low lamp burns in the vacant reception area, casting circular shadows like dropped coins. Mick waits behind a semi-partitioned area, potted plants around head height veil us from the front entrance.

Outside the doors are about fifty reporters, newspeople, and every nosey ass within a fifty-mile radius.

Mick, seated in the reception room, stands when he sees me.

His cufflinks are MIA, his shirt sleeves rolled up to his elbows.

My eyes follow the dots of blood speckling his shirt. They grows larger as he draws nearer.

The blood.

I'm suddenly pressed against his chest, trying to ignore the blatant evidence of our night while he strokes my hair.

"You're okay," he whispers.

I lean back, seeing the shadow of fire against his chin. His beard is so much more red than his hair.

"I'm fine."

I lower my head, inhaling deeply. "Actually, I don't know how the hell I feel."

I tilt my chin up.

"My mom wakes up the day a psycho manages to almost kill me in front of her. It's too much to take in."

Muffled noise like bugs swarming infiltrate where we stand.

I peek out at all the people waiting for us.

Thorn strolls up.

"Oh my god, Thorn!" I say when I see his face. "Where'd you come from?"

He jerks a thumb behind him at the back entrance where the silhouette of Henry patiently waits. "Laying low, girl."

A huge cut bisects his black brow. His upper eyelid is

swollen like a blowfish, and he's so full of piss and vinegar it's coming off him in waves.

He glances at the locked doors that hold back Paparazzi Hell. "Let's scat. There's a bunch of news whores out there waiting to make our lives miserable."

"What about the police?" I ask.

"They couldn't do much with me. I have a record"—he puts a hand to his chest—"I don't deserve. But Duffin and Largent had to turn on Tagger. All kinds of shit is oozing out of that woodwork."

Mick curls his arm around my shoulders. "Henry's waiting out back."

Then I see them. It takes a moment to understand. I'm a little slow from everything that's happened.

A couple who looks a lot like Mick and me walks up. Seeing someone who looks that much like me is surreal.

Though it's rude, I check her out.

"What?" I cover my mouth.

"Decoys," Thorn says, ambling toward the rear entrance.

"Yeah..." I say.

The girl's a little shorter than me, her hair a tad more blond, her eyes a pale green.

She smirks, and I know the resemblance is superficial. I can see how soft and young her eyes look.

But the reporters won't see that.

I shake my head. *It's damn smart.*

"Wow," is all I can say.

The guy looks a little like Mick in build but let's face it, how many men are running around at six feet three with dark auburn hair and rich chocolate brown eyes?

This guy's got reddish brown hair at best and his eyes are hazel.

"Close enough," Mick says, clapping the guy on the back.

"Thanks, Spence."

The guy lifts his chin. "Anytime, Mr. McKenna."

He and my double link hands as they move around the partition and walk toward the waiting throng

"Who are they?" I ask.

Mick caresses my newly injured face and kisses the tip of my nose. "Actors."

"Really?" I laugh. The night couldn't get any more weird.

He tugs me toward the back door that Thorn impatiently holds open.

I can feel the heat of the bulbs as lights snap and pop at the imposters.

Mick puts a hand at the small of my back and guides me quietly through the narrow back entrance.

I see Henry waiting in the gloom of the only streetlight for an entire block.

* * *

I USE my left hand for balance and slide in the limo.

Thorn hops in opposite me, and Mick follows. Thorn kicks out his legs, his hands loose and dangling on his thighs.

I say, "How can..."

Henry shuts the door and moves around to the front of the limo.

"Mick shelled out the big bucks so we could escape the bullshit," Thorn says.

Mick inclines his head. "It was either that or have you microscopically inspected after such a fucked up night."

Thorn chuckles. "I think there's a word to describe tonight, but I can't think of what it is."

"Colossal fuck up," I say.

They look at me, and

Mick bursts out laughing.

I bite my lip.

"How's my mom?"

Mick's eyes are compassionate.

"I'm in constant contact with Forrester. Tannin is sleeping."

"Damn, hasn't she been sleeping for years?" Thorn asks in his typical subtle way.

Mick shakes his head. "From what Forrester says, it's typical for a patient to exhaust themselves quickly after their first awakening."

Awakening.

I sigh, leaning into Mick's arm, and he presses me against his chest.

He is solid, real, and I close my eyes. It's a sort of simple bliss.

"You're coming home with me tonight," Mick says.

I open my mouth, and he kisses it.

Thoroughly... in front of Thorn.

I sink into him as though he's the last solid thing on earth. My rock.

Mick lifts his mouth from mine. "She's safe, Faren. I have two guards with her. One inside the room and one outside. They'll keep her safe."

I gnaw at my lip. I can't stand it if she's in a coma again. Her waking up once would be the worse tease in the world.

Mick nuzzles against my neck.

Hard stubble and warm breath send a riot of gooseflesh down my arms.

"It's normal slumber, not the kind she's been in for years."

"Good," I say, relaxing against him.

"We'll go see her first thing tomorrow morning. But right now, you need to be fed and watered."

I pull away with a laugh. "Like a plant?"

His eyes become molten. He grips my shoulders and

brings my mouth to his, crashing his lips so hard against mine it's almost painful.

"My plant," he whispers with possession so intense it should frighten me.

But I'm not scared of him. I'm scared of how I feel.

"Let my bro take care of you, Faren."

Both of us forgot about Thorn.

His grin is a slash of white in the dim light.

We smile back.

I settle into the circle of Mick's arms, with Thorn the perfect watchdog. Brutal, loyal, and cunning.

I feel safe for the first time in my life and try not to think about how anticlimactic that is. Instead, I revel in the moment like I've trained myself to.

I don't tell them I think Ronnie killed Rose.

He's dead now. He can't hurt anyone anymore.

CHAPTER 12

Thorn's eyes follow us all the way to the giant glass door's of the Millennium Tower.

He disappears behind the mirrored glass of the car window when Henry closes the door.

I flutter my fingers in a little wave but can't see if he waves back.

Mick guides me inside, both of us beat up.

His hands look terrible, brutalized with raw gelled abrasions where skin is completely gone.

My face looks like exactly what happened: I got slapped hard. With flesh and metal.

I'm beyond exhaustion.

"We got lucky there," Mick murmurs as he passes Tom the doorman. "Not having to deal with the media."

I doubt our lookalikes feel that way.

Tom looks at me with wide eyes that say he hopes he's got a job tomorrow.

I suppress a giggle by a hairsbreadth.

I'm sure he thought I was a permanent has been after the trumped up assault charges.

Now I might be semi-permanently here.

Mick lifts my hand to his mouth as the elevator moves toward the nineteenth floor.

As his soft lips migrate, the crook of my elbow comes to life. I spear the fingers of my left hand through the thick hair that sinks into the bend of my arm.

His mouth works upward until it reaches the farthest end of my clavicle.

When Mick finds the pulse at the base of my throat, the doors slide open. He picks me up, his hands cupping my ass.

I don't hear the keyed entry beep because my arms are wound around Mick's neck, and his hands are deep underneath the dress I wore for him.

He kicks the door shut and takes me straight to the shower. Mick sets me down in front of the glass walls.

I begin on the buttons of his shirt as he unzips the back of my dress.

The dress slips down my curves, getting caught on my hips. Mick's eyes flare at seeing the shimmer of fabric hanging on the widest part of me.

My naked breasts sway as I shimmy out of it and the dress glides to the floor in a glittering pile to join his ruined shirt.

Mick unzips his slacks and tosses them off with a flick of his foot. They cover my dress, then it's he that covers me with his naked body.

He steps on his underwear as he corners me inside the glass shower.

Mick throws a blind hand back and hits the faucet. The water sounds like rain as it steams the inside of the shower, the fog of heat insulating us together in a hot press of wet flesh.

I push Mick into the stream and it sluices around his head, stinging and hot against me. His hands flow over my shoulders and reach behind me to return filled with fragrant soap. It's not vanilla or citrus or something I'm used to but a fresh musk. It's watered silk over my body, his tongue is slick heat on my lips.

I gasp as he cleans me, first one finger then another dipping inside me as his tongue takes mine. Our kissing becomes so deep Mick moves out of the spray and hikes one of my legs up in a soft loop with his forearm as his fingers pump inside me.

Back and forth his fingers plunge in an expert slide.

Though exhaustion weighs my body down with fatigue, Mick's hands make me weightless with his tender persistence.

We need this.

No words, just water, soap, and our bodies in the humming quiet of a shower as big as my bathroom.

He doesn't break his pace, and my legs quiver around his fingers as they breach me, pull out and sink into my heat again.

I shudder as he drives me against the wall of my orgasm. I climb it and at the shivering top his hands leave my body. I stand quaking at the chasm of crashing release as he turns off the water and wraps me in a towel.

My core pulses. I look into his eyes for what I know he will do—what he'll finish.

Mick scoops me up, and kissing me, he moves to the bedroom. He lays me on the bed and stares at me.

Then unwraps me like a precious gift.

I want to replay this moment forever, the finest of my life: Mick's face as he looks at me as though I'm a found treasure.

It's a certain look a man holds for a woman. I know that because I've seen a lot of men look at me... and none has ever had that same look in his eyes.

My sex throbs in time to my heartbeat. His attentions in the shower erased a thin layer of filth I didn't know I owned.

Mick's love releases me.

He doesn't say the words, but I know.

He crawls over the bed, and I see the rose tat.

His mouth settles on my tender center, and I cry out, knowing he'll take care of me.

Mick takes his time, a slow revolution of his tongue moving down the side of my slit with a soft suction that causes my hips to flinch. He weighs me down with large hands on my thighs.

He spreads my body deliciously as he licks and sucks the other side. When his tongue finds my clit, he rubs the flat of his tongue back and forth.

My pussy gives a slow, deep pulse, and I know he'll shatter me.

Pieces of me fly like released doves, and I scream as the rhythm of his tongue slows perfectly. I become so sensitive even his breath makes me shiver.

A finger presses inside my pulsating core, diving deep, and I buck with want.

I open my eyes, satiated and languid.

I nod at him slowly, and he smiles, lowering himself into the well of my hips. His penis nudges me, and I widen my legs.

Mick enters slowly, his eyes on mine, his cock burying inside me with a smooth rock and retreat.

Mick dips his forehead until it touches mine.

I wrap my legs around his waist, pleasantly surprised by the smooth glide of his flesh inside me. All him—in all of me.

I croon against his neck, gently shoving against him as he rocks deeper.

"Don't you move a muscle," Mick growls.

I still.

Then I laugh—hard. I can't help it. My walls grip him like a glove.

"God, Faren!" Mick says. "I have to now..."

He pumps inside me, moving hard to the end of me then pulling out. I hike up my hips, and he slides his hands under my ass.

He fucks me with my own body, jerking my hips forward against his hardness.

He whispers, "I'm going to come in you now."

Those words split me open. His dick hardens even more, and I clamp him as I pulsate against his release.

I suck him down, and he gives me all. We're a circle of physical perfection I didn't realize existed.

We are suspended for that frozen moment of ecstasy, and when we can breathe again, Mick detangles from me and slides me in tight against him.

He smoothes my hair away from my sore face and kisses the abrasion Ronnie made.

I feel his heartbeat against my back. Strong. Sure.

"Don't you leave me, Faren."

My eyes close as I lie. "Never."

"I am who I was meant to be when I'm with you. I'm whole."

I feel the same.

I settle for the one truth I feel in my bones.

"I love you."

Mick turns me over, his hand mounding my breast.

"Not more than me."

I promise myself no more tears.

I lie.

CHAPTER 13

ONE WEEK LATER

I have a new hate for the news. I don't know which is worse: that we're all safe and no one went to prison or that every waking moment someone tries to accost me around every corner.

The paparazzi hang around the entrance to my mom's clinic like vultures with their sights set on carrion.

I can't wait until we move my mom somewhere undisclosed in the middle of the night under police escort.

Tannin Mitchell is awake, and she's looking at a full recovery—a new life.

Was it my almost daily vigil?

Was it her favorite perfume I wafted under her nose?

Was it the music that I played that had fed her soul before?

We'll never know.

All I know is that I have to tell her I'm dying, and I can't.

Kiki is being stalked almost as unmercifully as Mick and me, but Thorn scares them to a nice safe distance.

Tagger gets the grace of bureaucratic tape in his favor. His wound was superficial. All three cops are on administrative leave pending investigation, and we were sworn to secrecy under threat of lawsuit.

Tagger's agenda poisoned the waters we must swim in. While he recovers and his motives remain veiled in secrecy until the slow wheels of justice finish turning, we're under the microscope.

I'm healing up nicely, but wounds that can't be seen remain. Ronnie is dead by my hand.

Or heel.

I lean against Mick's shoulder as we drive to the clinic to visit Doctor Ludwig.

He has news.

I know exactly what it is, and I should be frightened that my lies are about to be uncovered.

Then those words come to me that Mick told me a week ago when he made love to me in increments.

The shower.

The bed.

I feel my face heat when I think about all the other places he's taken me to the moon and back.

Maybe he'll still take me there when he finds out I'm dying. Maybe there won't be a place in the world where he won't go.

Where I won't follow.

*　*　*

OUR HANDS ARE LACED, and I can't stop the dampness in mine.

Mick raises our hands and brushes his lips over my knuckles. "Dr. Ludwig, I'm not sure why you couldn't tell us over the phone if everything is fine."

His eyes are sedate; mine are wide with the news he'll receive.

My fear of my inevitable discovery crushes me.

"Faren?" Dr. Ludwig gets my attention.

I can tell I've missed the first summons.

Mick smiles at his distraction of me, and our hands drop.

"Your blood work came back, and there were some trace chemicals found."

This is not what I expect.

"What?" My voice sounds thick, hesitant.

"Are you taking any medication? For seizures or something else? You listed birth control pills as your only medication?"

I look at his pleasantly neutral face and rack by brain. I feel Mick's eyes on me.

I shake my head slowly.

Oh!

When I remember, I drop Mick's hand with a small smile.

I take Kiki's migraine medication out from my purse and hold it up for Ludwig's perusal.

The sun turns the orange bottle to fire, and a disquieting premonition flows through me.

My cell chimes softly from inside my purse, but I ignore it.

Ludwig's brows pull together.

"This is for a... Kandace King?"

"Yes, it's my girlfriend's."

His frown deepens. "It's never a good practice to take medication from someone else."

I shrug. *Like it matters?* I glance at my cell. Jay's name flashes in my voicemail.

It freezes me. But I ignore what that means, coming back to our conversation. "She uses it for migraines."

I used it too before I knew.

"Well, this is Topomax," he says.

Mick and I wait.

87

"I haven't used it for a little while," I explain.

"Often enough."

He's being cryptic. Mick says, "Just tell us what the problem is." His patience has thinned the normally deep rumble of his voice to a sharpened grate.

"Topomax is known for not mixing well with other medications."

My mind tumbles over his words like clothes in a dryer.

Birth control.

I grip the edge of his desk.

"I can see this wasn't what you were expecting," Dr. Ludwig says.

A horrible epiphany inserts itself in my brain.

"What the hell is going on?" Mick turns to me.

I jerk my face to his.

"I never skipped a pill," I promise in a rush.

He knew I was on them. I told him when he never asked.

Mick's brows hike and freeze.

Ludwig looks between the two of us.

"Topomax interferes with the absorption of certain medications." He inclines his head toward me.

His face is not so neutral now.

"You are pregnant."

Three words.

So different than the two words that began it all.

I slump back in my chair and exhale like a deflated balloon.

How can I be dying when there is a life inside me?

CHAPTER 14

The news comes as such a shock, it never occurs to me that Doctor Ludwig said nothing about my condition.

My terminal one.

Mick is quiet as he leads me out of Ludwig's office, but he holds my hand. He hasn't dumped me yet. The virgin who got pregnant her first time. Unheard of.

I know there's probably been someone else in the history of the universe who got pregnant with her first encounter, but why did it have to be me?

* * *

Henry grows larger as we solemnly make our way to the limo. His eyes tighten slightly at our expressions, but he's too classy to comment.

I don't risk a glance at Mick. He might ask the unthinkable.

To end the baby's life. It's early—doable.

It makes so much sense on too many levels.

But I can't.

I'm all for a woman's right to choose, and I'm executing my rights at this very moment.

We slide into the heated interior where champagne chills inside a bucket.

"I can't have that." I fold my arms and scoot across the limo seat.

Mick smirks, the first actual expression he's shown.

It makes me angrier.

"What?" I huff. I just want him to get it over with. *Dump me already.*

He leans toward the neck of the bottle and wraps strong fingers around it.

Slowly, he turns it until the label faces me.

Sparkling apple cider.

I blink. I can't rip my gaze from him as the limo pulls away.

He says nothing as he pops the cork. His dexterous fingers clink the long-stemmed champagne glasses as he fills them.

Golden bubbles tease the inside of the crystal as he hands me my glass.

My shaky fingers close around the chilly exterior and slide down to the stem.

Mick catches my tear with the pad of his thumb.

"What kind of man would I be if I didn't celebrate our child?"

The dam of my emotions bursts. Mick takes the glass back before hauling me into his lap. I fit so neatly, almost child-sized in his arms. He folds me against him tightly as though I'm a precious bundle, not just a woman.

"Shush, Faren," he murmurs, stroking my back. "I'm not going to leave you."

It's too much.

Too many revelations. Too much truth.

Too much of what I can never have staring me in the face.

I dry my eyes with the back of my hand.

I know what I can do. What I must do.

I have to live long enough to have this baby. I need to do it for Mick and the little he or she who's the size of a kidney bean right now.

His finger lifts my chin until our noses almost brush. "Listen to me."

I still under his touch.

"I love you."

I nod. I love him so much. My soul, my guts, my head... they're so in tune with my emotions, I feel as if my heart beats only for him.

Though that's not true. Now it beats for two.

"I knew from the moment I saw you I wanted only you."

His eyes love every plane of my face. Mick leans back to place his palm on my flat belly.

My shoulders drop, and I relax. "You're not going to dump me?" My eyes search his. "Because I wasn't trying to... trap you."

"I could have worn protection." Mick's brows rise as he assumes part of the guilt.

I shake my head. "Why didn't you? I mean—"

He puts his finger to my lips. "You said you were taking the pill, and I assumed that would be sufficient. And"—his eyes crinkle at the corners as pools of light slant across his face through the car window, a beat without music—"I wanted to feel you."

My head dips, and I snuggle deeper into the lap nest he's made for me.

Henry turns the limo as the Millennium grows closer, and Mick secures me tighter against him.

"So you always wore a rubber with other women?"

He doesn't hesitate. "Yes."

I look up. I can't believe I give a crap. "Have there been a lot of women?"

"Yes." His face is serious, eyes deep.

Shadows slay his expression, then the streetlights illuminate him in profile.

"Oh," I say in a small voice. Every insecurity I've had crashes on top of my head, crushing me.

Mick's hand finds my jaw, and he lifts my face level with his.

"I have never loved another woman." Those eyes probe mine. "I'm almost thirty years old, and I've had meaningless sex—a hundred times..."

I gasp, and he inclines his head at the number.

God, my goose is cooked! I feel ridiculous. He must have thought all my first-time throes of passion foolish.

Heat suffuses my face, and I jerk away from his fingers.

His hand slides from my jaw into my hair as Henry parks.

"No you don't," Mick says in a low voice. His grip tightens to just shy of pain. "Look. At. Me."

My eyes open, and I feel my gaze seethe at him.

"I've fucked a lot of women." His other arm snakes around my waist and jerks me closer, his breath hot against my face. "But you... you I made love to."

Henry raps on the glass, and Mick holds up a finger. A white glove appears against the dark glass, then Henry retreats, one hand crossing over the other as he waits for Mick's bidding.

I don't know what to say.

I've only been with him—I don't have another point of reference. "I haven't been with anyone else..."

"And you won't."

His eyes narrow. "I'm not about to share the only woman I've ever found who makes my knees weak. An expression I thought was a lie until I experienced it." His expression turns sheepish around the edges.

I laugh. "I do?" He's got to be feeding me a line of first-class bullshit.

"Why do you think I took you out of the shower without finishing you?"

My blood rushes back to the surface of my skin as I remember how expertly he worked me over in that cocoon of wet heat.

"I didn't know why."

"Because no matter how hard I hit the gym, it isn't enough to combat the Faren Mitchell affect."

A dimple on his cheek winks at me and is gone.

I'm very aware that we're keeping Henry, but I've got to know. I meet his stare, the ghost of a smile still touching his lips.

"Is there a difference?"

Mick's lips turn up at the corners. "Between fucking and making love?"

I glance at my hands.

He says nothing.

I take a deep breath. "Yeah."

"I didn't think so." His fingers slacken in my hair, unwinding reluctantly.

"And now?" I ask, though I know I shouldn't. It's torturous to think of Mick with anyone but me.

Like it was torture for him to walk in on Jay and me.

"Now"—he cocks his head—"I know that when I'm fucking you, I'm loving you." He grips my shoulders. "With you, it's synonymous. I can't take the love out of the sex, Faren."

His combination of crude words and raw truth undoes me. I fall forward, and Mick holds me.

Henry waits as the car purrs beneath us.

Mick says, "I've moved your things to my condo."

I pull back. "What?"

"I can't have you staying somewhere that's so easy to compromise."

It's too fast. My head's spinning. My stuff? Someone went through all my shit, and now it's in his place....

He's watching my expression. "Hold on." He grabs the handle as Henry finishes opening the door.

"Sir?"

"We're ready."

I'm not. But I let Mick lead me down that red carpet and through the glass doors. We traverse the elegant foyer and pass a doorman I don't know.

When we're in the elevator, I open my mouth to let him know how much I despise people managing me.

His tongue is there, stealing my thoughts before I can voice them.

I sigh, my resolve weak while Mick presses me against the hard elevator. His hands are everywhere, and mine wind around his neck.

"No," I say.

He sucks my bottom lip inside his mouth.

"Quiet."

I succumb as he whips me around and through the elevator doors as they whisper open.

He walks us to his door and slides the card through the keyed entry as I maul his lips.

"We're not talking right now, Faren." Mick groans against my neck, kicking the door shut.

"I need you... I need in you." His lips land on my throat again.

I plow through his hair, fisting it. "To fuck?"

He stops, and my flesh cools without his lips against it.

His gaze meets mine.

My bad hand spasms in his hair.

I watch his heart beat in the hollow of his neck.

"To love," he answers.

I don't catch the tears that leak out.

Mick carries me to the bedroom. My uncertainty stays at the door.

CHAPTER 15

Our clothes decorate every surface like bread crumbs as we move to Mick's bedroom. My bra hangs off the doorknob and his suit litters the ground in a discarded trail.

His face is somber as Mick lays my naked body on his bed. There is lust there, but there is also care. I rest my head against the pillow and look at him.

"You spend too much time crying," Mick comments. He slides between my legs, swimmingly close to my pussy.

I sigh with anticipation.

I could never have enough of what he gives me. I'm so greedy it feels like an addiction.

His face rests against my thigh, and the little bit of stubble rasps my sensitive skin.

I shiver as his breath steals over my center, and those brown eyes crest over my pubic bone as I gaze at him.

"I know," I say.

His finger runs up and down my opposite thigh until my breath catches, and he spreads me farther apart.

I groan as his finger enters me softly but without hesitation. It glides deeply inside then out.

He keeps up the gentle, insistent friction until I'm drenching his hand.

I try to move my hips to meet his rhythm, but his mouth is on my slit, digging against me, and I don't want to move.

His tongue finds my clit, and he strokes back and forth against it. I clench around his finger and pant with each brush of his tongue.

"No. More. Tears," Mick says softly, adding another finger until he forms a little scoop inside my channel.

He teases that sensitive spot up high, and I pause on the ledge.

Then his fingers move deeper and his tongue pins my clit even as he spreads my folds wide. I come hard, my hands fisting the sheets, my head thrown back as ecstasy floods my system. My core grabs at his retreating fingers.

His mouth stays hot and tight against my clit, lifting only to be replaced with his tip.

Mick uses my wetness to slide the length of him against my swollen nub. I move against him, riding the residual wave of my orgasm. A second wave crashes after the first, and Mick fills me with his cock, slamming it into my swollen depths. We're fitted together so deeply, I can't feel where he begins and I end—one flesh, a single consumption of need and lust.

As I think it, Mick holds my face and presses impossibly deeper.

"I'm not crying."

I gasp as he rocks harder.

So not crying.

Or thinking.

I'm a swollen, aching mass of need and sensation.

"I don't want you talking either." His low voice rumbles against my chest.

He moves his hands to my arms and pins them over my head, his hips moving, always moving.

I feel myself grow wetter, open more fully to his deep thrusts.

Mick meets the end of me and a low throb pulses from me to him.

"God, Faren." Mick puts his forehead to mine, his hands heavy against my wrists.

Our flesh slaps together as he rams inside me, and I meet each brutal stab with my legs parted farther. One of my feet dangles off the bed, and he releases my arms to put his hands on either side of me. He swivels his hips with slow, tantalizing precision, and I feel him against every part of me. My insides explode with the sensation of the hard length of him in me.

My eyes snap open.

"Oh God!" My walls clench down around him.

"Hold your feet and spread your legs," he says through his teeth.

I grab my arches, and my knees go beside my ears.

Mick slams inside me, filling me with his release. He's frozen above me, moving slightly to shift deeper, thrust more fully, and I grab his ass.

Our mutual pleasure is a symphony of groans as we grapple to connect more tightly.

I laugh as he begins to slip out.

"You can't get any deeper." I feel my goofy grin down to my toenails.

He kisses my nose and slides out all the way, tucking me half underneath him as he falls to his side.

"Can't blame me for trying."

I shake my head, my hair gliding across my naked breasts,

and he takes a nipple inside his mouth in a wet, languid pull. I thread my fingers through his hair, and he looks up at me, releasing my nipple with a pop.

Mick's hand moves to my flat stomach, caressing it over and over.

My hand covers his. "Are you sure you—"

His gaze locks with mine. "Yes."

My eyes slide away from the heat there. I might not be able to answer some of the questions I see.

"We should talk."

"Go ahead," Mick says. "I'm listening. But just so you know, I'm not having the mother of my child out of my sight."

I can't hide my smile at how overprotective he is. Even with Ronnie dead, he doesn't want to take any chances. Thank God he hasn't said anything about marriage. It's the island in the discussion, and we're the boats in the water. We've seen it, but neither one of us is going ashore.

My grin fades at how serious his expression is.

Mick's hand cups my face. "I didn't survive Rose's death and the debacle of Thorn's incarceration to lose you to preventable circumstances."

His lips close over mine.

"I won't."

He moves them over me softly.

"Ever."

My hand goes to the back of his neck.

"Okay."

A thrumming causes us both to turn our heads. His cell jitters on the dresser.

Mick frowns, bouncing off the bed and scooping up his cell.

"McKenna," he all but barks.

I slowly spread my legs as he listens to whoever's receiving his irritation.

One of my legs moves to one side of the bed then the other. I let my feet slide to the edges of the bed.

His eyes darken as he tracks my movements.

I wet my fingertip and place it on my still-engorged clit and slide it back and forth.

"Yeah," he answers in a curt syllable. His Adam's apple bobs as he swallows.

I use the fingers of my bad hand to spread myself so only my finger covers the little pink bundle of nerves.

I slide the hood back, my glistening secrets bare to him, and I watch him grow hard from ten feet away.

"I've got to go," he says.

Suddenly he turns away from me, plowing his fingers through his short hair. "Yes, I said I will."

My hands fall away from my naked glory, and Mick carefully puts down the phone.

He turns, and his half-erection gives a small lift at the sight of me.

"Fuck," Mick says without preamble.

I sit up, my playful mood expired. "What?"

He moves to the bed and grips my hair.

"I have to leave town for a few days."

The tip of him is so close I could flick it with my tongue. So I do.

His hold tightens, and I go all the way down to his base, choking myself.

Mick throws his head back in a moan that crawls out of his soul and it makes me grow wet again to hear something so primal.

He slowly fucks my mouth, and my hands cup his ass. I sit cross-legged, his hands buried in my hair, as he stabs half his length down my throat. I move his hips deeper as I grip his cheeks.

"Faren," Mick says, "you're going to make me cum."

I want it.

I don't want him to go, to leave me.

I cup his balls with one hand and deep throat him, fighting my urge to gag.

He stiffens under my hand, and his cock grows slightly harder. His release bursts between us, and I take it all.

His hands loosen from my hair, and I slide away, falling back.

He goes with me, soft and spent.

"What you do to me..."

He moves into the cradle of my body and kisses the mouth where his seed just went.

"I don't know how I'll leave you."

I meet his eyes. "Don't go."

"I have to." He groans and rolls over.

"Why?" I can't help my tone. I just found out the biggest news of my life, and I want to revel in it all weekend. I want to pretend everything's awesome and perfect, but if Mick leaves, I'll have time to think.

And I don't want to.

Mick holds me against him, looking down at my face.

"I've got this acquisition I'm working on."

I remain sullen.

Mick leans over and kisses me.

Again and again, so deeply I can't draw breath.

I shake as his finger breaches my entrance. He pumps me, and I relent, spreading my legs.

"I'm going to start up more Black Rose clubs—east coast."

Oh, that's good. For his sister.

He buries his fingers more deeply as my eyelids flutter.

I'm so close to coming again that I forget about him leaving and only feel him fucking me with his finger.

"Cum for me, Faren." He slides three fingers, like a tight triangle, inside me, and his thumb lands on my clit.

My hips buck as my orgasm pulses around his hand.

I gasp, and he catches my hoarse exhalation inside his mouth.

I gradually float down, and his fingers leave me.

His wet fingertips trail my arousal to my ankles and he grips them, easing off the bed.

"Better?" His eyebrows lift.

I nod.

Mick makes his way to the shower.

I admire his profile, the lean muscle perfectly highlighted in the light from the bathroom.

"Besides, I've been playing phone tag with this guy since we began negotiations." He shrugs. "I hear he's an asshole. At least, I hear that name more than his real one."

My heart speeds up again. I don't know why. Maybe women's intuition.

"Nothing worse than leaving you to meet Jay Hightower."

Mick whips a towel off an embedded granite peg in the tile of the bathroom wall.

"Cagey fucker," he mutters as the water turns on inside the shower.

He doesn't turn and see my expression.

I could never explain the shock.

CHAPTER 16

None of my stuff looks right in Mick's place. I put a heavy glass globe on a beautiful, glossy walnut shelf. Snow swirls around the St. Louis arch.

"You've put that in the same spot twenty times," Kiki says.

I nod. "It just looks so wrong there."

She moves behind me. "Faren."

I don't turn. I know what she's going to say.

"You've got to tell him. I mean... fuck me."

Her clothes rustle as she paces away. "I was all for pulling the wool over Mick's eyes when I thought it was a virginity toss, but now—you've got a bun in the oven, you're pickin' out drapes…"

"I'm dying."

Silence.

"Yeah," she says.

I face her. The gray of Puget Sound is my backdrop. I'm framed by the acres of glass that showcase the sea beyond and below us.

Kiki puts her hands on her hips. "Listen to me, girlfriend—he loves you. He didn't kick your hot ass out when you told him you were PG so I think you're in the clear."

My hands knot and I shake my head.

"Why didn't Ludwig tell him you're terminal?"

"I don't think they administered the tests that would give those answers."

Kiki rolls her eyes and flips her long hair behind her shoulder. "Just tell him the truth. You've come clean about why you ditched your clothes for dudes, and it was okay." Her eyebrows hike to her hairline.

"Yeah," I say slowly. Though it would never really be okay, I think I've reconciled the *why* of it.

She gestures at my belly. "And he's cool with your breeder status."

I burst out laughing.

Kiki forges ahead. "He still humping your socks off?"

I press both hands to my face to cover my blush.

She shakes her head at my obvious embarrassment. "How you ever lap danced is anyone's guess."

You do what you must.

My hands fall.

"So drop the next bomb and when he's recovered, go have lunch in Paris or something."

I really laugh then, bending over and holding my ribs. "What?"

"Moneybags is gonna have to make up for his *faux pas* of going to meet with that turd bird, Jay."

That sobers me.

He finds out your pregnant, then takes off when a pretty offer comes his way? Not cool."

My lips turn up. "I think that's 'pretty face.'"

She shrugs. "Whatever.

Kiki arrows her gaze at me. "So what's the peckerwood's story?"

I sigh. "I think he's putting me on notice."

Kiki scowls. "Oh, gotcha. He thinks he'll force the relationship with you?"

"Yes."

"You're pregnant with a billionaire's spawn."

I grin. "Yes, I'm aware."

"Well, thank Christ. Doesn't that make his little agenda go away?" She glances at her nails and picks the scarlet polish. A glittering flake falls to the glass table top.

The doorbell rings.

I turn, feeling my eyebrows cinch.

Who is it? I walk toward the door.

"Who's that?" Kiki asks, following me.

I shake my head. "I don't know... Probably Thorn."

The bell sounds again—insistent.

"Hold up, dumb ass," Kiki mutters.

I tap the code and unlock the door to Mick's condo before I swing it open.

Jay Hightower fills the doorway.

He's so much bigger when he's not beneath me in a chair.

* * *

"Well, hi, Faren."

I step back when I should slam the door in his face.

I never texted him back after the pregnancy news.

Kiki looks at my expression and turns to Jay. "Who the fuck are you?"

He gives Kiki a head-to-toe perusal of such comprehensive dismissal that she falters.

Jay doesn't answer her, giving me his attention instead.

"What…" I clear my throat. "Are you doing here?"

Jay says nothing. He looks around the condo, taking in the small touches from my apartment. The dog-eared paperbacks and the jade plant I've had since I was ten stand out.

The snow globe sits high and behind me.

I wish I could hide inside it, far away from the Jays and Ronnies of the world.

"I sent McKenna on a little goose chase with the promise of ten new flesh clubs for him. He's already where he needs to be with my assistant. It buys me time."

I feel less bad about Mick kicking his ass.

If they met, how well would that go? I'm certain Mick would recognize Jay. I notice his healing bruises are faded to vague yellow tinged smears.

"I think you need to get your rich behind out of here right now," Kiki says.

He curls his lips into a parody of her smile. It looks like a snarl.

I can't believe I thought Jay was the best lap.

He seems so bad now.

"Tell your black whore her commentary isn't needed."

Kiki's jaw drops, and I gasp, bracing for the worst.

She moves into his personal space like an exotic ebony leopard. "Your thoughts don't define me. Neither do your insults, your maneuvering, or your pompous prick bullshit. You're just a little man who wants to bully Faren for some fucked up agenda."

Oh shit.

I step forward. When Kiki gets mad, tact takes a back seat.

Of course, Jay isn't much for diplomacy. I wedge myself between Kiki and Jay as they glare at each other.

"Please, just go." I put my hand on Jay's expensive suit. His cufflinks remind me so much of Mick, it makes my mouth dry.

"Not until I have assurance that we'll continue our arrangement."

"What arrangement?" Kiki turns to me.

"He's blackmailing you?"

Kiki pushes me aside with a well-placed hip. "Listen you, *lap*. There's an assload of pussy out there that'd love whatever screwed-up shit you're selling, so go round up a bunch of hos and get while the getting's good."

Oh god.

Jay's chin kicks up as his eyes become slits. "I don't want willing pussy."

Kiki folds her arms, her chin jutting out. "So you're a rapist?"

Okay.

I walk to the door to show him out. Things have gotten way out of hand.

His strong arm snaps around my waist, and I cry out.

I'm afraid for the little bean inside me.

Jay grunts as Kiki works her magic. He releases me and turns on Kiki, his hand raised.

"You touch her, and I don't care what happens. I'll do nothing you want," I say in a low voice.

His fist freezes like an asteroid bent on landing.

Kiki's gaze stays on him. "Fuck him. If he wants to beat on women, let him. He can leave a mark, and then he's Right. Where. I. Want. Him."

His hand drops and stays clenched by his side.

Their chests heave as Kiki dares him.

Jay struggles with a restraint he clearly doesn't possess.

Finally he straightens. Jay's hazel eyes latch onto my face before moving down my body and back up. "I wasn't going to hurt you."

Right. I'm not convinced. "Following me around, coming to Mick's place—"

"Luring him away, you creeping stalker," Kiki says.

"I can be creative, *stripper*," he says.

"I've worked for what I have. I don't get all unnatural and infatuated with my clients. You're the pathetic one."

Enough.

"I'm pregnant." I drop the statement like the bomb I intend it to be.

I fold my arms.

The silence is so profound it has it's own zip code.

Jay Hightower stares at me.

Say something.

"See?" Kiki says. "Buzz off, ya parasite. Faren's already got a rich stud."

He steps closer, and I go to move away. His hand wraps around my wrist like a flesh-covered manacle.

"You don't have to be," he whispers.

"Let me go!" I say with real feeling. Warmth fueled by anger and fear rushes through my body.

"Okay!" Kiki says loudly. "I try to be reasonable, I try to be subtle."

Huh? It takes me a second to randomly acknowledge the impossibility of subtlety for Kiki.

Suddenly I'm coughing and choking. Jay's hand falls away, and I back up to avoid the brunt. My eyes water without mercy from only the residual as my hands cover my face.

"Sorry, baby," Kiki says, her index finger depressing her pepper spray. I'm lucky, it misses me directly by a millimeter. We're both coughing.

"Argh!" Jay screams like a pirate, clawing at his eyes.

"That's right, pal," Kiki says, advancing on Jay. The pepper spray is a constant hiss in the otherwise quiet condo. "Don't go away mad, just go away."

Mewling sounds crawl from his throat as his arms hit the walls.

Kiki lands a palm on his chest as he gets close to the threshold, and she shoves him through the doorway.

His puffy red eyes try to open, and slits of hazel hate us back.

Kiki slams the door and locks it.

"I'm calling the cops, numbnuts!" she promises loudly through the door.

I hear some shuffling and a low curse.

The distant chime of the elevator sounds.

Kiki places the cap on her spray and slides it into her huge handbag. She runs to every window, jerking them open as fresh air floods the condo.

I park my butt on the bench by the entrance, placing a hand over my belly.

Kiki snaps her purse closed and sets it down on a table. She sweeps a loose strand of hair behind her ear, swiping at her eyes as even the fresh air is barely enough to combat the spray.

"Wow... too many freaks, not enough circuses."

I laugh, and it comes out like an aborted hiccup.

"It's okay."

I cry.

I'm not sad, but terror makes me react strangely. I hug Kiki hard, and she strokes my back.

She pulls away. "I think he's a problem."

Yeah.

"Don't give me that look, Faren. It seems to me that you need to chat with Billionaire Boy, eh?"

"Mick," I say forlornly.

"Yeah. Tell Mick that this prick is stalking you and using the new strip club franchise deal to force you into doing him."

I shudder. I don't want to be with Jay. I can still feel my sticky dress from the last lap. I shudder.

The slimy memory coats the inside of my skull. Mick's face as he sees me betray him will be forever etched inside my brain.

I shake my head. "I can't let him lose that deal."

Kiki steps back, getting on her game face. "Ah, yeah. Ya can. That dodo bird might have more money than God, but he's cut from the same cloth as Ronnie was." Kiki squeezes my hand. "Y'know I love ya, but I have to say—you seem to attract the weirdos."

"Except for Mick."

"Yeah, I'll give you that."

We sit in silence for a few moments.

"I think Jay's going to skulk around licking his wounds for a while," Kiki brightens at the thought.

"And Mick will hightail it back here to give you some more action." Kiki swings her hips back and forth, and a shaky laugh slips out of me.

She bites her lip so hard a drop of blood blooms on her mouth like a ruby, and she licks it away. "Then you tell him that you're not long for this world. He'll hire his team of... everyone to deal with Jay, the press, and all the other clowns who want to give my bestie hell."

"And my baby," I say, my hand still on my stomach.

"Hell, yeah!"

Kiki jerks the strap of her purse over her shoulder.

"Now let's blow this popsicle stand and visit your mom."

She pulls me to my feet, our hands clasped together.

I have my mom.

I have Kiki.

I have a job where I give hope to the hopeless.

That silver lining is all I allow.

The storm cloud... I ignore.

CHAPTER 17

"Come here, Kandace," Tannin Mitchell says. Kiki moves out of the shadows until her thighs press against my mom's bed.

She takes my mom's free hand. "Hi, Tannin." Her skin is so dark against my mom's sun-starved flesh.

Mom clears her throat, and I release her hand to bring a cup of water with a bendy straw to her lips. Her clear gray eyes, just like my own, meet mine over the top of the cup.

"Thank you, baby."

She leans back against the pillows.

I look around her new room and sigh. It's beautiful and large.

Mom has her own private nurse and a physical therapist who sees only her.

It's all from Mick. He's a force of nature. He wouldn't say no, back down, or listen to any of my excuses. He can afford to take care of my mom, and he loves me. Therefore, it's my new reality.

Except sometimes it feels as though it's someone else's, and I can't say why.

"So what are you up to, Kandace?"

Kiki's smile lights up her face. "I'm a senior at the university."

Mom groans, slowly putting her forearm over her eyes. It's a monumental task for someone who woke from a coma a week ago.

"This is so hard."

Tears well. "Mom... don't," I say.

Her arm sort of slides off her forehead. "I remember when Kandace was barely eighteen."

I roll my eyes. "Me too." I try to keep the sarcasm away, but thinking about Kiki at seventeen is too much.

"Hey! Shut your pie hole," Kiki says. "If it wasn't for me, you'd still be in your turtle shell."

Boy, am I not hiding anymore.

My mom knots her fingers in the million-thread-count sheets. "I guess there's a lot for me to catch up on."

Kiki's eyes meet mine over the bed.

"What's going on?" Mom looks from one to the other of us.

I've visited Mom every day since she woke, and I've managed not to tell her the worst news.

I won't start now.

"You know that Mick and I are dating?" I ask.

Kiki's eyes bulge, but Mom doesn't notice because she's looking at me.

"Yes, I know who Mr. McKenna is," she says. She's heard all the stories about the wealthy playboy who owns strips clubs.

I take her hand again, and she gives mine a squeeze. The sun catches the strands of silver hair like tinsel around her face. I tuck a tendril behind her ear.

"Thank you," she says.

Silence beats us into the confession I begin to make.

"I love him."

Mom exhales deeply and says nothing.

She releases Kiki's hand and takes both of mine. "That's fine that you're in love"—she glances at Kiki—"and that Kandace is almost done with college. It's all perfect."

I hear a *but* coming. My forehead screws up in a frown I feel to my toes.

"But I just woke up, Faren." Her eyes search mine, trying to pound home a point she's yet to make. "Yesterday you were a senior in high school that my second husband disabled before he tried to beat me to death."

Hot tears brim and fall from my eyes onto the blanket. My breath hitches, and Kiki leans over the bed to squeeze my shoulder. She makes comforting clucking noises like a mother hen.

Mom lets me cry. "I wake up, and my daughter is all grown up, has a job mending those who are broken, and is dating a renowned player who owns strip clubs. Regardless of what he's done for me, he must be held accountable for his exploitation of you."

"What? No, Mom, he's not like that."

Mom shakes her head. "Yes, yes, he very much is. I can read, you know. The papers tell me exactly what he is. Assault charges? You've been a stripper?" Her voice holds the disgust I felt when I did what I had to do.

Kiki interjects, "It was my idea, Tannin."

Mom's head turns toward Kiki.

"Faren's financial ship was sinking," Kiki says. "She owed big-time debt for your care facility, and her PT wages weren't enough to cover it. They were going to move you to Evergreen."

Mom can't hide her shock. Slowly, she rests against the pillows. "Oh."

"And, Tannin, I talked Faren into working with me.

Neither one of us knew Mick—*knew him*, if ya know what I mean. He was just some hot rich guy who signed our paychecks."

"Why would you strip, Kandace?" Mom's trying to understand the incomprehensible.

Kiki's unafraid to give her answer. "I don't want any debt. No student loans, no mortgage... I want to get a place that's mine. Something fine."

"I see," Mom says with a sigh. My mom was never much for material things.

"Here's the thing," Kiki says. "Life is about options, and mine sucked. I don't know who my dad is, and my mom doesn't have the means. So it was up to me to make things happen. If men want to lust after me and fling money my way? Fine. I'm the one with the power. The pussy power."

Oh boy.

Mom looks as if she swallowed a goat, then she bursts out laughing. "Everything changes, but some things remain the same."

"Yeah." I give my foul-mouthed, true-blue friend a grateful glance.

I'd be so lost without her.

Thank God she never changes.

Mom blows another strand of hair out of her face. "Okay, so Mick's a good guy?"

I launch into an explanation about Rose McKenna.

"Oh my God, that's as wretched a story as ours," Mom says.

Kiki nods vigorously. "That's what I told Faren."

"Why doesn't he defend himself? He could explain that the clubs exist to give girls who choose that lifestyle a safe environment, a good wage, benefits. Why doesn't he make it known he's not a..."

"Silver-spoon trust-fund baby?" Kiki offers.

"Exactly. And an inventor...?"

I nod. "I don't think he feels he should have to."

"Wow," Mom says. "He's either a very good-looking dim bulb or a humble, deep-feeling introvert."

I know exactly what he is and what he can do to me with his hands and mouth. I feel my face heat.

Mom watches me closely. "Mmhmmm, I see that you're serious."

All that from my expression?

Mom glances at my wringing hands. "Out with it."

A soft knock sounds at the door. A woman with owl eyes, glasses, and white hair sticks her head in. "Tannin, it's almost time for our three thirty."

My eyes flick to the clock: 3:19.

Mom nods. "I'll be ready." She turns back to me.

"I suppose this revelation I feel brewing will have to wait until I get through another torture session."

I can't help but smile.

"Y'know, your daughter gives a pretty good hurt when she wants."

Tannin shivers. "I do hate my physical therapy."

"I know, but the atrophy is—"

"Acute," she says with a wry grin.

"Do you hate your therapist?" I ask.

I know exactly what my colleague will put Mom through, though it's an utterly different type of therapy for injuries versus head trauma recovery. Limbs don't always do what they're told after four years of deep sleep.

But atrophy is atrophy is atrophy. It's wasted muscle that needs to be reawakened, and it hurts like a bitch.

Mom nods slowly. "A little bit."

We burst out laughing.

"It's okay, Tannin. They say you'll be walking in a few months," Kiki says.

Mom looks at her hands. "Yes."

The hurt in her voice tightens my chest.

When her head rises, I see the same determination I possess, and I know exactly who it came from.

Mom grabs my hand, and I bring it to my cheek. It twitches a little.

"Can you use it?" she asks.

I think of lying, but I've had enough of that.

"Some."

Her smile is like captured sunlight. "I'm so glad, baby. I'm so glad."

We both know we're not talking about hands.

We're talking about how wonderful it is to be alive.

CHAPTER 18

"Where do you think the old blowfish scuttled off to?" Kiki asks. I bark out a laugh, almost tripping down the stairs of my mom's new care facility. "Jay?"

Kiki turns to me, bouncing down the broad concrete steps. "Hell yeah. He's the biggest prick of the moment. Although, there's always room for someone else to take top position." She winks.

"You're slaying me." I laugh.

"That's the objective, sweet thing."

We make our way to her car, a souped-up Fiat. I love it. It's small, new, and flaming burnt orange. Kiki loves it because it's a great downtown car. Seattle parking sucks, so owning a car isn't always bright. Better to take your chances with public transit.

I lift a shoulder, my hand on the passenger side handle. "I'm not sure that he's the *biggest*. But I think it's safe to say that he won't bother me anytime soon."

Her eyes meet mine over the roof of the car. "Yeah, but weasels like him always sleaze back around."

"I'll worry about that if and when it comes up."

We pile in, and Kiki turns on the car. It starts up like a tin can, the whole thing kind of rattling.

"So—prenatal?" Kiki asks.

I nod. "Next week."

"How far along are ya?"

I smile, shaking my head, and look at my hands. "Not even far enough to do the barf-o-matic."

"That paints a picture." Kiki gives me an assessing glance. "Does this mean you're gonna puke inside my new set of wheels? She twists to face me, putting her back against the door. Because"—she puts her hand to her chest, bright red nail tips flame against her white sweater—"I love you, but I draw the line at the bodily fluid share."

I laugh. "I think we're safe for today." I don't know when I'm going to start acting pregnant. Actually, I don't know where my headaches and dizziness have gone.

Of course, Doctor Matthews said I'd have peaks and valleys of symptoms. He even touched on the euphoria that I might experience and believe everything is normal.

"Okay, just sayin'. I'm prepared to go to the ground for our friendship, but cleaning vomit from the innards of my seat buckles holds limited appeal."

I snort. "Right. Like we've never had gross stuff to maneuver."

We glance at each other, thinking of the laps and their... leavings.

"Gross!" we say simultaneously and crack up.

We drive in companionable silence until Kiki breaks it, "I notice you didn't tell your mom you're knocked up."

Silence.

"No... I—it's not something I can rush. I mean..." I swivel to look at her then face the street again.

Kiki slams to a stop at a red light, engaging the door lock.

A swaggering drunk makes it safely to the other side of the crosswalk.

We sigh with relief.

"God, that was close," I say.

Our eyes follow the man lurching in between pedestrian traffic.

A horn beeps, and Kiki throws up her middle finger in an automatic salute to the car behind her.

Blue and red lights strobe on, pulsing through her back widow in a splash of vibrant color.

"Oh, fuck me running...." Kiki says.

I see the cop car pulling us over. She swings the wheel to the right and slides into a handicap parking space. It's the only spot open.

Just what we need. Almost home.

Almost free. I can taste a hot bath. I've had enough text messages from Mick while he's been away to know that he's going to please me until I weep.

But no pleasure now. Most likely a ticket.

My gaze sweeps to striding legs through the windows of the car.

Kiki's window slides down, and Tagger fills the hole.

Holy fucking crows.

I cringe before I can stop myself.

I might have made some gross errors in judgment, but my sixth sense works just fine. It's way past an alarm—more like a shrieking crescendo.

Kiki doesn't interpret my silence for the staggering fear it is.

Tagger almost killed Thorn.

He's on investigative leave. I do calculations in my head. *It hasn't been long enough.*

"Well hello, Miss Mitchell."

Kiki frowns. Her eyes move to my face then his. I know when she sees his name tag. Her face bleeds to hardness.

His hands fall on the car door. "Weren't you following the traffic a little too closely?"

"Aren't you going to ask me for my license and registration, *Tagger*?"

They have a stare off, and I realize, not for the first time, that Kiki's sometimes-crude snark hides her fierce intelligence. She doesn't trust easily, and she's already put together that Tagger popping up like a psychotic Jack-in-the-Box isn't good.

Tagger's lips flatten, his knuckles bleeding to white.

"You can't, can ya?" Kiki adds. "Faren's running around free because you blew it, and you think you can put her on notice by stalking her."

"What do you think you know, you cheap slut?" Tagger snarls.

Kiki smiles, pushing every ounce of charm she has into those big brown peepers.

"I know that if you lay a finger on either one of us before your bullshit 'internal investigation' is complete, they'll throw away the key and toss your corrupt ass in prison."

"You don't know dick." A cloud of uncertainty skims across his eyes.

"Oh yeah? Pre-law, douche." Her eyes rake him in supreme dismissal. "Might know a few things about your situation."

"Kiki..."

Tagger's eyes snap to mine.

"Tag!" a voice calls from behind him. He straightens, giving a wave that looks like a salute.

"Just a sec!" he bellows back.

Kiki looks behind her and squints at the other cop in the squad car. Her face is a jacquard of blue and red. "Be interesting to know how they let you out to run around and make a pest of yourself. I'm sure someone at your precinct would be stoked to know you're harassing the very woman this is all about."

Tagger looks at Kiki, his struggle for control reigning supreme. "Don't get involved, Miss King."

Kiki leans forward so her breasts brush his knuckles. His eyes flick down at her assets, and he doesn't move away.

Neither does she. Kiki's not above working it.

"I have two words for you, Officer."

Tagger licks his lips as I clench the strap of my purse.

"The first one begins with F." She bats her eyelashes. "And the second begins with a U."

Tagger jerks his hands off her car door as though he's burned. His eyes lift, and I see hate burning in them.

His fists clench as he locks on Kiki like a missile, but she's already pulling away.

She doesn't say anything until we're almost to the Millennium. "I hope you realize I misspelled on purpose."

"What?" I ask, still numb from the Tagger encounter.

"I think he's too much of a slack-jaw to get it."

Oh, *I think he got it.*

Those are two words that most everyone gets.

We slide into the underground parking garage, and Kiki turns off the Fiat.

The engine ticks in the silence as it cools.

"This intrigue shit is killing me."

I roll my head toward her. "I think it's me it's killing."

A moment later, I realize what I said.

Neither one of us corrects me.

We both know it won't be the two men who do me in.

CHAPTER 19

My arch fits perfectly against the rolled porcelain rim. As the razor glides up my leg, an errant bubble falls on the marble tile outside the tub. My hair is wrapped in a turban as I soak.

I'd kill for a deep, fruity, sweet glass of red wine.

My palm moves to cover my belly.

A small smile lifts my lips, and I let my head rest against the back of the tub. I wipe my wet hand on the hand towel beside a row of fragrant candles lined up like vanilla soldiers.

I stare at the text of Mick's penis thrust through the slim hole he's made of his slacks, and I feel my smile grow. It's a flesh handle I want to suck and play with.

Turnabout is fair play.

I lift my hips out of the water, take a picture of myself, and press send.

Mick: *Bubbles are in the way, baby.*

Me: *So greedy.*

I use my wet hand to push them away and send the pic of my hot pink goodness to him along with a pouting emoticon.

Mick: *Hang tight.*

I feel a frown form as I stare at the screen.

A noise startles me, and then Mick is in the doorway to the bathroom. I squeal, my phone skittering amongst the candles. I jump up in the tub, suds and water sliding off me.

"Hey, baby mama."

His voice purrs across my wet skin, and I shiver. He's says it as if I'm the sexiest thing that's ever lived.

His eyes eat me up, carnivorous—leaving no part of me unexplored.

Mick takes off his suit jacket, tossing it on the yards of marble vanity that are now cluttered with the mess of my femininity.

He stalks to the tub like a panther and takes me in his arms.

"Hey!" I gasp as his lips cover mine.

I soak his button-down shirt instantly.

I pull away. "I'm making you wet!"

"No." He dips his head and pecks my lips. "That's my job."

Moisture that has nothing to do with the bath floods my sex, and I crave what he offers.

"Yes."

"Wrap me, Faren."

I follow his erotic orders without pause.

He grabs my wet ass cheeks, as I twist my legs around his waist, ruining his perfect suit.

Mick twirls us around and walks past the bedroom into the living room.

The couch—where he first licked me into oblivion—grows closer. He places my wet body on a blanket.

"Spread them." Mick's already dark eyes appear obsidian with only the city lights to illuminate our encounter.

I part my knees, and his gaze falls to my center, a mirror of the text.

Mick wrecks another shirt, the damp material sucking off

him in a wet, tearing pull, and he throws it on the polished floor. His belt snaps out of loops too tight for the motion, and the waist band gives. His wet slacks fall even as he steps out of them.

"Show me," I say in challenge. That picture of his stiff penis fills my mind.

He smirks, popping his sizeable package out of the boxer briefs that are tight enough for speculation and loose enough for mystery.

I grab the length of him and sit up, flicking my tongue over the slit at the end of his dick. His ass clenches, and his hips move forward. I take him deeply inside my mouth, my smile allowing a swivel of his hips.

"Faren." He grips my hair and gently pushes my face down.

I relax my throat, letting his tip dive deep. He groans, fighting his instinct to hold me there. My lips are pressed to the base of him, and he lets the pressure go.

I look into his eyes, sink into them.

"Again," he says.

I glide back down, and he holds me. I repeat it over and over.

"Stop, Faren. I'll go if you keep that up."

"Maybe I don't want to stop," I say wickedly.

His eyes smolder. "I want to return the favor."

My hands slide away from him, trailing down thighs powerful from workouts he does as partial atonement for sins only he sees.

Redemption is ours together. His for me, and mine for his. We're each other's catharsis.

I lay back, and his fingertips press against my knees. Pinpoints of heat dot my skin as he pulls my legs back. His head lowers as his hands glide up my shins. His mouth hovers just above my most sensitive part, and I shiver as his breath heats me.

"Please," I beg.

Suddenly his mouth covers me in perfect suction, and I gasp, my hips flexing. But his hands are there, pressing my heels against my ass.

He laps at me, releasing pressure and sinking inside me, the tip of his tongue strong in my entrance.

When the flat of his tongue rasps against my clit, I moan, my arms flinging back across the armrest. Cool leather heats beneath my flesh as I writhe under his mouth.

My hips meet him as Mick flattens his tongue against my clit.

His finger replaces his tongue as it sweeps to the little nerve center that thrums with my building orgasm.

"I like that," I say when he inserts a second finger, curling his fingertips inside me high and deep, just a flick and I brim with fire. The taut line of climbing, the downward slope of my orgasm rides to meet me.

"Like?" he murmurs.

His hand exits my wetness, the other leaving my clit and my eyes snap open.

"You better fuck me now," I rasp, my mouth parched from my panting.

He gives no warning before he lifts my hips and sinks to the end of me.

Mick fills me so deeply and unexpectedly, I stop breathing, thinking.

Everything is that moment, where nothing matters but the joining of our bodies.

I blow a strand of hair out of my mouth as he throws back his head, his hips locked with mine. Mick's head lowers, and he looks at me.

He pulls out and thrusts back in. I moan, biting my lower

lip, and he tweaks my nipple. My ass is on his knees, but still he pulls me against him.

Mick picks up speed. His large hands cover the globes of my ass as he smoothly pulls me against him then pushes me away. Our rough breathing is the only music in the condo, the clock's ticking drowned by our noise.

He brings me to the brink of ecstasy and strains to hold back his release. I stop, and he pauses as well.

"What—"

"Shush," I say, reveling in the control, the power I possess over him.

I surge forward with him still locked inside me. Gripping his shoulders, I pull myself upright and press my breasts against his chest.

I bounce on him once, twice.

Shoving him in deeply from the new angle.

Mick groans as I ride him.

"God." His chin moves to my shoulder, and his breath scalds my neck.

I use his strong shoulders to position my heels on the sides of the couch and slam down. I grunt at the primitive sensation of being filled.

Mick shakes his head, the muscles of his neck straining against his release. I come down again, his balls pressing against my ass.

My core pulses hard, and I know I'm close.

I reach behind me, cup his testes, and gently squeeze as I move my hips.

The breath leaks out of him.

"I can't..."

Mick's release pours out of him, his arms convulsing around me as the wall crumbles against my orgasm.

He hardens as he dumps into me, and I throb against him,

our arms locked around each other in a tightness reserved for what's happening in this moment.

I don't pull away, and neither does he.

Minutes pass. When he slips out of me, he takes me onto his lap.

He chuckles. "Legs were falling asleep."

I rest my head on his broad shoulder, one arm around his neck.

"Wish I could stay like that forever," he admits.

"Like a naked pretzel?" My smile widens against the heartbeat that slows beneath his chest.

There's the barest pause as he considers what I've said.

"Yes."

His hand moves to my head, and he strokes my damp hair. Mick lies down on the cramped confines of the couch and tucks me against him, wrapping the excess blanket around us both.

Our breathing syncs in the silence. Words are unnecessary.

I fight sleep, but in the end, safety comes in many forms.

Mick makes me feel as though I'm home.

He is my home.

CHAPTER 20

"My secretary has left several messages." My doodling pauses at his words then resumes. I'm not sure how to respond. *Yeah, Dr. Matthews, I allowed myself to become pregnant after being diagnosed with a brain tumor.*

It doesn't matter that it was unintentional, an accident of drug-mixing in just the right coincidence of circumstance.

I'm dying.

I'm pregnant.

I sigh. "I'm sorry, things have been..." *Suicidal and surreal.*

Dr. Matthews says, "I understand you're accounting for your time differently now."

Yeah.

"However, your care is still important. We need to see how the tumor is progressing."

I blow a strand of hair out of my face and put the finishing touches on my stick family. I bite my lip as I fill in their faces.

I'm telling Mick today.

He's not flying me to Paris like Kiki theorized, but when

he mentioned New York City for a long lunch, I declined, feigning morning sickness. I need to be closer to home if things go sideways.

I still think it's possible he'll let me go when he discovers my biggest deceit of all.

"Miss Mitchell?" Dr. Matthews asks.

"Yes, I'll come."

"It's not urgent unless you're manifesting more symptoms. However, your care cannot be ignored." His voice rises at the end of his statement, a hidden question buried in there.

I feel myself frown. "Actually, all those symptoms have gone away."

There's pause in the open connection between my cell and his land line.

"While that's unusual," he begins slowly, "it's not unheard of. Remember, we discussed the possibility of a euphoric period, where all symptoms would seem to be in stasis?"

I remembered; I hate the falsehood of feeling well when I know the opposite is true.

"Yes."

"We'll do a marker test and administer another CAT when you come in..."

He rustles some papers.

"Friday at 4:00?"

It's Monday now, so I say yes automatically. That will give Mick plenty of time to figure out what he wants to do with me.

Or doesn't.

* * *

"THIS IS TOO MUCH FOOD!" I say, the catered spread goes on for miles.

Mick's eyes are hoods of lust as he maintains silence. "Open up," He dangles a fat strawberry by a short stem over my mouth.

I shake my head but can't keep the grin off my face.

"I'll tickle you until you pee your pants," he threatens.

"Not fair." I cross my arms underneath my naked, tender breasts. "I have to pee all the time anyway."

"Oooh." Mick crawls across the bed, dishes of every order strewn across the floor, dressers, and empty spots on the huge mattress. "A challenge."

I lay back, my legs opening to allow him between them. The strawberry is lifted high above him as he moves in for the kill.

"Open," he whispers.

My legs spread farther, and he groans.

My lips thin into a firm line, and he smiles. He dangles the berry in front of my opening, and I feel my eyes widen.

"I'm going to eat you now," Mick says, waggling his eyebrows.

He moves the strawberry back and forth, clit to entrance, and the nubby texture teases my soft flesh.

I moan. I know he'll stay true to his word. He tears the stem and top off with his teeth, spitting it onto a plate, and presses just the pointy tip inside me.

His lips circle the fruit, and he nibbles it little by little as his thumb moves to my clit.

"Oh my god," I whisper.

"You wouldn't be an obedient girl and eat the berry. Now *I* will eat the berry."

Mick licks and nibbles. I feel his slight stubble as his mouth works the succulent morsel, consuming it.

Eating me.

"All done," he says softly, landing on top of me gently.

My thighs quiver, and my pussy begs for more of his

sweet attention. But his mouth is on mine, and I taste myself and the tart sweetness of the berry.

I suck on his tongue as he enters me with his hardness.

"I'm going to be sore," I say, my legs spreading wider as he pushes deeper for a second round.

"A good kind," he answers.

I nod, smiling against his kisses. He glides in and out of me in a deep press of wet flesh.

Mick's pace is slightly desperate and needy, and my hips match what he offers.

He grunts against me as I meet him viciously, expectantly.

His eyes move to mine with the ferocity of our coupling.

Mick is so in tune with my needs that he doesn't question me but gives what I silently ask.

When our pace is at its most frenzied, he pauses, pulsing into me as I milk him of everything he spills.

We're frozen together, and I love it.

Love him.

When the tears come, he wipes them away.

When he asks what's wrong—I tell him.

* * *

"JESUS, YOU'RE NOT JOKING?" Mick asks, his shocked expression partially buried underneath his forearm.

I lean over him, still naked, and lift his arm off his head so I can see his eyes. The windows of the soul.

When his wasted expression is revealed, I almost wish I hadn't.

I shake my head. "I wouldn't after all that's happened."

He doesn't say anything for a long time.

Mick dislodges from me, and I let him go.

I've always been willing to release him. I never had a choice.

He paces, his limp penis looking sad and spent against his tense body. I sit up on my knees and watch him.

Mick turns, his anger riding him like a layer of fire. "This isn't fair, Faren."

I nod. I always thought so, but I never have enough time for a proper pity party. Too much rode on what I needed to do for my mom.

Now there's the baby.

"No." His eyes flash, and I frown. "I mean, this is worse than Rose."

I didn't expect that.

"Rose died senselessly." His eyes move off into a distant spot before that penetrating stare moves back to me. "There's no way when she woke up that morning, she thought 'I'm going to die today.'

But you, you always knew that you could not engage anyone permanently. Unlike the rest of us, you knew your time was almost up."

I shrug. That's all true. He's reiterating all the points I've turned over in my mind a dozen times.

He rakes a hand through his hair. "I can't do this."

My stomach flops over like an undercooked pancake. Doughy and soft. Unready.

I'm robbed of speech as I watch his expression harden.

His eyes roam my body and his Adam's apple bobs in a hard plow of flesh. "What are you going to do about the baby?"

I sink against my heels, staring at him.

My own anger boils to the surface, colliding with his.

"Do?"

I suddenly feel naked before him. Before, I'd only felt nude. Now it's as though my soul is laid bare under a microscope he controls.

"You can't think you'll go through with the pregnancy?" Mick's expression is incredulous.

My gorge rises, and I swallow down my emotions. "Yes, actually, I thought I might have enough time to get the baby to term before I..."

"Die?"

I nod miserably, my arm covering my belly.

His eyes track it, then rise to meet mine. They're black with his rage, my betrayal the ultimate lie by omission. "No. I'll do what I said I would do: Take care of your mom until she's well enough to function. I'll... see to your care until the end. But don't think for a second there's anything more between us."

I hang my head.

There's a smudge of strawberry juice on the inside of my thigh. It mocks me with the proof of my reality.

"You can't show me heaven, then toss me in hell, Faren Mitchell. It doesn't work that way."

I get up and walk past Mick. I collect my scattered clothes, dress, and gather my handbag.

Tears shatter my vision like broken gems as I smack the elevator button with my good hand. Great gulping inhales are the only sound in the hall.

I realize they're coming from me.

The doors mercifully whisper apart.

I don't look back.

Mick doesn't call me back, say he's sorry... or come after me.

This is more final than my impending death.

I feel as though I've already died.

CHAPTER 21

"*Oh my God.* What. The. Fuck?" Kiki asks as I stand at her door in a numb stupor. Kiki pulls me inside her condo and closes the door.

She leads me to her kitchen table. A place where I've told my secrets, shared my joy—my sadness.

"You—sit," she says. She races to the front door, throws the latch, and jogs to me, taking my hands.

Her hands feel so warm.

"Okay, do I need to go cut off a dick?"

My face crumples, and my stomach churns. I'm not nauseated because of the little one in my womb. I'm nauseated because the father hates me for leaving him. I hate me for leaving too. I'd do nearly anything not to go.

"Or two?" Kiki asks, stroking my palms, her fingers rough against my scar.

I shake my head, my hair sliding over the thin nylon shirt I put on.

Inside out and backward.

"Okay, let me think." Kiki taps a bright nail on her lip. Leaning forward, she pegs me with her all-knowing gaze.

"You told him."

"I did," I croak.

"And... he rejected you."

My tears answer her.

"Well, *that bastard.*"

We're quiet for a second.

"Okay, I know ya love him, but why do you look like you've been run over by another motorcycle?"

My laugh sounds like a sob.

"Oh honey," Kiki says, kissing my hand, "Kiki's here, baby. I don't care if you have two months or two hundred years—I love ya."

I inhale sharply. "I know."

She waits. A miracle for Kiki.

"He said that I brought heaven to him... then sent him straight to hell."

Kiki's face scrunches up. "Okay, so he's mad."

"Yeah," I answer softly.

"Well I'm steaming fucking pissed too!"

My face jerks up in surprise.

Her eyes search mine. "I dig you. You're my go-to girl-friend. You're steady, Faren. You've seen shit and survived. You're level-headed and put up with my shiny-thing problem."

I smile despite how awful I feel.

"I'd rather have you die and have known you for five minutes then to have never known you and not have this hole in my heart. The pain is real"—the devotion in her eyes is a balm to my shredded emotions—"but so is the love."

Kiki puts her fist to her heart, her eyes shining with tears.

Her hand slowly falls. "But this isn't about my anger. It's about how I love ya. And that's what Mick's problem is. He thinks it'll feel better to cut you off. Then he won't feel the pain."

Maybe... but she didn't see his face when he let me go.

"But the pain's going to follow his rich ass no matter what."

Kiki cocks her head. "Off-topic."

My head spins. "Huh? Okay."

"Why do you have red stains all over your mouth?"

I bawl then. Unglamorous, wrenching sobs that suck the fluid and snot right out of me.

I don't think I'll ever eat another strawberry again.

* * *

I SLEEP LIKE THE DEAD.

I have absolutely fallen into the early pregnancy lethargy. Vaguely, I notice Kiki come in and check on me, but I don't wake until I hear her arguing.

"Listen, asshole, she's not going to want to see you."

I sit up in her guest bedroom, barely more than a glorified closet.

My cheek feels hot from lying on the pillow for hours. Pale sunlight streams around the edges of the drawn curtains. My hair is tangled like a silken spider web.

"I don't care. I need to see her, to know that she's okay."

"What part of *fuck off* don't you understand?" Kiki says in a voice that means business.

I unwrap myself from the covers and pad out in a huge nightshirt.

A haggard Mick fills her front entrance.

"Faren."

I just stare, unresponsive.

He gives a loud exhale. "I'm sorry about what I said."

I don't reply.

I feel as if I'm having an out-of-body experience.

Kiki huffs and begins to shut the door.

Mick's foot wedges between the closing door and jamb. "Don't make me break your door down."

I do what I have to. "Mick..."

He looks at me. He's still angry.

Well, I am too.

I'm the one who's dying. I'm the one who danced on guys' laps so I could save my mom.

Now I'm the one who's pregnant. He can be all kinds of mad if he wants, but it's a luxury I can't afford.

I smooth back my tangled hair. "Thanks for checking on me, but I don't need anything."

His face imperceptibly hardens.

"Fine."

"Good, that's settled then, douche. Now skedaddle." Kiki moves to close the door.

"Wait," Mick says, frustration leaking through his pores. "What are you doing with the baby?"

I feel my sarcastic smile fill my face. "I'm not going to murder it."

Mick's chin jerks back as if I'd hit him. "I didn't suggest that."

Whatever.

I ignore Kiki rolling her eyes.

"We made it together. You can have him or her after... I deliver."

Mick licks his lips. "You know I... wouldn't want it any other way."

I look at my feet.

That was before, when I wasn't dying.

"Right," I say to my feet.

"Faren."

I look up. "I mean it," he says.

"I know." I know he'll take care of the child, even if he won't take care of me.

"Let me help with the prenatal."

"Can you help with all my care, Mick?" I slice into him with my stare.

He doesn't flinch.

He clears his throat. "You know I would do anything to take this away."

"Not everything," Kiki says. "Like toeing the fucking mark when my girl needs you."

Mick's knuckles turn white on the door's edge.

"I can't do that."

"Yeah, we got that, ya turd."

"Kiki, it's okay." My chin kicks up. "I've got this. Yes, I'll take your money to make sure our baby is born healthy. But stay away from me."

I hold my breath then let it out. "It's what you want."

Mick nods.

I manage to look in his eyes as little as possible. I can't stand his indifference staring back.

"Take care," he says and retreats.

I hate him.

I feel every painful beat of my heart.

I love him so much, this agonizing weight in my chest causes each breath to catch on the next.

***

"That was swell," Kiki says, putting hot tea in front of me. "Decaf for you, baby mama."

A lone tear rolls down my flushed cheek.

"What?" Kiki asks, concern straining her tone.

"That's what Mick called me before."

Everything now is Before Mick Knew and After.

"Oh." Her voice is small.

I fling a hand. "Don't worry about it."

We're silent for a space of heartbeats.

"So Mick the Prick will pay for the baby."

I don't deny her charge. "Yeah."

"And he's still gonna come through for Tannin?" Uncertainty taints her voice.

I nod.

A breath of relief escapes her.

"So... you just have to..." Kiki rolls her bottom lip into her teeth.

I say the words she doesn't want to. "Stay alive long enough to have my little peanut."

CHAPTER 22

TUESDAY

*K*iki's chin drops to her chest, and I see her shoulders shake. I stand and come around to the other side of the tiny kitchen table to comfort her. I hold Kiki as she cries. My tears have dried up for the moment.

She cries for us both.

I sit back and press my forehead to the commode rim. Gross—but the coolness offers some relief.

Morning sickness is bullshit.

It's all day-feel-like-shitness.

Mick blew me out of the water by dumping me, then I start puking my guts up the next day. A one-two sucker punch.

A gentle rapping sounds on the other side of the door.

Sue.

"Faren, are you okay?"

Just peachy. "Ah... give me a sec."

It doesn't matter that I'm sick. Sick and pregnant. Terminally ill.

Terminally heartbroken.

"I'll be right out, Sue."

A pause. "Just letting you know your two o'clock is waiting."

Work must go on. A job I loved is now something to endure. It's been an unnerving day of patients, throwing up, and heartsickness that takes my breath away.

I stand, my hand going to my flat belly. A shaky breath rattles out of me.

I remind myself I still have joy.

I'll see Mom today and tell her about the baby. There is no way I can tell her about my illness.

She's so happy to be awake. So relieved our mutual tormenter is dead.

My mind conjures up Tagger. I shudder. The fingers of my bad hand convulse on my belly, naturally protecting the new life growing there.

I rinse out my mouth, and my hunger rises like a phoenix. A gnaw begins in my belly, and I struggle to think of anything that sounds good.

Oranges and ice water appeals.

I glance at the commode and my stomach does a hot, slick roil.

God.

I walk out of the restroom, jerk the patient file out of the slot, and cruise through the door to the slave station while smiling at Brice.

Probably looks like a grimace.

It's his last session, and like Humpty Dumpty's men, I feel as though I've put him back together again.

"Wow, Miss Mitchell," Brice exclaims, a boy's face in a man's body. "You look like shit."

I scowl at his truth.

"I mean—crap."

I set down his patient file. "You know I'll work you harder

today because you noticed and commented." I feel my eyebrow pop. "Where's your filter?"

Brice gives a sheepish head-dip. "I guess it's on vacation."

I snort. "Must be a long one..."

He grins.

I grin back.

I'll survive the day.

* * *

Wednesday

Kiki: *Hey doll, whatzup?*

Me: *Nothing, just puking up all my food and torturing patients.*

Kiki: *Perfect. Want to come over tonight and I'll cook u supper?*

I feel a grin slip into place.

Me: *Ah... don't I live with u for the moment? Until I figure out my apartment....*

Kiki: *Lol—yeah, but I thought ud dig the invite anyway.*

Kiki uses anything as an excuse to check up on me. *I love her.*

Me: *Well, yes, thank you. 😊 I'll be there.... ?*

Kiki: *Late; I've got poles but have a break around 10-ish.*

The p-word elicits a sick feeling in the pit of my stomach that has nothing to do with the pregnancy. I stare at my cell for a second then tap out my response.

Me: *Okay, I'll be there.*

Kiki: *U know it!!! 🖤*

I swipe my cell, and the screen turns black.

Slipping it into my scrub pocket, I stack patient files and bring them to Sue. Her silent eyes hold questions I'm not ready to answer.

Any way I respond, I'll sound like a dumb ass.

"'Night, Sue."

She clicks them once on the counter. "Goodnight, Faren."

To her credit, she hasn't asked about Mick, Ronnie Bunce's death, or all the other media circus bullshit that's been surrounding me lately.

But Sue has noticed my bathroom worship. If I'm not squatting in the bathroom and barfing, I'm nibbling crackers and sipping ginger ale, hoping I can keep down a crumb of anything.

I guess it's good Mick doesn't want me. Who wants someone who has to use the bathroom for nothing but expulsion?

I walk out of the clinic and tilt my face to the dying sun. The sky runs blood red with ribbons of tangerine and gold, bathing my face in warmth. Soon it will be spring. Seattle is holding its breath for the next season; I can taste it.

I soak in the moment, then face reality.

I need to visit my mom, then go to Kiki's.

I didn't cry when I came home from work yesterday and my things were packed and stacked in front of her door. Courtesy of Mick's minions.

Instead, I did some pre-Lamaze breathing and ignored a tenant who missed her code-entry swipe while staring at an odd young woman who appeared to be hyperventilating.

Sighing, I chug down the stairs, car keys in hand. The noises of the city fill my ears, lulling me into that familiar comfort.

"Faren."

A thrill courses down my body like an electrical current.

I turn, and there Mick stands.

He's resplendent in a handsome deep chocolate suit. A terra-cotta-colored silk button-down perfectly accentuates his deep auburn hair. Cufflinks with the darkest royal blue sapphires glitter from his wrists.

The sun slants into the space between us, lighting him like a living six-foot-three flame.

I realize I'm staring and bite my lip, looking down.

My clogs have small scuffs from work. I analyze each one while I pray for composure.

"How are you?"

My head snaps up and the thread of restraint unravels. "What do you care?"

The words come out harsh, raw. That's all I have.

The wounds he gave me don't heal but fester.

Mick jams his hands in his pockets, dipping his head. "I didn't want this."

What the fuck is *this*?

I laugh like a seal barking. "Right..." I feel my eyebrows lift, and I cock my hip. "Me either."

Effing duh.

He grimaces. "I'm sorry, that didn't come out right..."

I put up my palm. "Save it, Mick. I don't want to waste my time."

A memory of him flexing above me as he's buried inside me rises like the tide in my mind. I close my eyes as it washes over me.

I'm drowning.

When I open them, he's closer, jaw clenched. He raises his hand, and I flinch.

He freezes. "I would never hurt you."

I nod. I didn't mean it—just habit. Killing Ronnie Bunce is fresh. What he's done to me is at the surface of my mind.

He cups my jaw, and I step out of a touch I want so badly my soul starves for it like food.

I hear a flash pop, and we turn to look. A reporter gives us a thumbs up, and Mick growls, spinning toward him.

He bashes the camera to the ground. Plastic shards fly across the cement sidewalk like black missiles.

"Give us some goddamned space," he snaps.

I don't wait but turn and walk away.

Like he did with me.

I don't know what he'll think when I just disappear.

I'm not waiting to find out.

* * *

I GROAN, and Kiki giggles. "I think," she says, "that you need to concentrate on being purely tactile right now."

The blindfold slides around and I try to peek.

Kiki slaps my hand.

"Ow, you bitch," I reply with a laugh.

"Open your pie hole."

I obediently open my mouth, and she pops a wiggling mess inside. But it's cool and pure.

"What is it?"

"Not until you have every bite."

I eat forever, and my stomach stays silent. No palace revolt.

Yet.

I lift the blindfold and look at the container.

"Oooh—Jello?"

"Don't diss it, baby. This is breakfast, lunch, and supper, right?"

I reluctantly nod. True.

I've already lost three pounds in the same amount of days.

"It's not like your skinny ass needed to take any pudge pounds off."

I touch her arm. "Thank you."

Kiki turns away, shrugging. "No biggie."

I watch her busy herself in the tiny kitchen, her stripper's dress giving me a show.

I'm unmoved. I know what goes into that job, and none of it is titillating, romantic, or otherwise.

It's a mess, and it attracts desperate girls at a despicable cost.

Every bit of her glitters—from her eye shadow, to the mandatory stockings, to the pointy heels that click against her travertine flooring.

My chin falls into my hand. Then my elbow slides on the glass table as I let my head fall into the crook of my arm. My eyes find the sea outside the huge windows, and I grow still at its beautiful apathy.

"Hey." Kiki's close.

"Yeah?"

The waves churn—deep and gray, moving ceaselessly. Immune to whatever happens, the ocean lives.

Her hand strokes my head. "Have you told Tannin?"

"Not yet."

"You're not telling her about... y'know."

"No," I say in soft confirmation. "Just about peanut."

I swear I can feel her smile.

"Peanut?"

I nod under her palm.

"I like it," she says.

I do too.

Our silence is broken by the doorbell.

I remain where I am.

"Who the hell?" Kiki's hand leaves me and I feel bereft without it.

I need to get a handle on myself. I'm such a needy sucker all of the sudden.

Hormones R Us.

Eight more months.

I can do anything for that amount of time. I can live that long—I know I can.

I have to.

"Oh, hi!" Kiki lets someone in.

"Hey, Faren."

Thorn.

I don't know if I'm ready for his condemnation.

Because it's bros before hos. I don't have a side for him to take. I'm just the girl who broke Mick's heart and lied about everything.

"Hey," I say.

"Get your ass up and stop feeling sorry for yourself."

Kiki groans. My head comes off my arms, and I swivel to meet Thorn's stare.

He's like a silent dark mountain of muscle.

Anger rears up. "No offense, but fuck off."

I hardly ever use the F-word, and Kiki gasps behind Thorn's broad shoulder.

He leans down into my face. "Don't you dare give up. Don't give up on Mick."

Kiki moves closer, dwarfed by his massiveness.

I lean right back. "He gave up on me!" Tears spring to attention, and I shake, my left hand bouncing like a Mexican jumping bean.

Thorn laughs and shakes his head.

"Ah, we didn't get the comedy memo, Thorn." Kiki crosses her arms.

He shrugs. "My boy—he's all kinds of torn up. And sometimes that's what it takes."

I swipe my tears away. "Well I'm more shook up."

Thorn swings his heavy arm, indicating the ceiling. "Nah, Mick's sidelined. Can't eat, can't sleep... ten shades of fucked up."

Really? I shrug. "Yeah? Why? *He* dumped me." I jab my finger into my chest. My lip trembles, and I bite it.

"He told me you're dying, that you're having his bambino." Thorn inclines his head.

"Okay?" I ask, irritation blooming through every pore.

So?

"He loves you."

I stare at Thorn.

I shake my head. "Not enough."

His smile is wide and genuine. "Now that's where you're wrong."

He leans down and speaks quietly in my ear.

It's not sweet nothings.

It's a nefarious plan.

CHAPTER 23

Doctor Ludwig squirts cold clear gel on my stomach, and I cringe from the iciness. I hold in the pee from the full bladder he insisted I have.

Sympathy lines his face. "I know, it's awful at first."

The sonogram lights up, and there's nothing but black and white fog.

Then a shadow so small I can hardly see it appears in the smog of my womb.

I look at Ludwig, and his eyes crinkle at the corners.

"Can't detect the heartbeat yet. Too soon."

He runs the wand over my skin, and it heats. Finally. Just as it becomes warm enough to bear, it's over, and he wipes down my stomach.

My bladder screams for release and I pop up.

The machine kicks out a photo and he blows on it, handing it to me.

My throat tightens and my eyes burn. *It really is a peanut.*

I forget my need to pee.

I open my mouth to ask my burning question and he says, "I don't know."

"How'd you know what I was going to ask?"

"Everyone wants to know if it's a boy or girl." Like, *elementary my dear Watson.*

"You can use the restroom now."

But my mind is elsewhere. I smile at the picture of my future child.

Mine and Mick's.

* * *

I visit the restroom on my way out, my new favorite place and whistle a tune.

I don't have Mick, though Thorn's plan is a good one. I don't have to trap Mick. I'm pregnant and won't live long enough to be more than a blip on his screen.

Thorn swears that if Mick doesn't spend my final months with me, he'll regret it.

After all, Rose McKenna left him with a wicked case of survivor's guilt.

His feelings don't make a ton of sense.

At seventeen, there was nothing he could have done. Thorn did what he could, and he still paid an unfair price.

The problem is—I don't want Mick to be with me out of guilt.

For the first time, I'll chase him.

Because of love. There's no denying it. I love him, and that's all.

Thorn promised me it was the last thing I could do to ease Mick when I'm no longer here.

And maybe it'll ease me.

Thorn has a sensitive streak. It's wide enough to accommodate mainly Mick. I don't try to talk myself into believing that Thorn gives a tin shit about me. He's worried over Mick.

I pause on the steps of Ludwig's swank downtown

complex and scroll through my messages. As I do, Mick should be receiving the image I carry in my pocket of our child via my matter-of-fact media text. No words, just the pic.

He can think whatever he wants.

I feel like ass, but I managed to change into my come-hither clothes before I left the doctor's.

I look at my texts, scrolling until I get to Thorn's message with the address.

I read the address again. Mick's offices are right where Thorn said they would be, within kissing distance of Ludwig's. For all I know, Mick owns the entire city block.

I remember Mick's offer of lunch in New York City. It's too surreal for words. What would it be like to go out of state for *lunch*? I laugh out loud, unconcerned about how crazy I look, laughing at nothing.

I pause at the stoplight, waiting for the white hand.

The orangey-red one blinks its angry rhythm.

The white hand appears, and I cross, a partial jog causing a spring in my step. A hot dog vendor's wares steal across the air and tickle my nose.

My stomach lurches at the rich, greasy smell.

A woman with exotic perfume strides by, her high heels mimicking mine.

It stirs my nausea like witch's brew. I cover my mouth and nose with my bad hand, hopping up on the curb and racing for the skyscraper that has *McKenna Enterprises* emblazoned across the front in elegant script. They're deeply embossed and black, solid copper piping making them stand out in subtle opulence. I briefly note the neon tubing in the crevice of each letter for nighttime.

I rip open the door and take a sucking breath in relief.

City smells don't greet me inside.

It's ultra-modern: glass, quartz, and an eternity fountain.

It smells blissfully like nothing.

Green plants swarm up the corners, begging to be a jungle. A pretty receptionist sees me and smiles.

I know I look good. I have on the outfit Kiki and Thorn insisted I wear.

It's the one I wore for Mick in the revolving restaurant of our first date. Meant to trigger nostalgia, provoke feelings.

Beads tickle my upper thighs as I move toward the sign that indicates where the elevators are located. Thorn told me to surprise him.

I'm not making polite noises of inquiry. The societal cues are no longer important.

The receptionist frowns.

Stripper wear is probably not normal attire here.

Or maybe it is. The Black Rose *is* owned by Mick.

I flutter my fingers at her in a feigned wave of confidence. Coached by Thorn, I act as if I'm expected.

"You're here to see…?" She seems a little frantic, as if she might charge around the desk and tackle me if I inch closer to the elevator.

I say what Thorn told me to say. "Audition."

She looks momentarily perplexed but nods. "All right."

She slowly sits down, and I move to the elevator, feeling expert in my high heels.

I feel her eyes on my back.

Inside the elevator that parted as I neared it, I push the 40th floor button and the elevator moves like grease through a goose. No lurching in this place.

I close my eyes, feeling weightless.

Feeling hope.

This is the last good thing I can do in this life.

No regrets for either of us. If it works out, everyone wins. Thorn told me he knows Mick will cave if I show up and remind him of what he's missing.

"You're that drop of water that's not the mirage in his desert," Thorn said.

The elevator stops with a small sway and chime, and my eyes open. The doors whisk open, and I move into an open hallway.

It's soft and dark—noiseless.

Pictures line the walls. Great men gaze dispassionately back at me—inventors, writers, and even a few presidents.

The door anchors the middle of the wall that I approach. I feel their eyes watch me from inside their imperious frames.

Mick's name scrolls in full across the door and I learn his middle name.

Jared Ulysses McKenna.

It makes me wonder what the baby's name will be.

Muffled voices reach me, and I hesitate as my tummy does a little flop.

Thorn had assured me he'd be alone, that he'd be receptive.

With effort, I shore up my weak confidence.

I move my hand from my rioting stomach to the doorknob. The metal grows warm as I hesitate like a chicken. I suck in a huge breath and open the door. I walk inside and stop in my tracks at the scene before me.

Mick stands in the center of his office, a wall of glass overlooking the city.

His city.

Soft music plays as a beautiful woman gyrates in front of him.

Her pendulous breasts sway to the rhythm of a song I don't recognize. Long chestnut hair touches the small of her back, a jeweled g-string bisecting her ass.

She must see his expression. She stops dancing, turning to look at me.

Cat-like green eyes run up and down my body. Dismissing me.

"I..." I stagger backward, almost losing my balance. From the front, I notice the triangle of cloth barely covers her goods.

The mystery girl smirks.

"Wait your turn, skank."

Skank?

"Christy!" Mick says in a sharp reprimand.

I choose that moment to have a morning sickness bout like never before. I drop to my knees, vomiting on Mick's pristine carpet.

"Faren." His voice is close.

At the moment, Mick's concern means nothing.

I've just seen him with a half-naked woman days after he dumped me.

When my stomach is empty, I feel a hand on my elbow.

"Oooh! Fucking sick!" the lovely bitch whines.

I'm too overwhelmed to notice. I'm dizzy and revolted.

Shattered.

I look at the mess I've made.

The sight makes me feel a little better. If I had the energy, I'd smile. There's a poetic justice to being sick in the middle of Mick's little soiree.

"Let go of me," I say, tearing my elbow out of his grasp.

His earnest eyes plead with me. "This is not what it looks like."

Oh, I'm so sure.

He makes me want to barf again. On him.

Gotta work on my aim. I bark out a laugh that sounds more than a little crazy.

I back away, glancing at the girl again.

I look at Mick.

I flip off the girl, smoothly channeling Kiki.

Another feel good.

I look at Mick as if I can light him on fire from my gaze alone. "I can't believe I misjudged you so." Angry tears run down my face.

"Faren!" Mick calls after me.

Fat lot of fucking good it does.

I spin back around to face him, and he stops inches from me.

I slap him so hard my wrist feels broken.

It also feels wonderful.

"Bastard."

He grabs my wrist and cranks my arm behind my back. I feel my body tense, waiting for the beat down. The one that Ronnie always gave me. His death has made old wounds and fears resurface like oil on brackish water.

I think of my peanut.

"Please, don't hurt me."

I know I smell like puke, and my fear made me stupid—reactive.

He leans forward, nuzzling my neck.

It's so unexpected, I flinch.

He ignores me, burying hot wet pleasure on my throat with his lips. "I will never hurt you."

Mick releases my wrist and steps away.

Our eyes meet, and the naked woman walks up to lay a possessive hand on his bare forearm.

I can't tear my eyes away from the sight of her fingers as they curl around his arm. Her ebony nails shout from his skin like beetles.

"Who's this dumb bitch?" she asks.

My spine straightens. I answer Mick, though his comment didn't require a response, "You already have."

I don't wait.
I vanish again.
This time for good.

CHAPTER 24

THURSDAY

I squeeze Mom's hand. She squeezes back. "Tell me, Faren." My chin dips. I thought the well of my tears had run dry, but one comes. Many others join the first.

When I've had a good bawl, I get out the first words. "I'm pregnant."

Mom smiles with benevolence. "I know."

I feel my shock register.

"Mothers know these things."

"How?" I ask.

She strokes my cheek. "I just do. And… you've been looking a little green around the gills."

I think that's the understatement of the year, but I say nothing. Her situation is so much more profound than my little bit of pregnancy puke.

"Is it Mick's?"

I give a single, miserable nod.

Her eyes are steady on me. "What is he going to do?"

"He doesn't want me."

I can't tell her why. She can't know I'm terminal.

My mom's eyebrow lifts, and she gives a small cough. I

bend forward with the sippy cup, feeling a sense of double vision that she's actually here now. A surreal doubling of reality and wishfulness collide. Her existence is a hope I'd left behind years ago. My heart soars to have this window of time with my mom.

"I find that hard to believe." She sweeps her palm at me. "Look at you, my gorgeous girl."

My face heats, and my bad hand closes around my cheek. "Mom..."

"I know you think I'm prejudiced, darling, but how many model types are running around with a set of smarts wedged between their ears, eh?"

I don't know how to respond to that. I'm a former stripper who can't keep food down, was dumped by her billionaire boyfriend, and has months to live. Things don't seem golden.

"When are you due?"

I do the math and come up with roughly Christmas Day.

"Fantastic!" Mom exclaims. "Just the gift I'm looking for."

She's too good in her assessments, not judging—all support. It makes me feel like shit for not telling her everything.

It makes me know that I can't.

"I'm not married... I'm going to be a single mom... I've made bad choices," I mumble. It doesn't matter that it was accidental. At the end of the day, another life is depending on me.

"Faren, look at me."

I slowly raise my chin.

"My grandchild is not a bad choice. You don't have to be married to be loved."

I open my mouth to deny Mick loves me. Old Tonka Tit proved it. My worth is so little that he was interviewing strippers in his office.

Her face becomes deadly serious.

"And if a young woman can survive Ron, become a physical therapist, and take care of her mother who's in a coma? Then I think she can manage to take care of her child. Besides"—she squeezes my knee—"you have me now."

"Mom..." I want her to concentrate on her recovery, not trying to bail me out of my unlucky circumstances.

"No arguments. Now I have a goal that will see me through the horror of my noodle appendages."

I sigh. "That's normal."

"Well, I don't have to like it, do I?"

I shake my head. She's got a solid six months before she'll walk unassisted.

But she will.

"When's Kandace stopping by for a visit?"

Between her studies and poles, she's barely free to breathe.

"Soon."

The silence is awkward, and I know Mom's going to ask me some tough questions. Call it a hunch.

"So—Mick?"

"Yeah," I reply, sounding grumpy.

Her eyes grow round. "Will he take care of the baby? Because he certainly possesses the means."

Yes, he does.

I think about his tender regard for me as he showered kisses like falling flower petals against my stomach.

"Yes. He's going to be a part of all of it. Even though we're not together."

"How did this happen?" Mom asks.

I laugh. I can't help it.

She does too. "Obviously, I understand the mechanics." Her dry voice reminds me of better times.

My smile fades. "I was on the pill and borrowed some of Kiki's migraine medication. The combo made me..."

"Fertile Mertile."

"Ah..."

"Just an expression." Mom smiles.

"Kind of a weird one!"

Her smile becomes tight around the edges before it fades. "You're looking too thin, Faren."

"I can't keep anything down but Kiki's jello."

Mom groans. "No more of that. When I was pregnant with you, I ate graham crackers and milk."

My lips quirk. Interesting combination.

"You get calcium, and the body's stomach acids are somewhat neutralized by the crackers; they're very neutral."

A thought strikes me. "Did you have cravings?"

"You're too early for that, but yes." She cocks her head to the side.

"Corn on the cob and peanut M&Ms."

I barely make it to the commode.

The remnants of Jello float in the water, and I slap the lid down to hide the sight.

"Faren!"

I sigh, my fingertips gripping the edge of the toilet seat. My bad hand covers my nose and mouth.

"Just a sec."

***

I DELETE another text from Mick after I tell him: *If it's not about my mom or peanut, I don't want to hear it.*

I don't want to hear lies and excuses or feel like I was never special.

I'm having a good day. I got dry toast down in the morning, glorious graham crackers and milk for lunch, and now

I'm looking in Kiki's cabinet for more of the gross/manageable Jello.

My cell vibrates on her granite island.

I read the text twice, wondering if it's a ploy. I decide it isn't.

I unwrap my damp hair from the towel, dab on minimalist makeup, and throw on clothes.

I get mad when I check the mirror before I leave, adding another layer of lipstick. *Who cares if I look pretty for Mick?*

I do.

I swipe my car keys off the counter to meet with the lawyers, Mick and Thorn.

I don't need the pregnancy to make my stomach churn.

* * *

"He'll go to prison," the first of four lawyers says.

It's a ping-pong match as the second leans forward, his black monochromatic ensemble broken only by a blood-red tie. "Even if that end is assured, we must erase all trace of Mr. McKenna's involvement."

The third lawyer looks as if he has Irish blood, his carrot hair and piercing green eyes are accentuated by an emerald bow tie.

Who wears those?

"It's a sordid clusterfuck. Sorry, McKenna, just saying it like it is."

He actually *is* Irish.

Mick nods. "I know how it looks. However, if Thorn and I—"

"Who?" the fourth mouthpiece asks in a lilt.

"Tyson Simpson," Irish supplies.

"Ah." He tilts his head back in understanding.

Mick sighs. "If it hadn't been for Ty and me, then Miss Mitchell would not be sitting here."

"And she carries your child?" Monochromatic inquires.

My head explodes in flames. I want a bucket of water to put out the raging inferno of embarrassment.

Irish assesses my expression. "Full disclosure, lass."

Oh Jesus, that somehow makes it so much better.

Not.

Thorn chuckles, shaking his head.

"I don't find anything funny at these proceedings, Simpson."

Thorn looks at the fourth lawyer. "Yeah? Well, your lack of humor doesn't stop me from thinking this whole thing blows." His looks at them with a sweeping scorn and gives a grunt of disgust. "This prick Tagger 'might' go to prison? That loose cannon has been gunning for Mick and me for a decade. He was using her stepdad as some kind of informant, and he tried to frame me. Can anyone say rinse and repeat?"

"Thorn—" Mick begins.

Thorn scrubs his head. "Nah, bro, fuck this."

Irish is the only lawyer who looks unperturbed by the colorful Thorn, who continues, unfettered by convention.

I wish I had an ounce of Thorn, I think wistfully.

Irish's eyes slant down on me. "You said that Tagger 'cornered' you and Miss..." Irish runs a perfectly manicured finger down his notes. He taps once as he reaches Kiki's name. "King?"

I nod.

Mick's face darkens. "When did this happen?"

He wasn't around for my deposition.

"A few days ago."

"See?" Thorn says, slapping his palm down on the table and I jump. "This prick doesn't feel accountable. He thinks because he's a boy in blue, he'll just get away with it. But no!"

His eyes scrutinize everyone there. "He admitted to going after me. He let Bunce go and did the kamikaze and hauled off Faren. Then he got shot by one of the other cops."

"They're claiming friendly fire," Monochromatic says.

"Bullshit," Thorn answers instantly.

"He still might walk. However, he's not locked down very tight until this comes to trial."

"Clearly," I mutter. I can't wait until Tagger's out of my life. Just the threat of him popping up tightens my stomach.

He and Jay. The worst complications.

Of course that's when I get a text from Jay.

Jay: *I need to see you. Make amends.*

Me: *No—Mick and I are over. So you can stop worrying about it. Just do your deal with Mick and never text me again.*

Jay: *I like that you're not with Mick. He's not worthy of you, Faren.*

I roll my eyes. *Creep.*

Me: *Stop texting me.*

"Faren?"

I look up.

"Are we boring you?" Mick asks, eyeing my phone.

I slip it into my handbag. "No. I'm not bored. I'm excited." I nod and stand.

Mick's eyebrows rise.

"I'm so excited to be here talking about a crooked cop and how he might skirt justice. So thrilled to be pregnant with a child whose mother isn't who McKenna wants."

The lawyers look at me as if I've sprouted a second head.

I'm on a roll like a locomotive without a depot.

"I'm so fucking stoked to be dying and still have to make everyone else feel good about it that I can hardly stand myself."

It's an epic fail. Full fucking disclosure, Faren-style.

I swing my purse strap onto my shoulder.

I look at the lawyers, then at Mick.

Their shocked faces are almost worth it.

"Now, I'm taking my excitement with me."

"Faren."

I hear a chair scrape.

I smell his clean sharp scent before I feel his hand on my shoulder.

"Get away from me, Mick. You have your life."

I turn and look at him over my shoulder.

"And I have what's left of mine."

I jerk my shoulder out of his grip and slip through the conference door.

It shuts quietly behind me.

CHAPTER 25

I swish smocks through the closet, looking for just the right one. I'm not one to complain, but Kiki's guest closet is even smaller than my old apartment's.

My work scrubs are crammed to the extreme left, and cardboard boxes are stacked floor to ceiling in every corner of the room. A twin bed and tall old dresser face each other, and a window absorbs the center of the wall that looks out over Puget Sound.

My mood is shit. The lawyer meeting and ensuing aftertaste feels as if I chugged a diet pop in ten seconds flat.

Just thinking about chugging makes me gulp hard against the gorge that rises.

I take out Spongebob. It fits my snarky mood. I have my CAT scan with Matthews and will have to fill him in on the pregnancy. That'll be the most fun I've had since this all began. I can hear his irresponsibility lecture now. And I can't really tell him who the father is.

I'm sure it won't be okay for my child's future for people to associate peanut with me. Mick would have to protect he/she from my past as a stripper. Dying. Bunce. I'm all kinds of bad news.

I blow hair from my face.

I don't let pity tears fall but they fill my eyeballs. I hold them wide so the tears gather but remain unshed.

I go through the motions of getting ready, deciding on a braid to keep my hair out of my face and not smelling the perfume from my shampoo is a plus.

I pack my lunch of crackers with my thermos of milk and set off.

I keep working my bad hand and manage to stave off the spasms with alternating applied heat and strength training for the most part.

I use it now to drive the key into my car lock and turn it fluidly. I slide into my car and turn over the engine.

I watch the crystal spin from the rearview mirror.

Shifting into reverse, I follow the arrows out of the parking garage.

I wait my turn as the arm moves up and down, allowing vehicles out.

The other side allows a limo in.

I'd recognize it anywhere.

My eyes meet Henry's for only a second or two, but I see what I need to.

Compassion, understanding.

I turn away, accelerating under the yellow and white arm.

* * *

I GO to my job by rote alone. I'm on some kind of autopilot. I wonder how Mick feels—is he robotic?

A vision of the bitch stripper fills my mind.

Probably not.

I park and head to the clinic.

I'm not so dead inside that I don't pause before opening the heavy glass door.

The cherry trees have buds in the deepest pink, like gems waiting to burst, and they lift my heart.

These days, I look for anything that does.

My hand covers my tummy, and I feel a surge of gratefulness for peanut. It gives life meaning. More than just me.

Just more.

Happiness comes in snatches, and I take every one.

* * *

"Excellent," I say and mean it.

Glory looks at me, her eyes narrowed from the strain. Her name's really Gloria, but it never took. She thought it'd be a good idea to go to the skate park and go toe-to-toe with her teenage son.

That's all well and good if you're seventeen too.

Unfortunately, Glory is forty-two. Her arm thought so too. But she's not a life-sized Gumby.

Her arm went one way and her body the other.

Now Glory is a semi-permanent patient of mine.

"One more rep. Really rotate the cuff."

I listen hard for the snap of overexertion, the telltale overextend. Sometimes that's a problem with hyper-flexible people. Their arm tries to cooperate as much as it can. Overdoing it is common.

Glory strains, the tension bleeding up her neck as the tendons stick out like guitar strings.

"That's it. Slow is better. Full motion... There. Done," I say. "Settle the pulley. Don't just let it go."

I receive my millionth glare and smile back with encouragement. Sometimes it's all my patients can latch onto.

At least, that's what they tell me when they're all done and better.

Glory leans back. Her recovering arm dangles along the side of the weight bench. "That is absolutely miserable."

"Yes." Because it's true.

Her eyes meet mine. "How do you know?"

Her tone accuses me of false empathy.

I raise my hand, palm out, and she catches the proof of my past.

"Oh."

I nod. "I get it."

She doesn't ask how. It's a wound of violence.

I wait.

When Glory's had her rest, she resumes.

Stronger than before.

Like I want.

Like she needs.

* * *

Friday

I haven't thrown up yet and I'm cautiously hopeful that the combination of crackers, milk and jello are keeping the nausea under control.

I enter Dr. Matthews's clinic and slide my insurance card through a slot a lot like the reception partition at my PA clinic.

The girl behind the desk gives me a bald smile of indifference as she makes sure I'm still insured.

A frown creases her brow.

"Miss Mitchell?"

"Yes?"

Please don't let there be a problem.

"Your bill has been taken care of by a private party."

Mick.

Of course.

I feel shame coat my cheeks like clown paint.

The first genuine smile she's ever bestowed on me flashes across her thin lips. "A guardian angel."

I used to think so.

I nod and say nothing. Mick said I made him know heaven only to toss him in hell.

I know exactly how he feels.

"Thank you," I say.

Her smile falters a little. Most people would be ecstatic that their health care bill of over three hundred thousand was null and void.

Not me.

The price is too high.

She recovers her composure and says, "Room three. The CAT tech will run you through."

* * *

"I'm not doing it." I'm so resolute I feel it clear to my toenails.

"Dr. Matthews has ordered a re-CAT," the tech states as though I'm being a willful child.

"Well, I have some news that'll change that."

The tech glares at me. "Fine. We'll get doc in here, and he can talk to you."

He stomps off, and I sit in the room, listening to the CAT's mechanical whir.

Ready for me.

Faren in a tube. Peanut getting radiation many times that of an X-ray.

I don't think so.

I carefully set aside the clipboard with its damning release form.

Doctor Clive Matthews breezes in.

"Faren?"

"I can't."

His brow wrinkles. "Okay... We discussed this on our latest phone conversation, and you were in agreement. What's changed since then?"

I feel myself grow lightheaded. I know what's coming.

"What is it?" My chart, caught in his curled hand, drops to his side, his gaze serious behind slightly convex lenses.

He studies me with compassion.

I take several breaths.

"I'm pregnant."

He just looks at me. Then he asks the same thing my mom did.

"How is this possible?"

I don't laugh, the question is posed so seriously. "I—I took some meds for my headaches and they negated the effectiveness of my birth control."

Matthews rocks back on his heels, chin down.

He's silent for a few moments.

His magnified eyes meet mine. "This changes protocol, Faren."

"I know," I mumble.

"Is the father..." He struggles to verbalize the terrible possibilities.

"Yes. He'll take care of peanut after... after..."

His hand drops on my shoulder, and I break apart.

Finally my tears shudder to a stop, and I wipe my sleeve against my face.

He says, "Peanut?"

I shrug. "I don't know if it's a boy or girl... I don't know anything, but the baby looks like a peanut."

He smiles. "They do in the beginning."
I give a watery smile back.
Then my doctor lies, and I love him for it.
He pats my shoulder. "It'll be okay, Faren."
I nod, believing him—if even for a moment.

CHAPTER 26

SUNDAY NIGHT

"Ta-dah!" Kiki says, spinning around a beautiful charcoal gray top. Skinny glitter threads run through it. It has a soft cowl neck and a fitted band at the tunic-length end.

"I love it," I admit, though clothing has always been way down the list of important stuff.

She judges my expression and pouts. "I know, I know. You won't be able to wear it for months. Until you get a Buddha belly."

"When I can eat actual food again."

She nods, a goofy smile plastered to her face. "Yeah."

Then her face changes. "I think you need to write me into your will or something. I don't want that asshat Mick saying I can't have auntie privileges with Peanut."

I feel my nose scrunch. "God, we need to get the baby a name or the baby will be named after food forever."

"I don't know," she muses, "I kinda dig Peanut. Ready for Jello?"

I make a face. "What flavor?"

"The flavor that doesn't make you do the puke-a-thon."

Yeah.

My cell buzzes.

A text from Jay, which I ignore.

"Jay again."

Kiki gives an explosive sigh of disgust. "Y'know, some dudes need the entire can of pepper spray. Just a squirt won't do."

I laugh.

My cell rings in my hand and startles me so much I almost drop it.

I yell, catching it midair with both hands. "Hello!"

"Faren, it's Doctor Matthews."

I fluster a response. "What?" He's the absolute last person I expect to phone me on a Sunday night.

"It's Doctor Matthews."

"Yes. Hi, Doctor..."

"I need you to come in right away."

My heart pounds. *What's wrong?*

"What's wrong?"

"It's something that needs to be discussed in person."

I feel my eyes widen.

"Okay..."

"Faren, let someone else drive you. Maybe the baby's father."

"No way," I answer immediately.

The open phone lines hum.

"Fine, but someone."

My eyes flick to Kiki, who's still as a statue. "I have someone."

She nods.

"Good. Come right away."

"I will."

The line goes dead.

Has the tumor grown? Can I no longer count on the eight

months I need for my baby?

"What is it?" Kiki asks.

"I don't know. It was Dr. Matthews. He says I need to come in."

Her brow furrows. "On a Sunday? Is he a quack?"

I shake my head, my lips quirked. "He's definitely not a quack."

Her brow furrows. "Probably bad news if he doesn't want to tell you over the phone."

Kiki's got a way of telling the truth that hurts. Those are the words I'm thinking but don't want to say.

"Let's find out," she says. "I mean, really? What can he tell you that's worse than dying?"

She shrugs, trying to ease me.

I accept that it's bad. My hand moves unconsciously over my belly.

I'm not giving up without a fight.

"Ready?" Kiki asks, car keys in hand, her other grips the doorknob.

"Yes."

Whatever it is, defeat will never own me again.

* * *

MATTHEWS'S FACE is like granite. *I'm* nervous by how nervous he is.

"First, I can't tell you how sorry I am. There's nothing I can do to give you back the time you've lost," he says.

Kiki reaches for my hand, and I squeeze it.

He takes a deep breath. "We've made a grave error."

Oh no... I don't have months. *I have days.*

"There is another young woman who has terminal cancer."

What? "Like me?" I'm trying to connect the dots and not making it work.

"No," he says.

Kiki gasps, and I drop her hand.

"Not like you."

"I—what?"

"You don't have cancer. I'm breaking every HIPPA code, but I owe you this. Farrah Michael does."

"Who?"

I've been slapped.

Beaten.

Trounced.

I don't understand.

"I know it's a lot to take in. There was a mix-up with the images. Your name was next in line, and somehow, it was placed on the wrong set of patient photos during processing..."

He spreads his arms wide, his face somber with injustice, regret, and a myriad of other emotions.

Kiki stands. "You mean to tell me you got Faren's photos mixed up with some other broad's because their names are alphabetically side-by-side? What load of crap is this? I couldn't make this horseshit up if I worked for it!"

"Kiki," I say quietly.

She turns, as pissed off as I've ever seen her. "What?"

"I'm not going to die."

Matthews gives Kiki a wary glance and nods. "That's right. I couldn't get Faren's pregnancy out of my mind. We weren't able to do another CAT to assess progression, so I did some digging..."

"Why didn't you accept the diagnosis you gave me?"

He lifts his hands in surrender. "I'm a man of science." He takes off his glasses, pretending to polish them with the bottom of his white lab coat. He slides them back on. "But sometimes even I want to believe in a miracle. It nagged at me. I trusted my gut."

His eyes shine.

Mine do too.

"I'm beyond mad at you."

"Me too," he concedes, inclining his head.

"Me three, jackass," Kiki trills, and he winces.

Doctor Matthews stands and walks to the lighted box for Cat images and X-rays. He clips photos in place.

"Here's your brain, Faren."

It doesn't take a rocket scientist to see that it's perfect.

He slides my X-ray beside my CAT, then does the same with Farrah's.

My one cavity looks like a solid block in the sea of my teeth.

Her teeth are dotted like a speckled egg.

"Dentition does not lie," he states quietly.

I meet him around the desk.

As mad as I am, Doctor Matthews is still the bearer of the news that completes me. Kiki's crying in the background.

I hug Matthews, and he hugs back.

I will live.

CHAPTER 27

I watch Kiki spin the wheel. Pools of light and shadow illuminate her face, large hoops glittering from her lobes as she rattles on.

"I say sue his dumb ass—god!" She bangs her hand on the steering column and winces.

I hide my smile badly.

"What?" she yells into the confines of the Fiat. "You've *got* to nail his ass to the wall."

"No," I say softly.

"Faren..."

Kiki turns into the entrance for the underground parking at the Millennium and swipes her card through the code slot. It pings, the auto arm lifts and she zips underneath. Parking near the elevators, she turns to look at me. The florescent lights turn her face a sickly yellow.

"You lived with a false diagnosis for over a month!"

I jerk my shoulders in irritation. "It's wrong. But, I think what it was is a gift in disguise."

Her brows cinch. "Come again? Ah—*no!*"

"Yes, it is. I mean..." I look into her eyes, cast in shadow.

"How many people recognize how precious life is? We hear it all the time, but they're just words people say without truly realizing the meaning."

I turn away and stare at the rows of cars. I place my hand over my heart, the beat of it inside my chest thrills me. I know that I'll live, that I have life—that I'm giving life.

I move my gaze back to hers. "That knowledge allows me to forgive. I don't want to spend one second wasting it on hate and vengeance. It's not about what's right and wrong here, but the chance I've been given."

Kiki blows a piece of hair out of her face, crossing her arms in a huff. "I still want to flog somebody."

I laugh. "Okay, *you* can be pissed."

"Well, I am."

"Okay." I touch her arm. "Let's look at the good junk."

"You be the optimist while I look for someone's ass to kick."

I ignore her anger. Kiki needs to compartmentalize stuff that hurts; it's how she's survived.

I love her.

"I don't have to tell my mom I'm dying," I say.

She nods. "Ya got me there."

"I get to live to see my child. Raise peanut. It doesn't get any better than that."

Kiki's lips twitch. "Well, now that you're off death row..."

I laugh. Her comment lacks any kind of tact or sensitivity, which somehow makes it better.

"You'll have to figure out your own accommodations. I'm not taking this auntie care very seriously. Give me the munchkin when said munchkin is fed, watered, bathed, and has a clean diaper. Ah-huh."

I grin. "Sounds a little conditional."

"Damn straight!" Kiki looks at me from under her

eyelashes. "I'm not ready for a screaming tornado of barf and poop!"

Nice visual.

"That's okay. I know your limits."

Kiki sits up on her knees and leans across the gearshift, hugging me so tightly I can't breathe.

"I was so scared, Faren."

I pat her back.

"I know."

She releases me.

"Y'know, if I swung for the other team, you'd flat out do it for me."

I hold her hand, loving the way she tries to ease my emotional roller coaster with humor that veils terror.

"You just haven't found the man who does it for you."

Her expression bleeds into the beginnings of sadness. "Like your Mick?"

I don't say anything for a breath of heartbeats.

My answer is awful.

It's brutally honest. "Yes."

* * *

I SLEEP ALL NIGHT. No nausea, no headaches.

Sadness and joy mingle in a paradox inside me.

When I open my eyes, dawn breaks through my window like prisms of promise. The first kiss of daybreak is almost colorless, a white almost-light that bathes my room in ethereal smoke. Dust motes swirl lazily in the rays that seep and deepen.

I stay in bed, listening to my heart beat. When I was little, I always thought the sound was a man walking in the snow. Now I know what that proof of life really means.

Hope.

Tomorrow will come, then the next day. And the next.

It's what I want to do with it that will matter in the end.

I turn my head at the soft knock at my door.

"Come in."

Kiki strolls in, a backpack with sparkles hiked up on one shoulder. "Gotta take off."

We look at each other and I see her struggle to fight tears. "It's weird not to have to be brave anymore," she says.

I nod. "Yeah."

"It's like someone turned on the tear faucet and it's a leaking nightmare." She huffs. "And where's that foxy plumber to come fix it?" She laughs.

I do too.

"Yeah." I frown, thinking how neglectful I've been about the details of her life. "How much time left for school?"

"Just two months until graduation, baby."

I feel my lips curl. "Right, then it's more school."

Kiki nods. "I like the torture. Closet masochist."

I feel my eyebrow rise.

"Okay," she admits, "maybe not so closet. I like to give and receive." She says and winks.

Kiki's told me about her activities. They sound dangerous. But everyone has an outlet, and as long as it's consensual...

"Don't give me that look. You might like a little tie-down once in a while."

"Not with... no," I say.

"Oh right, you're all bun-in-the-oven."

I laugh. "God, Kiki, it's not just that. I've had one partner..."

"The goddamned dodo bird." She sulks.

I say nothing, clenching my hands as I stare at them. I take my isometric handgrip off the small nightstand and work my bad hand.

Kiki's eyes go to my deft, rhythmic cycling through the strengthening routine. "Hey," she calls softly.

I raise my head.

"I *can* be mad at him. He had some ho with her dangling tits in his office about half a second after he tossed your pregnant ass out. I'm thinking he's a bird."

"Birds are nice," I say, thinning my lips to keep from smiling.

"Uh—they shit all over everything and carry a plethora of disease."

I bust up, grinning.

"Nice."

She waits. Finally, Kiki raises her cell. "Text me anytime."

"I will. But right now, I need to get my rear in gear and get to the clinic."

"And tonight we visit Tannin?"

"Yes."

"Things are looking up, girl."

I smile without tears.

"Yes, they are."

Neither one of us mentions that Mick will have to know that I'm going to live.

Not that it matters.

He didn't want me.

CHAPTER 28

I softly shut the door behind me and Sue is standing there. Her arms are folded underneath her ample bosom, and a scowl is plastered across her face.

"What's going on, Faren?"

My eyes dart around the four corners of the long corridor that leads from the reception desk to the three doors that house our facilities. No escape.

"You don't have the flu," she states.

Our gazes lock.

I shake my head. "No."

She waits and I exhale in frustration.

"I guess I need to come out with it."

Her eyebrow cocks, and her hands fist on her hips. "We have fifteen minutes before your first patient."

My teeth sink into my trembling lower lip, but I manage to spit out, "I think it'll take longer than that."

Her face fills with concern. "Come here and sit down, honey."

I think of the owner counting on me to do my job. "Grambley..."

"Grambley, shambley," Sue clucks. "We need to get you up to snuff. If a good chat-and-bawl session is the way to do it" —she spreads her hands from her wide hips—"that's what it's going to be."

"What do you know?" I ask.

Sue looks at me, and I duck my head at her expression. Her finger lifts my chin, and I bite my lip. "I see a young woman who has needed to shoulder too much, too soon. Who has worked hard, had tragedy and takes too much upon herself."

My shoulders round. "I—I'm pregnant," I blurt.

Sue smirks. "I figured. I'm not a dull tool in the shed, you know."

I fluster. "I didn't say that you were..."

"I know you didn't. But I have children. I was young once." She watches my face and chuckles. "Don't look so surprised."

I am, but I try to hide it. I feel shame at the level of my self-absorption.

I begin to speak. Slowly at first, then gaining momentum.

I talk past when my first patient arrives, and Sue holds up a finger and excuses herself.

She comes back and says, "Ten minutes."

I finish in eight.

Sue rolls her lip into her teeth and palms her chin. "So this McKenna is the father? And he has everything at his disposal... but when he found out you were terminal..." She shakes her head. "But you're not—god, a person could go insane with this. It's almost like walking through a funhouse full of mirrors."

I nod. That is my life.

"I think he was trying to take it back, to reach out. See if I—if we could talk."

Susan's face scrunches up. "Well, that man would have to

make a helluva apology to make up for that chasm of a *faux pas.*"

I agree. I'm not sure if I want him.

At least, that's what I convince myself of. I've never been adept at self-delusion.

Sue squeezes my shoulder. "Thank you for telling me. I want to be there for you. I heard about the assault charge, that was later dropped." At my nod, she continues, "And your mom's miracle."

We smile.

"And Mr. Bunce's perfect ending."

I feel my frown but there's relief mixed in.

She says, "Don't you dare feel guilty that awful man is gone from this earth. It's a better place with his absence."

I can't argue that.

She takes my left hand and turns up my palm. We stare at what Ronnie did to me four years ago.

"He didn't deserve to live another day."

I nod, but I wonder if I get to play God. If there's a price for what I've done.

* * *

My hand presses into my back, and I arch, stretching like a cat in the sun. Every kink pops, and I sigh with pleasure. It's been a strenuous day of cracking the whip on reluctant patients and nibbling at food I'm already sick of just to keep the nausea at bay.

I smile at Sue as I leave, and she lifts her huge smartphone. I lift my iPhone in return. We've exchanged numbers. She wants to be my support.

It's funny in a non-humorous way how people keep slipping through the cracks in my defenses.

I'm finally learning to accept help. I keep thinking I can

do it all. When really, it's been my pride all along that holds me back.

I walk down the broad steps into sun that spears through the pewter clouds like steel wool. All around me, the Fuji cherry trees have burst, and sprigs of cotton candy float on the ends of densely covered branches. A light drizzle falls as I move toward my car. My dampening scrubs cling to me lightly.

I notice the man then.

He reminds me very much of Thorn. But—he's not.

Ronnie is gone, but my paranoia remains. I slip into my car and take my lip gloss from my purse. I shiver once out of the rain and inside my cold vehicle. I adjust the mirror and pretend to put on the slug slime.

I'm really looking at him.

He appears to be talking into his hand.

Time to go.

I start the engine but before I take off I remove my cell from my scrub pocket.

My finger hovers over Mick's name.

I feel my pulse beat in my ears, the roar of blood is a river of noise. It carries my trepidation like shed debris, choking the waters of my mind.

My fingertip moves between *send* and *delete* contact.

I choose the one that feels like closure and slip my cell back into my pocket.

I look in the mirror, and the mystery hulk is gone.

I shake off the disquiet and drive to Kiki's house. A long shower and a visit with my mom sounds great.

I forget all about the stranger in my mirror.

* * *

I EAT strawberry Jell-O with sliced bananas, mechanically chewing as I cruise baby clothes at Nordstrom's online. I almost don't notice the light flash on for my webcam.

I hit the side of the laptop, and it turns off. *Stupid thing.* My Mac has been acting up for the last couple of weeks, and I haven't had the time or interest to worry about a malfunctioning webcam. I turn on my playlist and leave the computer on the dresser.

I walk to the closet and pull out my jeans and a new shirt. I run my hands over the pretty maternity top Kiki got for me, and I smile before putting it back. When I get a belly, it'll be cute. Right now, I've actually lost weight from my involuntary Jell-O and fruit diet. I pull out a snug long-sleeved tee in bright orange and a cream cami and walk to the bed, tossing off my work clothes. I sway a little to the music, remembering the only good part about poles—the dancing.

I flex my bad hand and pick up my hand grip. I tear through my reps and put the grip down on the nightstand. My hand trembles from the exertion. It took almost three weeks for my hand to get better after quitting poles. Even using my wrist and forearm wasn't enough to offset the physical challenge.

I shimmy my hips into all-lace tangerine boy shorts, put on the matching demi-cup bra, and squeeze myself into the whole shebang. I twirl in front of Kiki's built-in mirrors and decide I don't look too bad.

Knowing I'm going to live has something to do with it. My face has lost that perpetual pinched-with-worry look.

I smile and see the bloom of pregnancy casting its glow.

Maybe I can be happy without Mick.

Maybe living is enough.

* * *

"That's great, Mom!" I clap as she takes a sip of water unassisted.

She smiles. "I'm... I know it's silly, but just nourishing myself is a boon."

"Of course it is." I have no trouble seeing the truth in her words.

My patients are all impacted and hopeless to varying degrees when they come through my doors. Tannin Mitchell may be my mother, but she's still as human as anyone else. Maybe more.

"So when do you escape?" I ask.

I watch the whites of her eyes as she rolls them into her head. "I have at least another month here, then I move to the semi-permanent facility for walkers."

I think momentarily of that show, *The Walking Dead*, and shiver like a goose walked over my grave.

Mom laughs. "What's that face for?"

"Oh nothing... just something you said."

"Huh." Mom's nose scrunches. "Anyway, it's lighter assistance. Of course, your Mick says—"

"—he's not mine," I interject quickly.

She inclines her head, disbelief thick in the gesture. "Mick mentioned that I'll still have my personal physician, therapist, and nurse 24/7."

The silence is loud between us.

"Listen, Faren—"

"Don't," I say, holding up a palm.

"I won't be silenced."

I glare at Mom. I know she's fallen for Mick's charms.

"I know," she says.

What? She knows what? My bad hand twitches and I clench it in a loose fist.

"I know that you're dying." Her eyes are serious. Sad. Resolute. Brave for me.

Oh god.

I shake my head.

Her chin lifts. "I refuse the diagnosis."

I feel my surprise before I can say anything. "Mom—"

She slowly raises a palm. "Hear me out."

My mouth snaps shut.

"I did not wake up from this misery for my only child to be taken. I've spoken to Mick, and he says... He says that he didn't think things through, that he said some unkind words."

That's the understatement of the year.

"He says there's an explanation for the naked girl in his office."

I laugh out loud. I can't help it—it bursts out of me like a boil filled with pus.

"No." I wag my finger. "First, there is not an explanation for Tonka Tits."

Mom frowns at my name for the slut-with-melons.

I lift my shoulders without expounding. "Second, he let me walk out of his condo with my clothes on inside out and backward. I was crying so hard I couldn't see. While being pregnant with his child."

Mom sighs, and I hurry to finish my dialog—my truths. "There is no explanation that works, Mom. None."

I stand. I love her, but I can't talk about Mick. He's kept his promise of taking care of her. That's the most important thing.

But I owe her something. I lean over her face and kiss her cheek.

I release the air I've been holding. "It was a misdiagnosis. Mick spilled beans he shouldn't have." I meet her eyes, and there's triumph in them—a mother's faith. "You're right. I'm not dying."

She shakes her head, hands covering her mouth as happy tears spill down her face. "How?"

"They mixed up my name with one that was very close."

Mom's hands drop to her lap. "I knew He wouldn't take my gorgeous girl."

"Who?" I ask, feeling my brows knit.

"God, Faren."

I don't tell her that I'm not sure there is a God. I look at the small gold cross she wears around her neck.

I say nothing and smile.

As if to affirm her faith, my mom's hand closes around the cross.

I kiss her again and back away to leave.

She calls me when I'm across the room, and I turn.

"Don't shut every door that stands open."

I know she's talking about Mick. She's definitely chosen his side.

"Some should stay closed," I say and softly shut the door behind me.

CHAPTER 29

Kiki and I haul the last box of my stuff into my dump of an apartment. Old man Humphrey called and said I could come back.

I had four months on my lease. *Cheapskate*. Of course I can move back in.

We walk to the freight elevator for the fiftieth time, the Out of Order sign had been removed. It clanks its way up to my floor again.

Kiki plays with a large collarbone sweeper hoop. "So let me get this straight. You're gonna spawn for Mick..."

I roll my eyes and laugh.

Kiki goes on without pause. "And not try to lay the golden egg in the money nest?" Her brows come together as the elevator lurches to a stop.

I get out.

"Yeah." I glance behind me at Kiki bringing the last three boxes stacked on a wheeling dolly thing. "Mom is taken care of. I'll take his money for that. He can see the baby." I insert the key in my lock.

A man looms in front of me.

He comes forward as Kiki bellows like a pig on a skewer.
"Faren!"

I whip my purse into his head.

He swats my purse away and pushes open my door, ignoring me completely.

He speaks into his hand.

"All clear."

I watch him listen.

"Roger...th—" he begins.

Kiki moves in behind him and kicks him in the ass with her high heel.

"Take that!" She sinks her four-inch spike up his ass.

Muscleman howls and twirls around, his mouth an O of agony, one hand gripping his ass.

Kiki spills the boxes onto the ground and swings the lightweight dolly into his face.

"Fuck me!" he screams, swinging at her with the hand that isn't defending his face.

"Not on your life, dick hole!" Kiki shrieks back.

I back into the doorway, subtly dialing 911.

Muscles's eyes flick to my hand, and he bats my cell out of it. My bad hand obligingly opens, and the cell that cost me over two hundred dollars shatters on my wood floor. The battery spins toward his foot, and his toe goes over the top, halting its motion.

Kiki moves in for the kill, twirling the dolly around her head like a clunky lasso of metal.

"Stop, you crazy-ass bitch!"

"Ha!" Kiki screams, shoving the wheels into his chest like a charging bull.

"I'm her bodyguard!" he screams as she thumps him for the third time.

"What?" Kiki and I say at the same time.

She comically halts, wheels out and ready for another

stab.

A man who outweighs us by seventy pounds backs away from warily.

I glance at Kiki. Her hair's wild, her eyes are bright and filled with vicious intent.

I smile then cross my arms.

"Who are you?" I think I have a pretty good idea.

He swipes at his sleeves and tries to straighten his crumpled button-up. My eyes move to the black wheel marks on the shirt, and I feel my lips turn up.

"I work for McKenna Enterprises."

"I just bet you do," Kiki says, thrusting the dolly in warning.

He puts out a palm. "Jesus, lady, calm the fuck down."

Kiki grins like a shark. "No."

"I don't want to hurt you."

"Unless you want your balls for earrings, I wouldn't worry about pain inflicted on *me*."

He frowns then turns to me, the reasonable one. Yeah right. Every pregnancy hormone in my emotional circuitry is lit up. I feel as if I could beat him up myself.

"You're a bodyguard?" I ask.

He nods.

"Not a real Einstein though," Kiki notes, looking him up and down. He glowers, losing whatever patience he'd been working with.

"I don't have to protect you. Just Red here."

Red?

Kiki shrugs. "Man up and tell us what's doin'."

He rolls his powerful shoulders in a dismissive shrug. "I need to check out your apartment for issues."

I look around, thinking about Ronnie. He's dead but there's still Jay Hightower. And the unresolved cop, Tagger.

Somehow, those two running around make me feel less safe. I see some of what I'm thinking run across Kiki's face too.

"Fine," she says, waving him away. "Go skulk around and see what ya turn up."

He snorts, giving Kiki an eye flick that should make her crawl under a rock. Instead, she flips him off. "Sit and spin later, pal. Right now, be a good boy and find the bad guys."

His scowl is incendiary, but he marches off.

Kiki doesn't go up in flames though. Her lips curl into a smile as she leans against the handle of the cart. "That's kinda fun."

Not fun at all.

I don't appreciate Mick getting a meathead to shadow me. It freaks me the hell out, not to mention the zero-privacy issue.

Mr. Mountain of Muscle moves back into the living room and talks to his hand again. "All clear."

"Pfft," Kiki says.

He glares at her and she taps her nails on the top of the dolly. His eyes track her movement. "You're a violent broad."

She smiles like a feline in front of a bowl of cream. "Yeah."

He grins, and Kiki bats her eyelashes.

Unbelievable.

"Out!" I announce, pointing at the door. "You've scared the crap out of me enough for one day. I've moved back in, and I want you out."

"Don't have to ask me twice," he says, though his eyes travel to Kiki.

"See ya, stud," she says as he passes her. She flutters her fingers at him.

"It's Butch."

Her eyelashes flutter as much as her fingers. "Bye-bye, Butch."

Butch walks away with a slightly stunned expression, and I shake my head.

Kiki closes the door.

"That was fun."

"No."

"Oh yes. Did you see the pussy power in action?"

I had.

My lips quirk, and Kiki plops down on my couch, hoops swinging a millimeter above her shoulder.

"I had him this close." She puts her index finger and thumb almost together.

I feel my eyebrow lift. "To what?" I set the tea kettle on the burner and light it off with a struck match.

I hear something clank, and I turn around as Kiki rummages inside her purse.

"Anything," she says, popping open her compact and setting her lipstick to rights.

I'm quiet as I prepare our tea.

I turn to put a tea cup on the table in front of Kiki, her fingers are flying over her cell screen.

"Who you texting?" I ask.

"Thorn," she says without looking up. "I've got poles tonight. I'm asking for another hour."

I think of something. Something I've wanted to ask for awhile.

Kiki stirs her tea, watching my expression. "What?"

She blows, takes a sip, and grimaces. She sets the tea down and squeezes a ton of honey inside the cup, stirs, then takes another sip. Bliss covers her face.

"Have you ever... done anything with Thorn?"

I think of my little audition with him.

Kiki grimaces slightly and shakes her head. "He keeps threatening to give me a private audition. He was opening up a California club when I got my job at the BR. I lapped on a sub."

"Who?"

She shrugs. "Some dude who works the BR once in a while." Kiki stands and saunters over to the peephole in my door. She peers through and makes a small sound. "Brains is out there doing nothing."

I smile. Butch the bodyguard probably makes more in a month than I do in a year.

I shake my head. "I don't want him taking over my life."

"McKenna?" Kiki guesses, and I nod.

"You're gonna have to tell him."

I know.

Kiki jerks a thumb toward the door. "And for the record? I think it's great that oaf Butch is out there."

I lift my eyebrows.

Kiki gives a helpless little shrug. "You seem to be a magnet for bad shit, Faren. Ronnie's gone." She watches my involuntary flinch. "But his type likes your type."

"Oh?" My hand moves to my belly.

Kiki nods slowly.

"What type is that?"

"Fragile. You're like glass, Faren."

I'm not! I've been brave for years. I survived Ronnie. I'll survive Mick's rejection, being a single parent, and figuring out my future.

Kiki studies me, sipping the last of her tea. She looks a little sad.

"Glass breaks," she whispers.

Her words vibrate in my psyche.

CHAPTER 30

"Butch," I all but growl, whirling on him. His palms fly up. I can't take a pee without him up my butt.

He flicks a hand at his crotch. "Listen, Faren, Mick will have my gonads if I let you out of my sight."

I roll my eyes. "I *am* safe. Do you hear me?"

He just does a slow shake of his head. "That's what you think. McKenna is a powerful man. He's made enemies. If they knew that... if they *knew*, you could be used as... collateral."

Whatever.

This needs to end.

My phone buzzes. Another text from Mick.

He must've had a break from watching Tonka Tits flop her big watermelons around.

I'm about throw my phone when another buzz vibrates my palm.

I squint at my shattered screen, the Duct Tape's residue transferring to my fingertips from covering my battery sleeve.

Thorn.

Thorn: *I need to see you.*
Why? **Me:** *I think we're done, you and I.*
Thorn: *Girl—not by a long shot.*
I don't like it. **Me:** *Why?*
Thorn: *Just... Damn, come by the Black Rose.*
Seconds pass while I don't answer.
Thorn: *Please.*

I grip the phone, casting a surreptitious glance behind me at Butch. I jog and hail a cab instead of going to my normal coffee shop. I can't have caffeine anyway.

"Faren!" Butch yells.

I slip inside the cab, and a guy with a turban asks, "Where to?"

I tell him the address for the Black Rose.

His eyes condemn me, but I don't care. I lean against the back seat. Before I close my eyes, I see Butch in the side mirror, flinging up his hands.

I sigh with relief.

A moment of freedom.

The cab lulls me as I think. It jerks to a halt in front of the Black Rose, and I peek out the grimy window and give the cabbie a ten. I step onto the sidewalk, and he squeals away.

The entrance is subtle, a neon sign that's off during the day and bright purple at night. The rose lies on its side, as though discarded. A dim scarlet, its leaves are serrated and bright green that fades to black, as if it's dying on the vine.

My low heels click; my maxi skirt is elastic enough to stay up even though my frame has grown too thin. My light tunic-length sweater skims my hips and helps with the boho-vibe I'm trending on. I know my champagne hair burns like a low flame against the emerald of the sweater. I feel as good as I'm going to get, so I take a deep breath and walk through the glass door. I nod at the doorman who serves as a bouncer. My eyes adjust to the light.

"Faren." Gus nods.

I say hi. He'd always made me uncomfortable. Some men have a sheer physicality that's intimidating, and he's no exception. He's six feet five and muscular. I've seen him toss a guy barely smaller than him the length of the sidewalk.

"You quit the poles?" he asks.

I nod with a hard swallow. "Yeah."

His eyes move down me, my curves hidden by my flowing outfit. "You were good." he says, his eyes flicking to mine.

Yuk.

I back away with a small smile. "Yeah, thanks." My eyes fling around the dim hall, searching a little frantically for Thorn.

His hand wraps my wrist, and he pulls me to him. "Why don't you give Gus the time of day, Faren?"

Oh god. *Really?* Could my luck be this bad?

I open my mouth for a scathing response.

"Fuck off, Gus," Thorn says from nowhere.

Gus drops my wrist as if it burnt him. "Just playing with the girl here."

"Yeah?" Thorn asks and telegraphs nothing. His fist is suddenly in Gus's nose, and Gus howls, staggering back.

"She's not the girl. She's McKenna's girl, fucktard." Thorn turns to me.

I step back.

Way back.

Thorn's black eyes glitter at me, and I see Gus rise behind him like the sun.

Gus lands on Thorn, but he's already in motion.

"Fucking. Slow. Learner," Thorn says, jerking his knee into Gus's chin.

More howling that sounds like a slow gurgle as it leaks to a stop.

"We done?" Thorn asks, chest heaving.

Gus gives hate from his hands and knees. His shattered nose is swelling up into the wells of his eye sockets.

"No, you cock suck."

I can't back up any farther. My butt is against the wall.

"Stay down, you dumb fuck," Thorn warns in a growl.

I notice Thorn's hand is bleeding. A drop distracts me as it trembles off his knuckle and splatters to the black granite floor.

The front door opens, and my palms smack the wall. I yelp.

Mick moves into the foyer. His face shows nothing. His eyes move to my face—probably tight with my fear—to a bleeding Gus on the floor, and then Thorn.

"What's going on here?" He's calm, but it's a facade. Mick's body is tense, spread legs and loose fists dangling by his side.

I guess some quality control is in order.

Gus doesn't respond. Instead, he charges Thorn. They crash next to me, and I scream, trying to get out of the way.

Suddenly Mick is there, putting his body in front of mine like a shield.

My nose is stuffed between his shoulder blades. I smell him: clean male, cinnamon, and the undertone of his suit, fibers of silk and the faint touch of cleaning solution. It's a bouquet that is uniquely Mick.

I barely stop myself from hanging onto his back for dear life.

I push him away when every bit of me screams to cling.

He isn't expecting that and stumbles forward. I squeeze out between the wall and his body, and Gus's hand hits my mouth.

My face goes numb, and I see stars. I feel the wall again as I slide down it until my ass hits the floor.

"Faren!" Mick yells.

It's the first time I've heard true panic in his voice.

And rage.

Gus is getting the better of Thorn, and I'm just collateral damage.

I watch Mick from my stupor on the floor. Mick steps in like a dancer, his fists coming from his shoulder as though he'll drive through Gus. He delivers a one-two punch to Gus with a precision born of practice.

Thorn steps back and remarks, "Looks like you're McFucked, Gus." He spits blood on the floor.

But then Thorn's face changes. "Mick! Hey! No!" Thorn lands on Mick, who can't, or won't, stop hitting Gus.

Thorn hauls him off. "She's okay, buddy. Faren's okay."

Mick's chest heaves, and his eyes move to mine. His fancy shirt is covered in blood. Gus lays moaning and rolling around on the floor.

Mick's eyes flick over my body, landing on my sore face.

"You're fired, Mr. McKinney."

Thorn chortles, his arms still around Mick. "Surprise!"

"Let me go, Ty."

Thorn's eyebrows jump. "You sure, bro? 'Cause you still have your game face on."

Mick stills. I watch him cram that ready rage back down inside wherever he stores it.

He's just shown me that he can be scarier than Ronnie ever was.

CHAPTER 31

"Faren." Mick crouches down and stares at my face, his fingertips lightly brushing my wounded skin.

I pull away from his touch.

"Thorn texted for you to come."

I glare at Thorn like he's the enemy, and I walk myself up the wall with my palms.

"Yeah." I toss razors at him with my eyes. "Thanks."

Thorn just smiles.

Prick.

"We need to talk," Mick says.

I shake my head as a low moan comes from Gus. I turn away toward the doors, and Mick grabs my arm, spinning me around.

I open my mouth, and he crushes his against mine.

I'm starving.

For him.

I hate him. I hate that he had that naked girl in his office. But my mouth moves under the press of his lips as though hypnotized, operating under a will of its own, eating at his lips.

My arms wind around his neck. I bite his lip and taste his blood.

He groans against my anger, taking me deeper into his body and lifting my feet off the ground.

"Hurt me if you need to, Faren, but love me."

I grab his neck and squeeze, trying to choke the life out of him.

I hear a grunt. "*Damn*. You two are so many levels of fucked up."

We turn to Thorn. I see Mick's mouth bleeding out of my peripheral vision.

I wipe my own mouth and turn to Mick. He brushes my hair out of my eyes and cups my chin. I cast my eyes away from his damaged lip.

A mouth that's loved every part of me.

And maybe her, my mind whispers into that deep part of every woman. The part that knows no matter how right something may feel up top, something profoundly wrong might happen.

"I set it up. I set ya both up." Thorn's palms sweep out from his body as he casually steps over Gus's form.

I follow him, ignoring Gus.

We move to that office where I auditioned on his lap, where I collected my first paycheck at Mick's feet.

I gulp back my shame and anger in a lump of regret.

Thorn continues. "I thought if I got Christy to show her wares for my boy and you walked in on it, you'd get jealous and make things right with Mick."

Mick puts his hands on his hips. "I believe she thought there was more to the bargain than an audition."

I look between the two of them.

"A lot more." I seethe. "Why?" I ask Thorn, trying to make sense of why he thought his mess of a plan would work.

"You're one of those chicks who needs a dose to get your ass in gear."

I open my mouth to deny it.

But I can't. I'd been ready to pull out the stops that day. Instead, I'd gotten a load of the skank, assumed the worst, tucked my tail between my legs, and gotten the hell out of there. Mick had been texting me ever since. When I wouldn't respond, he put Butch on me.

Oh my God—*Butch.*

"I left Butch somewhere," I confess.

Thorn rolls his eyes. "He's dumber than a box of rocks, but at least I didn't use Gus."

"Yeah." I fight not to glance over my shoulder.

"How could you let someone like him work for you, Mick?"

Mick looks at Thorn.

"I did a background check," Thorn says, defending his choice. "He had no priors. Some dudes just like to victimize."

"Or take what they don't deserve." Mick's eyes drill into mine.

"Yeah, he won't be doing dick for a while."

I have to ask... "Where'd you learn how to fight like that?"

Thorn and Mick look at each other.

"What?" I ask.

"Remember, I'm a self-made man, Faren."

Thorn grins. "Not everyone you run with is."

Mick smiles back. "True, but I like some of my associates a little rough around the edges."

I fold my arms as they discuss the benefits of solving everything with violence.

"Chet's an asshole," Thorn says.

Mick shrugs, dismissing the topic.

I wonder why Chet, whoever he is, was the first one who came to Thorn's mind.

Mick turns to me. "Christy means nothing to me. She was just the woman who kept us apart for too long."

I look at my feet. I can't believe Thorn set me up. He got that dumb bunny to run up there and tear off her clothes for Mick so that when I walked in... well, it looked bad.

"Faren, look at me," Mick says.

I lift my head.

"I could never be with someone like her."

My lips quirk. "She had crappy boobs."

Thorn shakes his head, dimples appearing as he tries to stop his laughter.

"Haven't met tits I didn't like."

Mick says, "You're not helping."

Thorn turns away, and I want to hit him as his shoulders shake.

"You are beautiful to me. Every part of you," Mick continues.

"Come back to me, Faren."

A tear escapes my eye. "Why?"

Is it the baby? Is it guilt?

"I love you. If I only have this window of time to do it in, let me love you now. Because tomorrow will come, and if you're not in it, I can't live with knowing you could have been."

I walk into his arms and run my hands down his back, his heartbeat against my cheek. His body warms me to my toes, in places I didn't know were frozen. Mick thaws my resistance.

I tilt my head back and notice Thorn quietly left. I don't know when or how.

My vision closes like a tunnel until it's only Mick's face I see.

"What if I tell you it isn't a window but a lifetime?" The breath catches in my throat. Knowing that I've bared that part of me I keep hidden.

His smile is like the sun breaking through storm clouds. "Then you'll be mine for longer. Mine to hold, cherish and keep."

I still don't breathe until spots fill my vision. I inhale deeply to keep upright.

Mick bends his head to kiss me, a press of warm breath and skin like heated paper, and then it's gone.

"What are you saying?" I ask.

He doesn't answer but tows me. We walk through the labyrinth of halls that lead from Thorn's to his office.

Mick opens the door and walks to his desk. With a flick behind a drawer, it bounces open a crack, then he slides the drawer out fully.

He places a velvet box on the desktop.

Our gazes lock. "What is this?" I ask.

Revelation mixes with disbelief.

It can't be. It can't.

Mick taps it once. "Ask me how long I've had this?"

I shake my head, my vision fuzzy. I don't think I've breathed properly since Mick came through the door of the Black Rose.

"That first night." His dark eyes hold my gaze, keeping me prisoner.

My hand moves to my chest. I have to hold my heart in. It's trying to escape. "Which?"

"The night I thought you were... acting out the virginal scene."

I walk forward and snatch the box off the desk while Mick's eyes gleam with anticipation and another emotion I can't name.

I pop the lid and gasp, sinking into the chair in front of his desk.

Moments lengthen like hot taffy.

"Do you like it?" he asks quietly.

Like it? Love is too soft a word.

Nestled in black velvet, a deep-pink heart-shaped stone the size of a large pea glitters like rose-colored ice. Every facet fractures a prism back at me. A narrow platinum band holds it in six prongs. A secondary band has baguette diamonds flush-mounted in a ring that's three times the width of the engagement ring.

My eyes flare to his.

I can't speak.

Or move.

Finally, I do the right thing. I stand and throw my arms around his neck across the desk.

"I didn't know."

Mick pulls away a little. "I didn't either."

I feel my frown.

"I didn't know I loved you. Then I met you and realized I always had." His gaze burrows into mine. "Marry me, Faren Mitchell."

His words are barely above a whisper. It's Mick's eyes that convince me.

They hold mine.

And don't let go.

Instead of answering, I say the words I'd alluded to before.

He blinks.

"What did you say?"

"I'm not dying."

His eyes close for a moment.

It's more than the *yes* he's hoping for.

Men who cry are not weak.

Sometimes tears are bravery that leaks out when there's too much to hold in.

CHAPTER 32

Mick pulls my hand up for the hundredth time, admiring the ring on my finger. He brings my fingertips to his mouth and kisses each one while looking into my eyes.

We're naked in his bed, a place I didn't ever presume to grace again. His hands run down the length of my torso, and he puts the side of his face against my tummy.

"Are you going to get sick of moving my stuff back and forth?" I ask, my naked breasts brushing the top of his head.

"Ah, I think so."

I frown. I can't decide if he's teasing me.

He laughs, the sides of his eyes crinkling as he looks up at me. "The construction for the new penthouse is at the bitter end." His face takes on a coy cast.

"What have you done, Mr. McKenna?"

He jerks me underneath him, and I squeal. Our faces are almost pressed together.

"I've made sure my family will have a special place."

He leaps out of bed, and I enjoy his nakedness. Mick's eyes become hooded when he notices me watching him.

"Let me show you," he says.

Mick pulls me out of the bed we've just made love in. I wrap his robe around me, and it trails behind me like a cape.

He snuggles it underneath my chin and grins. "You look great in my clothes."

"Funny," I say, "I never wear any when I'm here."

"As it should be." Mick slaps my ass through the terrycloth.

He puts on some black nylon work-out pants, and I see his abs flex into lines of striated muscle. He laces his fingers through mine as we walk to the front door.

He looks at my feet. "Get your shoes on. There's a lot of construction debris that could hurt you."

I slip on my clogs, feeling a little exposed out in the hall.

He sees my expression. "Don't worry. My neighbors only care that I'm rich. They don't care if my... fiancée is walking around in my robe with her work clogs on."

I flush, thinking about being his wife. I like the new title of fiancée very much.

It's not shame, but happiness. An entirely new feeling.

Hope.

Joy.

Ecstasy.

It's a heady combination.

We take the elevator up. I'm like a lovesick puppy, nuzzling against his bare chest. I don't even notice when Mick moves me out of the elevator.

He pushes back the plastic tarp that covers the front entrance, and I take in the view.

I thought his view in the downstairs condo was amazing, but it's nothing compared to this. Every wall is glass. It feels both private and exposed. I weave between stacked molding, nail guns, caulking, and the other finishing products that line the subfloor. I stop in front of windows that have only an eight-inch ledge between their bottoms and the floor. My eye follows the seam to the twenty-foot ceiling and it stretches the length, running without a break to the top where it transitions into the ceiling and runs the perimeter. The corners meet in a thickened forty-five degree angle of glass.

"It's almost... a little nerve-wracking," I say, pressing my hand to my belly.

My eye catches the sparkling pink diamond on my left ring finger as Mick wraps his arms around my waist. "It's supposed to seem like we're floating in the sky."

It does. I feel as if I'm borrowing a slice of the sky and standing on a magic carpet that's invisible.

I step away from the glass, and Mick thrusts his sneakered foot forward in a martial arts move. His instep beats the glass with a burst of sound, and I jump back.

His foot smoothly drops. "Tempered, baby."

"Oh," I say, nervously scooping the robe closed at my throat.

Mick chuckles. "It's specially made for"—he waves a palm at the windows—"height, atmosphere, viewing aesthetic, etc."

"Right," I say softly, not looking down at the people and cars that scurry like ants beneath us.

"I have a surprise," Mick breaks into my thoughts. He grabs my hand and leads me through the chaotic mess of the penthouse.

It feels like it takes a year, it's so big. I realize the penthouse is at least twice the size of his condo. "How big is... all this?"

"Eight thousand," he replies as he pushes open double doors.

A sea of creams, buff, and *cafe au lait* greets me. There's a beautiful crib in the corner, not too near the windows. A breath of relief escapes me when I see only half the wall is comprised of glass. Light coffee covers the walls with a beautiful cream on the ceiling. Mini-crystal chandeliers dot the ceiling in two spots, dripping their prisms, and fluffy chocolate and caramel clouds appear to float between them. Built-in bookshelves line the interior wall from floor to ceiling, and every child's book a person could wish for is neatly stacked on them. A soft animal mobile floats above the crib.

The plush carpet gives beneath my feet as I walk across the variegated espresso-speckled pile.

My hand runs over the exquisite bed linen of the crib sheets. An antique toy chest in cherry hardwood softly glows like brandy in a crystal sniffer. It's nestled in the corner beneath a huge bank of windows.

Overwhelmed doesn't describe my feelings as I soak in the opulence. My mom and I have always worked hard. To experience this level of luxury is surreal.

Mick watches my expression "You like?"

I slowly nod.

He steals behind me and layers kisses up to the tender spot behind my ear and back down again.

I don't know how I feel about the extravagance, but the subtle wealth in every detail is understated. I can't help but love it.

"I guess it doesn't matter if it's a boy or girl," I say.

Mick shakes his head.

He kisses my swollen face where Gus hit me. "He hurt you."

It hurts to smile so I just tilt up the corners of my lips. "You fired him."

His expression darkens. "I wanted to do more than that."

My eyes flick to his scraped knuckles. "You scare me sometimes."

Mick glances away. We're quiet for a moment.

When he looks back, his body is tense. His memories share space with us; they crowd our intimacy.

"I am a different man than I could have been."

"Because of Rose?" I ask.

He nods and looks down at me. "I'm the right man for a woman like you."

I search his eyes. "What kind of woman am I?"

My heartbeats pile on top of each other in anticipation of his answer.

"The woman I love," he says slowly.

I believe he meant to say something different. I stand in the circle of his arms, taking in the only finished room in the penthouse, and ask, "What were you going to say?"

I feel his hesitation.

"Fragile."

"A man who wants to possess a woman as breakable as you has to be willing to do things that others might not."

I lean back. "Like hurt Gus?"

I see something move over his face as the shadows shift. His expression makes me shiver.

His head gives the barest shake. "No. That's the least of what I'd do if someone threatened you."

"Oh."

He kisses the top of my head, and we leave the nursery.

His revelations have made me heavy inside. Not in sadness but in solidness.

Mick turns off the light, and I glance behind me. Some of the city lights stream in through the bare windows.

I can see the mobile from the front entrance. Shadows from the animals dance on the walls, disproportionately bigger that what they really are.

They look like monsters in the dark.

CHAPTER 33

"So..." Kiki peeks at me from underneath her falsies. "Everything's all hunky-dory in the Land o' Mick?"

I take a deep breath.

"Can't take back the pause."

I laugh. "No, I guess not."

I've had a lot to work through emotionally, and I know I'm not done reconciling the past month.

We look at the huge sparkler on my finger.

Kiki grabs my hand. "I've never seen a pink diamond before."

I smirk. "I think it's safe to mention neither one of us has seen that big of a diamond before."

"Right," Kiki says, gently putting down my hand. She's in day-off chic of bright pink yoga pants with the obligatory *pink* across the ass, mocha cami that exactly matches her skin, signature hoops, and a topknot of spiraling ringlets.

Kiki's eyebrows lift.

I swallow. "He knows."

"Yeah. I figured."

A disgruntled sigh slips out of me. "The girl was Christy, some skank Thorn sent up to make me jealous so Mick and I would get back together."

Kiki rolls her eyes, throwing up her arms. "Thorn!" She plants her elbows on the kitchen table, and her huge hoops swing forward, catching the light from the window. "He's like a meddling sister! That would never work with you."

I smile. *True.* "Didn't work too well." I think about spewing vomit on his carpet.

Not at all.

Kiki flops back against the chair and takes a swig of Red Bull.

It's ten a.m.

"God, that's rank," I say, giving a chin dip toward the energy drink.

"Jealous?" She waggles her brows.

I snort and cross my arms. "Yeah."

"Figures."

We smile.

"I hate this lethargy," I say. "I feel like I've been on spin cycle for about a year, and then someone enlisted my butt for a marathon."

"Charming. Where do I sign up for getting knocked up?"

"You'd never have an accidental pregnancy."

Kiki's face gets serious. "I do like practicing."

"Not the same."

"I don't *want* a permanent dude."

I think she's scared to fall in love and that she hasn't met the right guy. I say none of that. "I know... but—"

She wags a glittering pink nail tip at me. "There are no buts. Well, that's not entirely legit. There are lots of asses, just not that many exceptions in Kiki's world."

"I don't think we live on the same planet."

She nods. "You got that right. But it's interesting as hell."

I look at her ensemble. "You're going to have to class up your act when you get all lawyer-y."

Kiki shakes her head. "Nope. Going to do an Erin Brockovich on everyone's collective ass."

I draw a blank.

"Y'know? Julia Roberts?" she prompts. "The chick with the awesome rack who everyone thinks has a room temp IQ and blows them away with her intellect while wearing club wear?"

Ah.

"Yes." I laugh.

"I'm going to channel her. I think I'm up for it. Kiki's going to stay Kiki."

A memory threads through me. "That reminds me of Thorn."

She scrunches her face, giving a not-so-delicate sniff. "How? Because—girl, he is *so* opposite of me."

I shake my head. "Not so much. He talks about himself in the third person too."

Kiki pouts. "We don't get along." She flings a hand out and bangles that match her earrings tinkle. "I mean, he's a stand-up dude."

My eyebrows jump. *Stand-up dude* would not be how I'd describe Thorn.

She notes my expression. "Not the kind you're thinking of. He's all Thorn, all man. But he's had my back at the BR. That's what matters."

"Something's not quite right about Thorn, Kiki."

She shrugs. "His setting on the dryer isn't dead center on normal, I'll give ya that."

I bark out a laugh. "Yeah."

"He's a limited-doses guy. Whenever we're together for longer than five minutes, I want to tweak his dick."

I hold my sides as I laugh. "Nice."

She shrugs.

"Who's this Chet guy?" I ask, remembering the guy Thorn mentioned in passing.

Kiki frowns. Finally, she snaps her fingers. "No offense—he's another richie like Mick."

I scowl. Mick and I don't have smooth sailing ahead of us, but I hate the way Kiki thinks that's all Mick's about.

"Mick invented his way to wealth. And he's the father of peanut."

Kiki's lips twitch. "We gotta get that kid a name. Chet Sinclair is a rich player who's buddies with Mick. He's a trust-fund weaner."

I feel myself frown. "I'm surprised Mick would hang with him."

"Birds of a feather..."

"No."

Kiki lifts a shoulder, smoothly changing topics. "So when's the wedding?"

"We want to wait until my mom can walk."

"Not going to make peanut legit?"

I smile. "Empire waistline, it's a beautiful thing."

"Tannin does need to be there," Kiki muses.

"Yes. I mean..." I clamp onto my bad hand. It twitches in my lap, and the ring scratches me. I'm not used to wearing it. "I want to get married right away, but having Mom back—and my life..."

"What did Mick think about the clinic screw-up and you thinking you were going to kick it for over a month?"

I bite my lip. "He's pissed, wants to sue."

Kiki jerks her head in a nod. "Damn straight."

I put up my good hand. "No. I don't want to spend that time."

"But—"

"I want to live *now*. I don't want to spend time going after people. As I pointed out to Mick, we don't need the money."

Kiki's face lights up. "Have you heard from that prick, Hightower?"

She's making me dizzy with her subject changes. Classic Kiki, fifth gear all the way. "No. And that's a little weird."

Kiki frowns. "What about stupid Tagger?"

I plop my chin in my palm. "Nope, still under investigation."

"Huh." Kiki blows a wisp of hair out of her face. Then she grins. "But ya got yourself a body guard. Things are looking up."

I draw swirls with my finger on the table top. "He's kind of a doofus."

Kiki cackles. "Yeah. But he's better than no one." She takes my hand. "I heard about Gus. That fucking creeper. His ducks were never quacking all in a row."

I squeeze her hand and let go. "It was weird. Like he flipped his switch."

"Mick too?"

"Yeah. God, *that* was scary. He beat on him hard." I didn't say *like Jay*. The words stood between us.

"Good to know he'll protect his woman." She winks. I remember Mick's eyes when he told me he'd do more if anyone ever threatened me.

I shiver. "I think he's good on the protection thing."

"I like it. Don't give me a pretty boy. Give me a man."

"With a penis," I add.

"Pfft. They all have one."

"And you like them all."

"Not all." Kiki deliberates for a moment. "But a girl has to try new things."

We laugh, and her phone buzzes. She scrolls through the text and frowns. "Weird. Thorn's calling me in."

That is weird. He's always up on schedules.

"That skank—Christy?"

"Yeah?" I'm still angry about nasty titty.

Kiki smirks, easily reading me. "She didn't 'show.'"

"What does that mean?"

"In a word: hung. That's my best guess with that hobag."

"Oh."

I search her face and see discontent. "Getting tired of the poles?"

She nods and sighs. "A little. I mean, it's a good gig. It got me this." Her palm sweeps the condo with a view that won't quit. "It's paid for my schooling through graduation."

She sulks. "I need a sugar daddy."

I laugh. "I fell into mine."

"No—he fell into you."

"Touché. Icky but true. You don't like the rich, Kiki. You're prejudiced against the wealthy."

"I'm an equal opportunity girl. If he's got the hose to put out my fire, I'd consider it."

"God... you're doing a Thorn again."

She scrunches her nose. "I like to think I'm unique."

"No offense," I say.

She stands.

"Gotta go shake my thing."

I hug her. "Thank you."

"Congrats. I knew he'd get his head out of his ass and claim you," she says.

"Claim me?"

"Yeah." Her eyes are serious. "The good ones do."

CHAPTER 34

THREE WEEKS LATER

His hand grips the open window frame of my car door. "Come on, Faren, stop busting my balls."

"I'm not trying to." I look up into Butch's face.

His features are all mashed together. His eyes are sunk into a tanned but doughy face, like partially risen bread with raisins pushed in. He's one of those guys who's worked out so much he doesn't have a neck.

We're having a "discussion" outside my mom's new clinic. My engine's running, and I'm ready to make my escape to Mick's place.

"I can follow you in my car, but I'd rather ride with you," he says.

I sigh. Butch has been following me for almost three weeks, and it's getting old.

"How much longer?"

He shrugs the mountains that are his shoulders. They roll like an earthquake under his tight suit.

"I don't like it any more than you do."

"What?!" I half-shriek, and he backs up a step. My hormones roil like lava trying to erupt.

"I mean…" He scrubs his crewcut, backpedaling. "What I mean is… I'm just doing what Mr. McKenna wants."

I feel shame light like a torch. "It's okay, Butch." I pat the seat next to me, and he exhales in relief, jogging around the front of my VW.

He slides in, and my car dips.

"Thanks. I don't want to catch heat because I can't protect the mark."

"What?" My stomach lurches, and I realize I'm out of crackers. I think I'll breathe fire next. Forget baby mama, it's *pregnant dragon.*

His neck turns brick red. "I… Shit—shoot!" He turns his miserable eyes to me.

"Forget it, let's just get home."

I PULL out into bumper-to-bumper Seattle traffic. Not even my mom's awesome progress can lessen my foul mood.

I'm just pissed because I can be.

I'm aware I'm being an unreasonable snit, but I can't seem to help myself.

I think back on my conversation with Mick. He told me Butch will shadow me—period—and that I don't need to work anymore. His future wife won't need to. He said our baby needs its mother, and I get that. I do.

But I won't be told what to do. Just the thought of leaving the affirmation and fulfillment I gain from dealing with people who, like me, were survivors of injury? I don't think I'll be able to throw that away. My job is about more than money. I'm helping those who struggle to take back what's been lost.

I yelled at Mick, and he kissed me until we landed in bed.

He wants to make me happy and keep me safe. But sheltering me won't make me feel like anything but a kept bird in a gilded cage.

I know we have things left to sort out before the wedding bells chime. I glance at the shimmering pink diamond. Nothing is perfect. The last month of my life has been so emotionally chaotic, I need time for everything that's come to pass to settle.

I catch Butch in a texting marathon beside me. I turn several times, making my way to the Millennium Tower.

We get close to the garage, and Butch puts away his cell. I don't bother to make conversation. I'm not being aloof on purpose. I just don't want to rain my shit mood down on him any more than I already have.

My stomach growls and churns at the same time.

"Hungry?" Butch asks as I park in Mick's extra stall.

Einstein speaks.

"Yeah," I say slowly, exerting a patience I don't have. I can't believe my baby, the size of a kidney bean, can make me feel like a frayed electrical cord.

He looks chastised. "Listen, I know you don't like having a guard. That after your stepdad," he seems to reach for the right term, as death-by-stiletto probably won't work, "*died,*" he finally manages, "you feel lax about your safety. But you're dating a very wealthy man."

Wow, I didn't know Butch could puzzle that out. He seems to sense my surprise. "I'm not stupid, Miss Mitchell."

I cast my eyes to my hands. "I'm sorry for judging you."

"I'm not great with words. My face hasn't gotten me anywhere, just my instincts and my fists. But I think just fine. My body thinks faster, if you get me."

I raise my head, thinking of Ronnie. *I get it.* "Yes."

"So we understand each other." He stares, unashamed of who he is and daring me to try to make him feel small.

I feel really bad about my assumptions and ill treatment of this guy Mick hired.

Because he wants me protected.

And the guilt deepens. I haven't even told Mick about Jay's threats. About the deal that still rides on my acquiescing to something I can't give. How Kiki pepper sprayed his face. I don't know if it's relevant anymore, but I can't talk myself into believing Mick wouldn't care about it if he knew.

It's sort of a mess.

"Yes, we understand each other," I answer, burying my thoughts.

He scrutinizes my face. "Stop fighting my protection. Just roll with it. McKenna will feel better, and after the baby is born, maybe he'll calm down."

My lips twitch. "Doubt it."

Butch gives me a small smile. "Me too."

"So I'm stuck with you?"

"Looks like." Then he cocks his head. "But we're good?"

I nod. "I think so."

"Good," he replies, slipping out of the car. "Now let me do the circuit and text you. Work with me. I can give you better protection and be less..."

"Invasive?"

He nods then slams the passenger door.

Our uneasy alliance is better than being silent enemies. I ease my head against my car seat and close my eyes. I'm so tired from the emotional roller coaster I've been on. The pregnancy—everything.

I decide to wait for Butch's text that Mick's condo is free of bad guys.

Next thing I know, it's dark outside. The buzz of a text lights up my phone. The screen is bright in the dimness of my car.

Thorn.

I'd fallen asleep.
I'm disoriented and stare at the picture Thorn sent me.
I blink.
I spread two fingers over the glass screen, enlarging the image. The features of a face I don't know stare at me, coming into sharp focus.

What the hell? Who's this?

I dig at my eyes a little, trying to clear them and look at the caption.

THORN: *Faren —**this** is Jay Hightower.*

I feel my heart thud against my ribs. My bad hand does a little leap in my lap.

ME: *That's not the Jay Hightower I lapped for at the club. The one Mick is negotiating more clubs for....*

I WAIT A FEW SECONDS, watching the screen grow dim. I don't get a response. I feel my brows pull together.

I scroll back to his message. The text came in two hours ago.

I groan and throw my head back on the seat.

I rub my eyes, trying to clear my head.

I sit there in my car, thinking. I tap my screen and it lights up. I get on Google and search for Jay Hightower.

I go from *web* to *images*, and a face fills my small screen that doesn't vaguely resemble the man who's been stalking me. It resembles the pic that Thorn sent.

Hightower appears to be over sixty.

I kill the image and message Mick. I feel shaky. I don't know what's going on, but it's some kind of identity mess.

Mick told me he'd be at work late tonight.

He's catching up after neglecting everything to attend to me.

Me: *Hey.*
Mick: *Hey baby. Did you see your mom?*

I NOD and realize he can't see it.

Me: *Yeah, she can eat on her own. She's on the rails* 😊

THAT's my nickname for the poles that rehab patients drag their legs between as they relearn how to walk. Mom's been doing arm exercises for weeks to strengthen herself so she can hold up her body weight.

She cried today because she couldn't.

I told her she would soon. Her progress is better than anticipated, but she's impatient. Everyone always is. That part is always the same.

Mick: *I'll be home late, maybe nine.*

I THINK ABOUT JAY HIGHTOWER. It's possible I can get answers without Mick knowing about what I've kept hidden. Even though it's for his benefit, he wouldn't like it. Call it a guess.

Me: *how'd that deal go for the east coast clubs?*

. . .

IT'S ALMOST a full minute before he gets back.

MICK: *it's in the works, everything went smoothly. Why?*

MY HEART RATE TICKS FASTER. I feel my thoughts circling an elusive epiphany but missing it by a fraction.

ME: *so, he wasn't as much of a prick as you thought he'd be?*
  Mick: *lol—more. But with enough money, even an old geezer like Hightower can be made to see reason.*

WHAT'S GOING ON?
  I tap out my response. Neutral, casual.

ME: *thought I'd ask, know it was important.*
  Mick: *you're important.*

I STARE AT THOSE WORDS. He met the *actual* Hightower. So who the hell is the one who claims to be him? The guy who threatened me with a deal he was privy to but didn't actually make? The guy who got his butt kicked by Mick?

ME: *love you.*
  Mick: *love you more. I'll show you how much when I return.*

. . .

His parting words cause a thrill to zing through me.

When my heartbeat returns to normal, I rifle through the glove box. I find what I'm looking for and tear open a package of animal crackers. I mash a handful into my mouth and swallow the dry load. It settles my stomach. I breathe a sigh of relief when my tummy quiets.

I finger through one more text before I make my way to the condo I share with Mick.

Me: *that guy that you lit up with the pepperspray?* **Not** *Hightower.*

I press *send*.

I don't hear back from Kiki. I glance at my cell. After seven. She must be at the Black Rose.

I take the elevator to the lobby. I exit, deep in my own thoughts over the Jay Hightower identity mystery. Mainly I don't like it because I don't know what it means. What does the fake Hightower hope to gain from impersonating the real one?

My eyes travel through the lobby. I don't see Thomas, the flaky doorman, anywhere. Disquiet settles over me and I hesitate.

Ronnie's dead, I remind myself.

I'm irritated by my paranoia. I need to pull up my big girl panties and get over myself.

I mentally shore up, slipping my cell inside my pants pocket and adjust my purse on my shoulder.

I walk to the bank of interior elevators and press the glowing number for our floor as the doors sweep closed behind me. Someone else is already in there, and we share the three-second sliding eye contact everyone who gets stuck in an elevator together does.

He gets out at the seventh floor, his work-out clothes giving away where he's been. I relax when it's just me. I close my eyes, still feeling groggy. My catnap doesn't refresh me, I feel like I'm still pulling myself through mud.

I take my cell out of my pocket and check for a message from Kiki.

Nothing.

I frown and put it back.

The elevator pings, and I step out. I glide though the dim hall to Mick's door and get my key card ready. A sliver of light glows along the seam of the door.

It stands slightly ajar.

Time wavers in the pocket of my indecision. Everything happens quickly, but as though in slow motion. A paradox of the moment.

I should turn and go back the way I've come. My earlier disquiet returns like alarm bells inside my head. I realize I never got that a-okay text from Butch.

Like a scene from a bad horror movie, I push open Mick's door and walk through.

Actually, I fall.

Over Butch's body.

CHAPTER 35

My palms hit the floor, and I skate across the wood like I'm riding a Slip'N Slide from summers' past.

The floor is slick with blood.

It feels like a slow-trickling river underneath me. My momentum as I stumbled over Butch's still form was enough to send me on a forward tumble.

I hear a muffled scream and flip over on my back, my palms slapping the tacky surface in a muted smack.

He fills my vision as he comes for me, his only clothing is underwear and a coating of Butch's blood.

I react without thinking. My foot strikes the hand that carries the knife and it clatters away, spinning and striking the kitchen island with a twang that sounds like a discordant note.

Then my bad hand gives out.

Fuck.

Jay, who isn't Jay, moves in. The fading twilight strikes his hazel eyes and they appear to catch fire.

He looks like a demon.

My elbow collapses without the support necessary from my hand. It cracks on the wood, and I yelp, scrambling as Jay lands on me.

His erection settles into the crack of my ass and my scream sounds like a howl.

Kiki's round eyes meet mine, a gag stuffed in her mouth.

She shakes her head and I fight instant tears. Instead of giving in to defeat, I dip my head forward then slam it backwards, my neck shrieking from the angle.

Jay bellows and rolls off me.

I stand, then trip and fall on my ass. The blood's so thick I can't get a foothold.

Kiki's eyes slide to a point behind my left shoulder. I duck.

The breeze of a hand moves over my head, and I run.

I sprint to my bedroom and slam the door, flipping the lock.

He hits the door.

It shudders.

My eyes charge around the room and light on the glass towel bar in the bathroom. It takes seconds for me to see it's all I have.

I run in there as the door cracks behind me.

I take a marble vase and toss the flowers out on the floor. They scatter like a rain of petals. I bash the vase into the towel bar holder embedded in the wall tile.

The glass bar slides out of the broken holder, the end sheared off into a jagged point.

I drop the vase, and it shatters the tile floor, fissures running from the center in a haphazard web.

I grab the rod before it hits the floor, but Jay is there, scooping me up from behind.

Peanut!

The maternal protection instinct crushes me. It sets my

teeth and leaks out in a growl so primal Jay pauses in his assault.

I can hardly breathe for it.

I don't need to. I wrap my hands against the opposite end of the towel bar and stab backward.

He screams and staggers away.

I glance behind me and see I've nailed him in the groin.

Our eyes meet.

I see the end of me in his.

I tear out of there, and he rushes after me.

I move by Kiki. Tears are streaming out of her eyes as I leap over Butch's body. Jay's maybe twenty feet behind me and bleeding like a stuck pig.

Stuck dick, I think with a hysterical bark of laughter.

I'm on the edge of losing it. I smack both buttons on the elevators. One leads to the penthouse, the other to the lobby.

The elevator doors open and I jump inside.

Thomas's dead eyes look up at me. His skin is already turning gray.

Adrenaline surges to my extremities.

I look up. Jay's ten feet away, and he looks as though he's peed his pants.

In blood.

I hit the button with my bad hand. The doors whisk shut. The elevator travels up to Mick's unfinished Penthouse. No escape.

I back into the corner, pressing my face against the cold walls.

The mirror reflects Thomas on the ground at my feet.

Oh God, help me.

Kiki's down there.

I cover my mouth, choking back a sob.

Survive.

The chime pings, and I rush through the opaque tarp

hanging in the entrance of our soon-to-be penthouse. The carpenters have done more work in the kitchen. A granite top graces the island, and carved corbels adorn the underside, making it appearing to hold up the surface.

A nail gun sits hooked to a compressor. It has a fully loaded clip of finish nails. My eyes skip to the compressor. They haven't left it on but it holds air. I can hear it leaking out in a faint hiss.

It's all I have.

Why didn't I use the lobby elevator?

What if Jay has the knife again?

I hear the flap of the plastic at the entrance, stealthy, like unopened candy as Jay pushes through.

***

"Do you believe in bad seeds, Faren?" Jay's voice touches the emptiness of the space and bounces back to me.

I can't help cringing. My left hand flops like a fish out of water. I grab it with my right, clenching my eyes.

I don't respond. He'll know where I am.

I let go of my hand and grip the cabinet door for the kitchen island, moving inside it. I listen to him walk around the mess of the construction.

"I do. I very much believe," he says.

What is he talking about? My eyes move to the nail gun. Almost within reach. A balanced lean out of the cabinet, and it's mine.

"You might not be aware of our connection, but I continue our father's work."

What?

"I was there on that special night."

I should be thinking about escape, but his voice holds me. I'm hooked. Afraid. Riveted.

"There is more than one Bunce. I was only a mistake. One of dear old Dad's many prostitute dalliances. But then I found purpose. I almost had this entire thing wrapped up. Then Father died by your hand."

My breathing stopped. My mind sifted through memories like sand through an hourglass.

I touch on one that tumbles into place like a puzzle piece.

A boy with dark hair. Looking at me curiously as he rides away with Ronnie. I was five.

He would have been around thirteen.

I remember how pretty his eyes were. They glittered through the back window of the car like the sun.

Or the devil on fire.

His face leans down into the hole of the cabinet. I'm a rabbit caught in a snare.

"Or your foot," he says, referencing how I finished Ronnie.

He jerks me out of the cabinet.

My arm flails behind me. I scoop up the nail gun. It's heavier than it looks. My left hand sings with displeasure and the klutziness that all non-dominant hands possess.

My prayer to a God I don't believe in takes half a second.

I stab the tip of the nail gun into the back of his foot as I spin behind him. It bites deeply against his Achilles tendon.

I depress the trigger, and nothing happens.

Then a symphony of jagged beats pop like a shuddering strike of firecrackers.

Jay drops me, jumping up and down as he yells, grabbing at his ankle.

Ignoring the pain he turns, dumping to a straddle on top of me. I throw my hands in front of my face as his fist smashes into me.

"You fucking bitch!" he howls, his hands wrapping my throat.

"You don't deserve anything," he grits through his teeth.

He slams my head against the wood floor. Stars burst in front of me and I choke, gasping for air.

My hands try to find his eyeballs but I'm too far away.

"He fucking took me instead of you. He pimped me out to men instead of you! You were his fucking princess and I was his prince whore."

Whack!

My vision begins to dim.

"He said someone had to be sacrificed."

His voice lowers as his thumbs dig a pathway into my neck. "Rose McKenna was the first whore I got rid of."

My eyes fly open and he smiles, his teeth like a wolf's.

"That's right." His fingers press down.

I grab the hose of the nail gun and jerk it toward me.

He's so intent on killing me he doesn't notice.

"This entire time, I've been taking as many flesh whores as I could. Daddy's favorites."

He grins as he presses. My fingers loosen on the hose.

"Imagine my surprise when the flesh tycoon fell for the biggest whore of all."

The metal heats underneath my hands.

The hissing of the compressor threads through me.

"Two birds with one stone."

He leans forward, and stale breath and day-old sweat tickles what's left of my breathing.

"I'll make it slow for Miss King. And the knife is an abortion tool of sorts. You don't get to have anything. That baby's coming out."

Adrenaline surges. My fingers wrap around the handle of the nail gun, and I drive the tip into his knee.

His eyes widen for a moment of frozen time.

There's a click as the gun does one more hiccuping fire,

driving a slim two-and-a-half-inch finish nail into his kneecap.

Jay falls over in a shrieking pile. His fingers are gone and my lungs fill with air powdered with sawdust and drywall flakes.

It's the best air I've ever breathed.

A face appears above me. As Tagger fills my sight, I try to swim away on my elbows. My bad hand is spasmodic and unusable.

My killer screams so loud, he drowns out all other noise, even Tagger's shouting. Cops fill the room with the black barrels of their weapons clearing holsters.

Mick is there, his hands hovering over my body as his eyes move to my neck.

His lips form words. I strain to hear him over all the people and noise.

I open my mouth to tell him to get the imposter.

Then my lips close, and sleep rolls over me in a dark wave of nothingness.

My body claims me into the unconsciousness of traumatic injury. Protecting me from more.

CHAPTER 36

I don't wake up and see the face I want to. Lance Tagger stands over my bed, and I push myself deeper into the pillow.

Pillow?

I look around, dismissing Tagger for a moment, and see that I'm in a hospital.

I sit straight up.

"Where's Kiki?" I croak. My fingers move to my tender throat.

Tagger leans forward and I shy away.

Thorn and Mick move into my line of sight.

Now I'm ultra-confused.

Mick kisses my forehead, and a breath I didn't realize I was holding slides out of me.

"She's fine," he answers.

My hands move around his waist, and he grabs my elbows, holding me tightly against him.

I swallow hard. "Butch?" He's an oaf, but my body tingles with the thought that the blood I tripped on was his life slipping away. Nobody deserves that end.

Thorn dips his head around Mick's body, putting a large hand on the back of his neck.

"He's going to be okay. Lots of blood transfusions." Thorn and I look at each other around Mick's body.

I shake my head. "No. You're on... investigative leave."

Why he's in the same room as me, Thorn, and Mick?

Tagger gives me a lopsided smile.

"Tagger's been holding out on us," Thorn says.

"This was much bigger than just you, Faren," Tagger says.

I slip out of Mick's embrace and fold my arms. "I've obviously got time."

Tagger drags a metal chair over as Mick gives me some water. He strokes the back of my head, and I grab his hand.

Like Jay's voice in the emptiness of that unfinished space, Tagger's words are a freight train of information, lies, and years of police work. I wait for the train wreck I know is coming.

Finally, I respond. "So Jay Hightower had an assistant..."

"Dmitri Bunce."

"His natural son?" *Ronnie had a kid. A biological one.*

Tagger nods. "He ingratiated himself to Hightower, became indispensable."

"He was intimately aware of Hightower's business dealings," Mick adds.

That's how he knew about the Black Rose expansion.

"Then after years of systematic childhood sexual enslavement..." Tagger trails off.

Oh god. I cover my face with my hands, thinking about the innocent boy in that car almost twenty years ago.

He blames me. He holds me accountable for the deeds of his father. Little did Dmitri know the tyrant that Ronnie was to me and mom.

"Powerless to stop being pimped out by his own father, he became fixated on punishing those he saw as being in a better position. The strippers his father paid, the prostitutes he pimped to high-paying clients… They were first on his list." Tagger's eyes flick to Mick. I feel his body tense underneath my fingertips.

"Mr. McKenna's sister was the first of many."

Tagger tosses a photo on my bed.

A glossy pink scar bisects the left side of the torso, directly underneath the ribs.

The skin does not have the blush of life, but is gray like molding parchment paper. I remember Thomas the doorman.

"Dmitri?" I ask and look at Thorn.

He nods. "Finito." He makes a swipe with a finger across his throat. A breath slides out of me.

Bright spots of color appear on Tagger's face. "We know now that Mr. Simpson was never guilty. At the time, we didn't have our current technology, and he was at the scene, holding a knife—a dead assailant at his feet."

"All that time, it was Ronnie Bunce's screwed-up prodigy," I say.

Tagger sighs. "We've matched Dmitri's DNA to the scene. The wound he had is exactly where Mr. Simpson claimed it would be."

"But why?" I look at Tagger. "Why were you after Mick and me? Why did you treat Thorn like he was guilty?"

Mick and Thorn look at each other.

"Go ahead," Tagger says.

Thorn smiles. "I've been dying to say this."

Tagger rolls his eyes.

"I'm the fuzz, baby," Thorn says.

What he just told me doesn't compute. "What? You're—you're Mick's manager at the Black Rose."

Thorn shakes his head. "I'm deep undercover. But not no more." He winks at his butchered English.

"We recruited Ty when we realized the mistake that had been made and let Mr. McKenna take the credit for exonerating him."

My mouth drops open and I turn to Mick. "You knew."

"Yes." His eyes are steady on mine, his hand gripping me.

"He couldn't tell anyone," Tagger says. "There's never been two men who were so much of the same mind. McKenna and Simpson wanted Rose McKenna's killer."

My head is reeling until I think of something. "Dmitri kept killing?"

Tagger nods. "It's a horrible fortune that a human being's compulsion to murder is what ultimately gets him caught."

"There were so many related murders of known prostitutes and strippers with the same modus operandi," Thorn spreads his arms wide.

"We needed someone with Ty's street knowledge. The killer would never look at him. We know now, his eye was on fooling Hightower, infiltration of the revolving lap clubs and in the end—you. In the beginning, all we understood was the perp was after pole dancers."

I roll my lip inside my mouth. Ronnie is dead, but his legacy lived on regardless.

The sins of the father.

Thorn nods. "We thought we had him at the raid."

"You thought it was Ronnie," I guess.

"We did."

Mick's hand clips Thorn in the arm. "I'm still pissed you let Faren do laps in that shady fucking mess."

Thorn rubs his arm. "We didn't know Faren was related to Bunce. I've explained that, bro."

Mick and Thorn exchange a stare full of heated reprisal.

"The tangled web we weave," Tagger says.

Thorn shoots him a look.

"Shud-up, Tag."

It's so strange to see their interaction.

I shake myself. "So that college degree you have?" I ask Thorn.

"Criminal justice."

"Huh."

"Of course, we didn't know Bunce was wanted for the attempted murder of your mother. Once we discovered that... we had to watch him. He had about a hundred different aliases. We wanted to catch him in the act."

So they had been drawing him out while my mom languished in a coma.

I open my mouth.

Tagger holds up a palm. "We had you under surveillance."

"Butch?" I ask.

Tagger smiles. "One of ours."

Mick's forehead rests on the top of my head. "I wanted to tell you a million times. The sting had me in knots."

"Ronnie almost killed me."

I remember Mick and Thorn showing up at just the right time.

The cops breaking up that horrible lap dance.

Mick showing up just as the fake Jay, who was really Dmitri, came all over me.

I narrow my eyes. "What about that time you showed up and kicked Dmitri's ass?"

Mick looks sheepish.

"That's all me. I couldn't stand that you were an unwitting part of the operation."

"We didn't know Dmitri was the perp," Thorn admits.

"Then..."

"Yeah?"

"How... how did you find me?" I ask.

"Butch. He discovered the condo wasn't secure."

Before Dmitri went medieval on him with a knife. I remember the bloodbath I tripped over with a shiver.

"How'd Dmitri know you were on to him?"

Tagger shakes his head. "He didn't. He was making his move."

I think about all the texts where I blew him off. Not caving to his demands.

Kiki pepper sprayed his ass.

He was a killer.

My eyes touch on Tagger. "Is he… dead?"

Thorn nods. "He rushed the guys with a weapon."

Tagger shrugs. "Suicide-by-cop, Faren."

But Thorn's gaze glitters with malice. That stare tells me Dmitri would have been dead regardless.

My mind whirls with the revelations. No one is who they seem.

Even me.

CHAPTER 37

I'm okay. Peanut is too. Thorn is way more than a manager of expensive flesh. Our initial encounter is seared into my brain. If he was deep undercover, would that explain the private lap dance he insisted on? Maybe Thorn played the role a little too well.

That Thorn had to go to prison at the tender age of eighteen doesn't seem justifiable. That his freedom became the sacrifice.

At the end of the day, both Bunces are dead—that's what matters.

I almost died as well. No one knew Dmitri Bunce's obsession for payback until it was almost too late.

* * *

I SWING open Kiki's door, and there she lays, a dark shadow against the off-white bed linen. My chest feels tight as I walk forward.

Her face turns toward me, and she holds out her hand.

I take it and fall on her.

Her arms wrap me.

"I thought he had you."

I pull away. "Nah, you were giving me some pretty good body signals."

She gives a shaky laugh, and I notice she still has a hoop in her ear.

Only one. I touch the dangling circle, the diamond cuts are sharp underneath my fingertips.

"That was so fucked up, Faren," Kiki says.

I nod, my hand dropping. "*So*."

I watch her think. "Is peanut okay?"

I smile.

Then I cry. I nod over and over.

"Come 'ere, girl." Kiki sits up, and I perch at the bed's edge and she holds me while I cry.

When all my stuttering cries are done she says, "Like I said earlier, should've used the whole can of pepperspray on his ass."

I laugh. "Yeah, one can was not enough for him."

"It's crazy, y'know?"

Our eyes lock.

"It is. I can't believe who he was..."

"What he did," Kiki says.

I nod.

I move a long curl behind her ear. "Are you okay?"

"Me?" Her hand splays on her chest, two nail tips torn off. "Hell yes! That peckerwood didn't have a chance."

She sees my face and looks away. Kiki sighs. "Bruised some of my ribs... but he wanted to tie me up worse after that text you sent me."

I grimace at the thought of Jay, a.k.a. Dmitri, roughing up Kiki. Then tying her up. Gooseflesh swarms my arms.

"The one where I say it's not Jay?"

Her finger goes up. "Yeah, he didn't appreciate that

memo. And why the hell did you come inside when you saw the door was open?" She puts her hands on her hips, her face moving side to side in indignation. "You should have called the boys in blue. 9-1-1 duh."

"Ah..."

"You were like some dumbass girl from one of those hack and slash movies."

Yeah.

Kiki's lips turn up. "I guess you kinda saved me."

I almost touch my index finger and thumb. "Maybe this much."

"Team effort."

We high-five instead of crying again.

Tagger walks in, and Kiki crosses her arms. "I'm not quite on board with you being a good guy yet." She gives him the stink eye.

He grins.

"It's all in the name of justice."

Kiki makes a rude noise. "Would've been great to know before dipshit Dmitri Bunce almost wiped the floor with my ass."

"Yes. Well, he's done now."

"Good," Kiki says.

I ask, "How's Butch?"

"Still in ICU, but things look good. He's a tough SOB."

Tagger's eyes move from me to Kiki full of amusement. "You're in good hands, I'll be seeing you soon."

She scowls at his back. "Don't bet on it," Kiki mutters as Tagger exits.

"He's a good actor," I say.

"Hmmm... I still think we were fed shit like mushrooms."

I give a sideways smile, though I'm not nuts about how we were kept in the dark either. "Ready to go?"

"No. My ass has a perma-breeze. Let me dump this ugly-ass hospital gown and get into some tight jeans and I'll be good as gold."

I wait as Kiki gets dressed.

Lost in my thoughts.

* * *

HENRY INCLINES his head as Kiki and I walk toward his car.

"This is so many shades of surreal. Like an out-of-body experience," she says.

I don't tell Kiki how many times in the past six weeks I've felt the same way.

Henry opens the car door, and I glance back at the plainclothes cops behind us.

We slide into the limo.

Henry gets in the driver's seat and slides the partition window open.

"Miss Mitchell?"

"Home please, Henry."

He gives a Mona Lisa smile as he slides the glass shut.

Kiki wears a grin. "You're getting all used to this, Faren."

A little bit.

I put my hands in my lap to stop the left from shaking.

"I need a pill," Kiki laments, leaning back against the plush seats.

I cock an eyebrow. "For what?"

"I won't sleep a wink after psycho coming after me, almost killing you and seeing that poor bodyguard laid out with a plastic tent over him."

Kiki shudders at the memory of Butch in ICU.

"Yeah."

A lone tear escapes down my cheek.

"He'll be okay, Faren—don't worry."

Her eyes lock onto my face, easily discerning my conflicting emotions.

"It's not that. I was a stinky ass to him."

"You were, were ya?"

I nod miserably. "He was just doing his job and I was a big fat walking prego hormone. I beheaded him with a butter knife." I balance my elbow on my knee as I cup my chin.

Kiki laughs and claps. "Oooh... don't make me laugh. It hurts like hell!"

I feel myself frown.

"Look at us! All giddy and shit because of our near-death experience!" She cackles as I stare at her.

She's lost it.

Kiki busts up again, alternately howling and crying.

Finally she collapses, gasping. "God *damn* that sucked! If Bunce wasn't dead, I'd kick his ass!"

"Morbid, Kik."

"Whatever."

We slow in front of the Millennium garage. The limo sinks under the concrete, and Henry crawls toward the elevators.

He lets us out, and I have an overwhelming urge to hug him.

There were moments when I thought the last human contact I'd have would be death by Dmitri Bunce's hand.

Henry must see something in my face because he squeezes my shoulder. "I'm glad you're well, Miss Mitchell."

I nod as he makes every effort to not notice the tears rolling down my face.

* * *

KIKI and I hold each other for a long time outside her condo, my damp locks from the shower cling to her arms like angel's hair.

"Is stud waiting for ya?" Kiki asks.

My face heats. "Yes."

She smiles, then grabs her side. "No poles for awhile."

"I guess you're going to have to go legit," I say, not bothering to keep the humor out of my voice.

"Who? Me? Nevah!" She slips her card through the entry slot and turns to me. "I'm going to go lick my wounds in private. But text me when you get to Mick's. I have to know you're okay."

"I will, but I need to call my mom first. I'm sure this is all over the news. She knows I'm alive, but she'll worry."

"Yeah, she will."

We look at each other, so many things unsaid. The current of our friendship has changed course, gotten deeper, braver—more.

"Love you, girlfriend."

Not more than me. "Love you too."

* * *

HE'S THERE WAITING for me when I slide through the front door. The people who made his condo return to normal have left.

I move past where I tripped over Butch. My eyes flick to the location where Kiki was bound to a chair.

Mick's eyes watch me. Letting me get used to it.

I walk into the bathroom. The remaining towel holder sticks out of the wall like a broken tooth the repairmen must have missed it. My gaze sinks to the spot where the tiles were broken and are now whole again. They skip back to the towel holder.

I back away, trembling.

"I can't."

His arms go around me. Then I'm in the air and being walked out of the condo.

I close my eyes because Mick has me. I'm safe.

I feel my body float as he takes me to the elevator and I cling to his neck, breathing in a smell I associate with sex and safety.

Love.

My eyes are open as we walk through his new penthouse.

I don't know how Mick did it all when I was in the hospital for barely twenty-four hours, but he and his army finished it. The place went from eighty-five percent complete to one hundred percent in a day.

I begin to breathe again.

There's not a nail gun in sight.

CHAPTER 38

I lay underneath Mick as he smooths both hands down my head. Trapping me.

I'm willing beneath him. So very willing.

"So?" he says as he presses his mouth to the tip of my nose. "How is my Faren?"

I close my eyes in a long blink. They're full of water when they open to look at him.

Mick shuts his eyes and sighs. "I wanted to tell you. I didn't know Bunce was after you. I thought he was my sister's killer, that this would come full circle. Justice, revenge—all of it."

He swipes his thumbs over my cheekbones as the water of my sadness spills over.

"It seems more than coincidence."

He fans my hair around our bodies. "Yes. Our fortuitous first meeting."

"When you ran into me with your bike."

I suppress a smile with effort.

Mick grimaces. "Looking back at everything I don't know why you're with me."

"I do," I say.

The very air holds its breath.

"Why?" he asks, as though afraid of my answer.

It's the simplest one I can give. "Because I love you."

Mick circles me with his arms, bringing me into his neck. "I don't deserve you, Faren."

I breathe him in, his sharp, clean male scent. "I deserve a chance. A second chance." It's not an answer, but they're the words I want to say.

He lowers me into the softness of the bed. "I still want to kick that doctor's ass."

I put my finger over his lips. "There's been enough ass-kicking for a lifetime for me."

"Let's do something more constructive then." His eyes darken, studying my face.

I wind my legs around his waist and he gives a small shake of his head, easily scooting out of my hold.

"What?" I half-laugh, my legs falling apart. The laughter dies in my mouth as Mick skims my yoga pants off my hips, bringing my panties along with them.

There's no pause, no slow time-release of our passion.

His mouth dives to my entrance in a sweep of desperation, as though our bodies have been lost to each other and found again through circumstantial luck.

I don't believe that.

We were meant to be. Fate is a fickle master—it played with my life like a fine instrument and smiled on me.

By all rights, I should be dead—twice.

But for a meeting of a motorcycle and a killer whose ambitions lay at my feet, I survive.

To live another day.

Mick jerks my hips against his face as his mouth moves from the top of me to my entrance. Worshipfully, he brings me to the peak with just his lips and tongue, his precision so slow and deliciously evocative. I yell into the unfamiliar room with an abandon born of pent-up emotion and relief. My thoughts fly away like wisps of smoke.

He glides up my body, my heartbeat still racing, the juices of my arousal coating his face, and he kisses me. I taste myself on his lips and writhe beneath him in anticipation.

His hardness comes against the center of me, and I dig my heels into the bed, my hips rising to meet his first thrust. Our bodies line up, and he sinks into me, his shoulders rippling with tension. We shout out together.

Mick goes to his knees as his hands grip my hips, and he pulls me deeper against him. I groan at the tight fit, our flesh married together as if it has never been apart.

I push up as he pulls, our flesh smacking in our frenzied lust. His large hand comes around the back of my neck, and he pulls me upright.

I sit for a frozen moment, perfectly impaled on him. I look down into his face and he rocks within me until I gasp.

Deeper still he moves, swirling his hips as he pushes upward, and I feel myself spiraling out of control. I release my inhibitions, closing my eyes and concentrating on the sensation of Mick inside my body.

"Look at me, Faren."

My eyes snap open, and Mick's hands land on my shoulders. He pushes me down as his hips lift, hitting me exactly where I need the depth, the friction, the pressure.

Mick's hand slides down my sweaty back, holding me against him, and I feel the answering throb of his own release. We cry out together, his hands spasming against me as my arms convulse around him.

He nuzzles my neck as my cheek rests against the top of his head, my fingers pressing into his sides.

We hold that position until pie wedges of light move across our skin, fading to shapelessness, turning to shadows.

Mick's arms curl around my ass. He walks us across the bed, gently lowering me beneath him.

Right where I began.

Right where I'll always be.

* * *

Four months later

"Oh my god! Mom!" My hands cover my mouth then clap. I'm near-hysterical, tears springing to my eyes.

She's walked the rails.

Sweat runs down from her temples, dampening her tee, but her smile is all joy. All accomplishment.

"Slavedriver," she accuses.

I nod. Accurate assessment.

I grab her at the end of the railroad and hug her fiercely.

"Hey, careful with your old mom," she says.

I lean away. "I think you'll be okay."

"Somebody's got to walk you down that aisle."

I put the sweaty strand of hair that's escaped her hair tie behind her ear. "You're very non-traditional, you know."

"I know, gorgeous girl." She glances down at my growing belly. "And gorgeous boy," she whispers.

"Did you tell anyone?"

She shakes her head. "Not for a lack of Kandace trying every way she could think of to wheedle it out of me."

Kiki's so determined to know the sex. She's turned into a surprising mother hen.

Could be the lack of mothering she had when she was growing up.

But I turn away from sad thoughts.

Today's my baby shower, and I'm going to have happy ones.

I no longer allow sad to find me. I choose happy.
Each day.

* * *

"You can't peek, Faren," Kiki says, loving the suspense.

We're on our tenth kitschy baby shower game, and she promises this is the last one.

Liar, liar tits on fire.

The blindfold makes me hot, and I squirm in my chair. I'm wearing the beautiful gray tunic-length top Kiki got for me months ago, even though it's too warm.

I love it.

A good memory from when everything was bad.

"Ready?" she asks.

I nod.

She tears off the blindfold, and I take in the quilt hanging from a wood pole.

Pictures of me.

Mom.

Kiki.

Mick.

Each snapshot represents my past. They also represent my future. I have one now.

My eyes run over each photo, applique stitching expertly twining the perimeter of each square to secure the memory forever.

The square in the center holds my most recent sonogram.

I look at Kiki. "You're so sneaky."

Kiki stands and points at a tiny penis. "It took some doing."

I laugh.

"I don't know what you had to do to get ahold of that photo."

She winks. "You don't wanna know."

We laugh.

Sue from work brings out the food. Mom shifts in her chair, doing ankle rotation exercises as she smiles at me.

I stare at the proof of life in front of me.

Mine.

And my baby boy.

CHAPTER 39

"Stop squirming, you pain in my ass," Kiki reprimands. I bite my lip, staring at the three images of me.

"I don't know if I should be wearing white, is all."

"Oh, horse puckey." Kiki rolls her eyes, and the seamstress wisely says nothing, rolling the hem as I stand on a dais-like platform. "It's off-white anyway."

"You know what I mean."

The seamstress smiles. I see her traitorous expression in the reflection. I grump, folding my arms.

"Arms hanging, please," she says from the floor.

I sigh and drop my arms.

The waistline is slightly empire. It's very fitted and flares only slightly below my huge breasts.

The bodice offers them up like two pieces of succulent fruit.

Kiki's eyes follow mine.

"Girl, you do have the tah-tahs now."

"Hmm..." I think I look kinda... I don't know... oozy.

"You look awesome. Mick's gonna pop a boner when he sees you in that."

"Ouch!" the seamstress mutters.

We watch her suck blood off the finger she stabbed.

Kiki smirks.

I stare at the reflection. My hair spills along the short-sleeved top.

Kiki walks up behind me, lifting my heavy hair into a twisty temp up-do.

"There," she murmurs softly.

My creamy skin contrasts with the light coffee of hers. She lays her cheek against my shoulder, one hand buried in my hair.

I watch my hand rise in the mirror and cover her head, tucking it against my neck.

"I love you," I say.

Her large brown eyes meet mine in the mirror.

"Love you more."

The seamstress fusses at the hem, but Kiki and I stay wrapped together. Our gratefulness for life supersedes everything else.

Kiki promises I'll be the most beautiful bride who ever lived.

I agree.

There probably isn't anyone more grateful for the chance.

* * *

Thank God I'm awesome on heels because Kiki's choice are skyscrapers.

Mick's so tall that he still has me by a couple of inches.

I'm so cliché. I want June, and that's what I get.

Mom pushes her walker forward, and I take a step.

The music plays softly, a song that's been heard for a

hundred years. The bridal march keeps time with my mom's tentative steps. I'm her adoring sidekick as I draw closer to my future husband.

Thorn is a dark shadow alongside Mick. He smiles at me and I clamp down on the urge to wave.

And run to the altar.

It's a small affair. A few dozen people. Mick pulled in favors from everywhere and got the air above our heads classified as restricted air space. Our vows would have been drowned out by the noise of chopper blades as they slice the air. Instead, they'll be spoken and heard at his palatial estate in the countryside of Redmond.

The silence is not oppressive but pregnant with anticipation, closure.

We finally reach the steps that lead to a gazebo. Ribbons of icy blue grace the lattice work, woven through with the blush of deep pink roses. Their fragrance overwhelms me as I release my mom's hand and look at her for the last time as a single woman.

She smiles through the tears and sweat that brought her to this moment. I hug her and turn.

To look at my man.

His eyes move from my upswept hair, curls cascading down the deep back of my almost-cream wedding gown.

A small gold chain encircles my throat. His eyes pause there then move to my cleavage.

What I see in his gaze causes heat to infuse my skin.

Thorn chuckles and the minister inclines his head just as Mick takes my hand.

The stone in my engagement ring echoes the colors of the blooms that will witness the words we speak next.

My bad hand is quiet as Mick says the words he's made up for me. It is still as he slips the slim wedding band encrusted with square-cut diamonds onto my finger. They glitter like captured ice, the large heart-shaped pink stone rising above them like the first blush of a frozen sunset.

We don't let the crowd keep us from being real, intimidating us from the public display of affection that will announce us to the world.

The minister tells us we're married and announces me as Faren McKenna.

Mick ignores the hooting and hollering from the audience. Instead, he scoops me into an embrace so tight I feel the baby move between us.

His lips brush over mine and he pulls back. "What was that?" he asks a little breathlessly. His eyes search my face.

I smile, the feel of his hands are warm on the small of my back.

"Our son."

CHAPTER 40

AUTUMN

"This is stupid as shit," Thorn announces in a classic Thorn-ism. Mick pops the cork from the wine bottle, and I sigh with jealousy. Everyone can have some but me.

"Don't pout, baby, or your nose will stay that way." Mick pinches my ass.

I jerk a little and glare at him. He puts a stemmed glass of sparkling cider in front of me.

I don't think I'll ever have another glass of something resembling apple juice for as long as I live. I balance the bottom of the cup on my belly.

"You're ready to pop, Faren," Thorn says, reaching for a beer and chugging half.

"Gee, ya think?" I roll my eyes.

"Oooh, testy I see."

Mick says nothing, but he chuckles, and I narrow my eyes at him.

Thorn smirks. "When's Kiki coming over?"

"Soon," I reply with a huff.

Thorn scoops his beer bottle into his lap. I've found out a lot of things about Thorn besides him being an undercover detective.

That he has refined tastes was the most shocking.

He's a true beer connoisseur. He's also a little bit of a clothing whore. He pulls his slacks up from his ankles as he leans back, a sliver of black is revealed between his dress shoe. His shirt cuff pulls back to reveal the tat sleeve.

"Y'know, Kik and me?" Thorn says. "We're just not..." He threads his fingers together. "Cohesive, if you feel me."

I think they're too much alike.

"That's why you're here."

His eyebrows shoot up. "You're not setting me up?"

I take a sip of my non-alcoholic bubbly and shake my head. "Not in the way you think."

He scrubs his face in irritation. "Okay, tell Thorn."

I smile at his third-person speak. "We have someone else coming, and Kiki will split if she thinks it's a blind date."

"Or any kind of date." Mick makes a sound in the back of his throat.

I raise my glass and our eyes meet, his have heat. "What he said."

Mick smiles and it holds promise. It says it all. How creative he'll be later in loving me. My smile in answer has the knowledge of a hundred nights where he already has.

"So I'm some kind of Walt Disney?"

I remember the rumor of the animator tycoon having a frozen crypt and frown.

Thorn freezes, mouth partly open, beer held stiffly in one hand.

"Nice," Mick says.

Thorn relaxes. "Damn. So she's going to show, and some other dude's gonna get up all in there?"

I make a face, and Thorn laughs. He points his beer bottle at me. "You're great to get going, Faren."

I glare at him.

"Y'know, Thorn..." He lifts his eyebrows, taking a swig, and I continue. "Someday some girl is going to hit you between the eyes like a two by four, and you'll be singing a different tune."

"Uh-huh," Thorn says, clearly unconvinced.

The doorbell rings.

I set the glass down on the coffee table and waddle over to the door. Before I get there, the door flies open.

"Hey, baby!" Kiki screams and throws herself in my arms.

I almost topple over, my center is so unbalanced now.

Front heavy, I stagger underneath her enthusiasm.

"It's criminal that I live in the same building and you guys are too busy humping like bunnies to invite old Kik over. What's with that?" she asks, ignoring the awkward pause as she sweeps inside like a tornado, dumping her handbag, scarf, lightweight jacket and kicking off her five inch platform pumps.

Her eyes land on Thorn, and she looks wary.

"Hey. Was I supposed to bring like special stuff because He-man's here?" Kiki jerks a thumb at Thorn.

He grins as if to say, *told ya.*

I untangle from Kiki. "No. We're—it's just a casual get together," I say.

Kiki's eyes narrow to slits.

"Hmmm." Her gaze moves to Mick, and he shrugs.

Kiki pads to the island and taps a nails on the mirror-like surface of the crushed quartz. "Set me up, stud."

"Your wish is my command," Mick says, winking at me.

"I like a compliant man," Kiki says.

"Then you won't like me," a voice says from the door.

Kiki's frank appraisal of him is met by an equally bold one.

"And who might you be?"

He cocks his head to the side, longish hair surfing over eyes so pale, they fight between a cool white and gray. "Chet Sinclair. No e."

I swallow as I watch the maelstrom.

Thorn sits up straight, and Kiki comes to herself in a rush of assumptions, defensiveness, and indignation.

She opens her mouth, every person watching her.

Mick moves in with perfect timing, putting a drink into her open hand. "Stay awhile, Kiki."

Her mouth snaps shut and she openly glares at me.

I can't help it—I laugh out loud. I hadn't really grilled Mick when he said that he had the perfect man for Kiki.

I didn't know that one existed, but Mr. Player here? He might not be the right one.

Kiki takes a solid sip of her drink and manages to fold her arms across her considerable boobs. "So, you're the Chet Sinclair? No e."

Mick gives Chet his drink, and I watch him swing his honey-colored hair out of his eyes and take a sip of a martini. He takes the olive off the plastic spear with a practiced twist of his tongue.

It's obscene.

Kiki can't look away.

"That's right," he finally answers.

"I think I'll just call you No E." Kiki nods vigorously.

I'm amazed to see she might be nervous.

Kiki never gets nervous.

Very interesting.

Chet looks at her over the rim of the martini glass. "Whatever. I've been called worse."

Thorn laughs.

Chet turns to him. "Hello, Thorn. I hear you're quite the celebrity?"

Thorn looks at him for a beat. "Depends on how ya look at it. Is every Tom, Dick, and Harry knowing I'm a good guy good? Nah." He brushes a hand over his cropped hair. "I'm thinking that's the kind of notoriety Thorn doesn't need. Infamous I don't want."

Chet smirks. "I'm not sure you're right on that score, Thorn. Fame is one and the same; a person can have fame for the wrong reasons and still be well-known."

He looks directly at Kiki when he says that last.

"And what is your name?"

"Kandace King."

Chet looks at the ceiling, seeming to consider her. "Alliteration at its finest. Tell me... is it Kandi?"

"Pfft—no! What kind of name is that?" she asks, insulted.

"A name that reminds one of something sweet."

Thorn chortles, and I want to punch him.

Kiki flashes Thorn a look that should burn him on the spot, but he keeps on grinning.

Flame on.

Mick clears his throat. "Soup's on."

"Excellent," Chet says, "I'm famished."

"Me too," Kiki says.

Chet moves toward the kitchen. He's graceful, tall, and very lean. The angles of his cheekbones could cut paper. He's not so much handsome as striking.

His features would linger in a person's memory far past the idea of beauty. When Chet looks at you, everyone else melts away.

Chet puts a casual hand on the back of Kiki's neck, and she startles, trying to pull away. His grip tightens as he looks down at her.

Something passes between them, and I glance at Mick.

"What may I call you then if not Kandi?" he asks.

"My friends call me Kiki," she says, and her voice sounds breathy.

He squeezes her neck, and I watch Kiki's eyes tighten. Then Chet releases her. "Well then I shall call you Kandace."

Her brows come together.

"Not into friendship, Chet?" Thorn pops a cherry tomato in his mouth and grins at Chet like the Cheshire Cat.

A secret smile curves the corners of his mouth. "No. I think Kandace and I might be destined for other things."

What a pompous asshole.

I give Mick an *I can't believe you did this* look.

He doesn't respond.

"I don't think so," Kiki says.

He puts a finger under her chin, and her rich dark skin blooms with color. "I do."

My water chooses that moment to break.

"Mick!"

He flinches, looking at me as he rounds the kitchen island.

I grip his forearms. "My water broke."

A look of pure panic washes over his face, but it's gone as soon as it starts.

"Okay." He moves in one direction, and I go in the other.

Thorn grins as the usually unflappable Mick strides around the penthouse looking for the hospital bag.

Chet only has eyes for Kiki.

Thorn scrutinizes them as he mows through the vegetable dip.

"I'll take you two to the hospital." Thorn swipes his keys off the counter and pockets them.

Mick jogs back into the kitchen with the brightly colored bag he's had packed for two months.

"You're a week early."

As if that's going to stop the baby from coming.

"I think the baby has his own timeline," I point out.

"Let's go," Thorn says.

I move toward the door, Mick's anxious hands cruising all over me.

"I'm fine," I whisper.

He glances at me with a tight smile before he turns toward Chet Sinclair.

"Can you take care of Kiki?" Mick holds up the bag helplessly, pregnant me under his arm.

"Oh yes," Chet says while he stares at Kiki.

She shakes her head and moves to leave.

Chet's hand closes around her arm. "Stay."

It's spoken like a command.

Kiki never listens to anyone. She told me this guy was a rich weaner.

Yet... she stays.

And I go.

My baby is coming. The proof of life, of my continued existence.

The love I get to keep.

THE END

But - the gritty journey doesn't stop here! [Love *The Token 2?* Grab book 3 of *The Token Series*, *Obsession* **HERE**] **and continue with this dark romantic thriller series**] If you loved Token 2, you won't be able to put *The Token 3 - Obsession* down!

⭐⭐⭐⭐⭐ "... Great book - love Marata Eros's books..."

📖 NEVER MISS A NEW RELEASE! Join TRB News for exclusive updates, early access, and special offers.

📚 YOUR WORDS ARE POWERFUL! If you enjoyed *The Token 2 - Absolution*, please share your star rating and thoughts to help other readers discover their next favorite author. *Thank you!*

Continue your journey with more of TRB/Marata Eros' thrilling novels:

THE PEARL SAVAGE

⭐⭐⭐⭐⭐ "A real page-turner!"

NOOSE

⭐⭐⭐⭐⭐ **"Raw, edgy... graphically** painted."

BLOOD SINGERS

⭐⭐⭐⭐⭐ "One hell of a ride!"

CLUB ALPHA

⭐⭐⭐⭐⭐ "It's action-packed and so suspenseful....

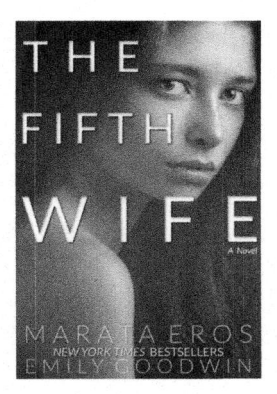

THE FIFTH WIFE

⭐⭐⭐⭐⭐ "Absolutely fantastic dark taboo toxic romance. Loved it…"

THROUGH DARK GLASS

⭐⭐⭐⭐⭐ "One of the best and I have read many!"

BROLACH

⭐⭐⭐⭐⭐ "...oh hot hot **hot**..."

The Token 1 - Provocation

⭐⭐⭐⭐⭐ "**Crazy good.** It draws you in..."

EMBER

⭐⭐⭐⭐⭐ "This story is... **explosive**!"

HER: A LOVE STORY

⭐⭐⭐⭐⭐ "Emotively moving - gripping and *sensual*..."

THE REFLECTIVE

⭐⭐⭐⭐⭐ "'...futuristic writing, hard characters, **powerful**..."

REAPERS

⭐⭐⭐⭐⭐ "One of the **best**!"

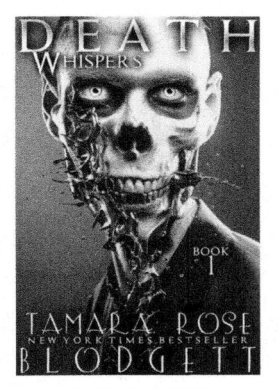

DEATH WHISPERS

⭐⭐⭐⭐⭐ "HUNGER GAMES, 50 SHADES and DIVERGENT, anyone?"

A HARD LESSON

⭐⭐⭐⭐⭐ " ... **HOT! HOT! HOTTT...!**

PUNISHED

★★★★★ **"Unputdownable from Start to Finish!"**

Enjoy a special treat! Read on for an **exclusive bonus chapter** from one of Tamara Rose Blodgett's unforgettable stories...

BONUS MATERIAL

GRETA

CLUB ALPHA
Billionaires' Game Trilogy
Book 1

New York Times BESTSELLER
MARATA EROS

Copyright © 2015 by Marata Eros
All rights reserved.
No part of this book may be reproduced in any form or by any electronic or mechanical means, including information storage and retrieval systems, without written permission from the author, except for the use of brief quotations in a book review.

* * *

*C*ompletion.

That's what it is to graduate with honors, and finally go after what I'll *be* in this life.

Marketing. International travel, stretching the bounds of the four languages I've mastered. Perfection.

Hot guys.

My eyebrows flick up. *Speaking of which.*

I track a handsome specimen right now.

A man moves across the room lithely, coming to stand at the exact opposite of the huge bar. His crystal tumbler full of amber liquid catches the light. His coloring suggests he's Latino or some exotic Spanish mix. At six feet three-ish, he's built to move, dance— and do other stuff.

My lips curl at the *other stuff* part of my internal monologue. I'm *so* wanting to find out what the sex fuss is all about. By all accounts, it's pretty life altering. It's beyond time.

My studies are through—it's Greta Time now.

His gaze locks with mine, and he smiles. A deep dimple winks at his cheek, and a cleft bisects a chiseled, square jaw.

Beautiful green eyes with thick black lashes rim the windows of his soul.

He pauses, and I say *yes* with my eyes.

Please approach me.

My breath catches like a trapped bird in my throat.

What a beautiful man.

My hand grips the smooth curved wood of the high-end bar I find myself in; the other holds a low ball of peach schnapps.

I take a sip, grimace slightly, and set the drink down.

People flow between us as we stare across the room, and I lose him momentarily as the moving scenery of bodies blocks my line of sight.

I crane my neck, swinging my head side to side, searching. I remind myself that I'm not here to meet a man. I'm here to meet my fellow graduates and celebrate our graduation from the most prestigious university in Washington state.

Someone sits down beside me but it's not *him*. I look around the other man.

Tall, dark and handsome has vanished.

I take another absent-minded sip then knock back the rest of my sweet drink. Disappointment burns alongside the alcohol inside my stomach. *Where'd he go?* I restrain myself from pouting.

I stand. Against my better judgement, I'm brazenly determined to seek him out, then a wave of dizziness hits me.

My hand flies out to the bar and latches on. Frantically, I look toward the entrance, hoping my friends will arrive. Though I'm known for being frighteningly punctual, none of them share that trait.

I lift my fingertips from the polished surface and touch my forehead. My hand comes away clammy and shaking.

Alarm sweeps through my system. *What's wrong with me?*

I forget the man with the deep-green eyes—and my drink and friends—as another wave of dizziness follows the first.

I stagger backward toward my seat, my knees hit the stool, and I sit down abruptly.

"Miss?" a low voice murmurs from my elbow.

I turn my head, but my neck feels loose, as though it's made of rubber.

A man's face wobbles in front of me, his features coming together and shattering in the field of my vision.

"Are you well?"

Well? No. I shake my head, and streamers of color flow across my eyes. I groan, feeling nauseated as the dizziness grows.

I feel pressure at my elbow then a grip. I'm walking?

"Is she—" a deep melodic baritone voice inquires.

"I have her." Curt. Final.

"Okay?"

"Fine," says the disembodied voice at my side.

I'm gliding. My head tips back against a warm chest.

Everything fades to black.

* * *

Paco

STANDING at the edge of the bar. I sip the sparkling cider.

My bodyguard, Robert Tallinn, remains by the exit while eyeing the entrance.

Though I've attended school in the states for many years, I still believe America is the most aggressive country in all the world. I remain vigilant while traveling.

My jet is scheduled to leave for Costa Rica early in the morning, and that is why I partake only of the non-alcoholic beverage in my hand.

Tallinn fought my spontaneous urge to visit the lounge within the elite hotel we're staying in.

Coffee is *grande* in Seattle. Very. I am here to romance the local coffee barons for their money, in exchange for my beans—a perfect trade, in my estimation.

Tallinn hates the lack of protection the hotel offers. I told him it's his job to keep me safe.

His smile was tight at those words.

I raise my glass to him now, and he glowers.

Laughing, I take a sip then set my glass on the smooth polished surface of the wooden bar.

That's when I see her, and my back goes ramrod straight.

The crowd is thick. Beautifully attired people mingle with others they consider to be of equal caliber.

But she stands out like an angel among demons.

Her head is tipped over a pale-amber drink. Her platinum hair is twisted into a loose bun at her nape. The size of the knot tells me its length—but not how it would feel in my hands.

Her graceful neck is bent as she studies nothing at all. She appears to be frozen in time. Waiting.

I stand, drink forgotten, and stare at the most beautiful woman I've ever beheld.

She lifts her face as though she has become instinctively aware of my gaze on her. Eyes like a late-summer sky fall into mine, and my chest grows tight. Light-pink color rises to her fair skin, and I feel myself harden inside my slacks at just a look. The attraction is beyond casual lust.

I feel as though gravity has asserted itself and I am being pulled into her orbit.

I must meet her.

As we continue to stare, people move between us, and another man sits beside her, large enough to block my view.

I set the tumbler at the edge of the bar and begin walking toward her.

I see her searching face for an instant as she appears to swing around the torso of the man who blocks our mutual appraisal.

I understand in a vague way that my approach isn't casual.

Someone steps in front of me.

"Oh, pardon me!" a woman says.

I move around her impatiently.

The angel stands. She appears to look shaken and unwell.

I stop.

The man beside her rises, his back facing me, and takes her elbow. She remains hidden behind him.

I vacillate, thinking of the connection, the electrifying chemistry from a glance. I begin walking again.

I intercept them, and the other man is half-carrying her, his arm locked around her narrow waist.

My eyes are for her, though, as I pose the question to the man, "Is she—"

"I have her," he says in a closed tone. Final.

"Okay?" I finish my question.

Her cheeks are flushed, and her head has fallen back against his shoulder. The blue eyes I so admired are hidden by closed eyelids. Dark-blond lashes fan against her high cheekbones.

He is clearly with her. I should drop it.

I cannot.

"What is wrong?" My eyes still rove the woman, not giving the man my full attention.

The man turns. "Drunk."

I look fully at him.

He winks; a deep sense of oddness surrounds the gesture.

Turning, he ushers her out. And I let them go.

Tallinn suddenly appears at my side. "What the fuck was that?"

I shake my head. "I am not sure."

Tallinn stares after them thoughtfully. After a full minute has elapsed he says, "I didn't like that dude."

Neither do I.

I stare at the empty space they had just occupied.

* * *

Greta

BRUTAL FINGERS GRIP my butt cheeks and pry me open. A hoarse cry escapes my cracked lips.

He plunges inside me again.

My muscles instantly tense around the intrusion, though my virginity is long gone.

Slick wetness covers my inner thighs to my knees.

Later I find out it is semen.

Sweat.

And blood.

His thrusting continues.

Silence is the only noise. The screams fill my head because my mouth is gagged.

Panting.

The only break in the quiet is the grunts of their ecstasy.

I'm unceremoniously flipped over onto my back. Four faces with masquerade masks loom above my warped vision.

"No," I say in muffled agony for the hundredth time, lifting my forearm to cover my battered face.

One of the men hits me, smashing my face into the stained mattress.

Another lands on top of me, stabbing inside my wounded vagina. "Yes," one of the assailants says as he uses me.

I slide back and forth on the mattress as he pounds into my unwilling body. Another pries my jaws apart, forcing my lips open. He jerks the gag out then thrusts his length inside my mouth.

Vile salty essence fills the space. My chin is jerked back and the hot liquid glides down my throat.

I choke.

He removes himself from my mouth and clamps it shut, pinching my nostrils together.

I have to swallow, or I won't be able to breathe. My throat convulses, and he releases my jaw.

I scream as I suck precious oxygen, gurgling through his semen. "No!"

The next blow slams my other cheek into the mattress as my hips are lifted and a new man assaults me. His stabbing penis tears and burns where no one has ever been.

I can't live through this, I think.

But I do.

* * *

Paco - Two Years Later - Present Day

Francisco Emmanuel Lewis Castillo.

I set the pen down and lean back, regarding my good friend and co-conspirator.

It is *terminado.*

I've signed my soul over to the devil. He no longer chases me from the dark corners of my mind. This particular demon stands in the sunlight, taunting no more.

Zaire chuckles, running a hand through hair a shade of blond so dark that it flirts with being brown. He sets his ten-gallon cowboy hat on top of all that shaggy hair.

Clear hazel eyes regard me with amusement.

I say nothing.

Zaire Sebastian has been after me for the five years he's run the enterprise I finally succumb to.

Club Alpha.

He flat-palms the paper, spinning the sheets until they face him. His eyes flick down, and a fingertip stabs my signature.

"Careful, you might cause it to bleed, *amigo*," I note softly.

Zaire laughs. "Always so cryptic, Paco." He makes a low sound of chastisement in the back of his throat. "How long have I known you?"

Forever.

He reads my expression and nods. "It's just now I find out you have a hundred names?"

I dip my chin. "Just four."

He grunts his answer and I'm struck by how different Zaire and I are.

He perpetuates fantasy.

I manufacture exotic coffee for exotic tastes, my own not excepted.

It is the taste for the very fine and my need for something extreme—a thing not within my control—that has finally driven me to Mr. Sebastian.

Zaire stands, offering his hand. "Are we clear on the terms?" He studies my face. "Humor me," he adds as I give a single shake of his hand.

I spread my hands away from my body, enjoying the slide of my linen suit, which is tailored perfectly to never impede my movement, as though I'm wearing a second skin.

I lift my shoulder. "You wish for me to recount the particulars?"

"Hell, yeah, Paco. You're a particular kind of guy."

True. I smile and Zaire grins.

"I will have three months for this fantasy to come to fruition. I have three days from the time of this signing to submit the twenty-page questionnaire about the things that make me—uniquely me."

Zaire's eyebrows pop to his hairline.

"It will be an honest disclosure," I say.

"Nice. I like how my telepathy always works well between us."

Zaire's rough-around-the-edges manner is a *fachada*, a clever front for the smart-as-a-whip man who swims beneath the surface. He twirls his fingers, encouraging my continuation.

"I have agreed to a no-liability clause against you, even in the case of my death, pursuant to the... *activities,* which might or might not present themselves."

"And?" Zaire runs his fingers down the brim of his hat, where the evidence of the habit is in the curvature of the rim.

"I will tell no one. I understand and have agreed to the non-disclosure."

Zaire makes the universal symbol for money, moving his thumb against his four fingers.

"I shall pay half in the moment listed therein, and the remainder at the end of the three month term, regardless of the outcome."

Zaire slaps his palms together. "Hot damn!" His eyes glitter at me like captured stars. "I look forward to putting you through the paces, Paco. I ain't gonna lie—I've been wanting to get you like a fox in a trap since the beginning."

I stroke my chin, my fingers finding the cleft at the end and squeezing it together. "I am aware, Zaire."

"Yet you still agreed."

I nod.

"Why? You've signed, now I *have* to ask. Why would you take this kind of chance? Because I'll be straight with you. I don't care about your money." He pauses, his eyes moving to the ceiling. "Yeah, I do. What I mean, buddy, is you have *so much* to lose."

I shake my head. "When a man has every need met, and ones he did not think he had are satisfied, then he is left with a void." I cock my head, moving my hands to the pockets of my slacks. "You act as though you would talk me out of our arrangement."

Zaire shakes his head. "No. You said, and I quote, 'Your heart beats, but it does not live.'"

"Yes. I am familiar with contentment, but I am not on intimate terms with contentment's distant cousin, joy."

A slow smile spreads across Zaire's face as a flutter of emotion skates across the deepest part of me. Unease.

I embrace the uncommon feeling. For too long, I have felt nothing besides the slow, rolling river of time's passage. I welcome any emotion that causes my soul to surface through the murky waters of my complacent mediocrity.

Zaire shakes his head, and a low chuckle breaks the seam of his lips. "You're going to make a fun subject." He gazes around the room before his eyes land on the wide expanse of glass that flanks the entire wall. From this vantage point, seventy stories aboveground inside the Columbia Center, the clouds appear touchable. The gray Puget Sound churns like angry boulders of water beneath us.

I walk over to stand beside Zaire. Our heights are similar, though our heritage is different. "Why do you do this?"

Without turning, Zaire places a forearm on the glass. He gazes over the city, at the raging sea beyond. "I know what it is to be rich. To be so rich you could park an incinerator in the house and burn money twenty-four hours a day."

I say nothing, waiting for the point. Zaire Sebastian will have one.

He rolls his head on his forearm, facing me. "This isn't a game, Paco. Once we start, with the exception of the one-month markers, it's your new life. I have people everywhere. They can get to you anywhere in the world."

I nod. *I'm counting on it.* I travel extensively to oversee the manufacture of my beans. I can be in Costa Rica one day and Brazil the next.

He straightens from his slouch against the window. "Your preliminary physical came back as outstanding, by the way." His lips quirk. "My techs were making bets on how much time you spend on that build."

"Oh?" My eyebrow hikes.

"Yeah," Zaire turns and throws a punch toward me. I

stiffen my gut and arch backwards, capturing his wrist and twisting as I dance into him.

"Shee-it!"

"And?" I ask. He struggles and I nestle his fist between his shoulder blades, cupping my opposite hand on his elbow.

I apply pressure.

Zaire taps my leg.

I drop his limb and step back, out of arm's reach.

We stare at each other.

"They said two hours—every day." He's breathing hard.

I'm not at all. "They would be wrong."

"How long, Paco? How much time do you devote to physical perfection?"

I cast my eyes down. *Too much.*

When I look up, he's massaging his arm. A wicked grin slashes the solemnness of his face.

"I don't worship my body; I use it. I have trained it to be used. There is a difference between doing one thousand sit-ups and forcing the body's compliance."

"Have you forced it?" Zaire asks.

"Absolutely."

Zaire snorts. "You realize I have you as a level-five risk on the form?"

For the first time since our meeting began, I get a thrill like an electrical current. Singing tension winds through me, causing my toes and fingers to tingle with anticipation of the unknown. "Yes."

"That means you're rating at the highest level for hand-to-hand combat, knife play—"

My lips twitch. "There is no such thing as *playing* with knives."

He stares at me for a moment before going on, "Stylized weaponry and a variety of martial arts background."

"Yes."

"Is that accurate?"

A beat of silence presses between us like a bomb before detonation.

"Yes."

"I will personally oversee your submission and handpick the girl."

I open my mouth then close it.

Zaire's wide grin angers me.

"Cat got your tongue?"

I'm unfamiliar with the idiom, though I speak several languages.

"You have utterly no say in this fantasy, Paco. This is what you're paying the big bucks for. This is a match-making enterprise of the highest order. We will find your love match."

I believe love to be an impossibility for me. However, I remain silent about my skepticism. "You trivialize it," I say and hear the sullen tone in my own voice. I can't shake it.

"It's not about what you can *get*, Paco. You could have a bevy of the finest tail on the earth. Hell, chicks smell money a mile away, they'd swarm you like bees to honey. That's not what's at stake here."

Zaire strides to the door, and I stroll after him.

He turns and gestures sweepingly, using the arm I didn't leverage behind him. "This is about a wealthy man—or woman—knowing the one who says *I do* really wants them for *who* they are, not *what* they have. This fantasy is engineered to pull out every stop to prove their worth. No one can pretend through the circumstances I provide at Club Alpha."

He meets my silence with his own.

"Three days, Paco. You have three days for dissolution. If I don't hear back, you can assume I've gone through your questionnaire, found it to be sound and withstanding further legalities, your fantasy will begin."

"And your failure rate?" I ask, though I know.

"Zero."

Neither one of us mentions some of the candidates have sustained injuries during their unique fantasy trials.

I've interviewed each one personally. Their answers are the same: they would do it again.

"I would never guess you were a lawyer in charge of fantasy matchmaking for the wealthy, Zaire."

He gives me a hard look. "And I would never guess you were an exotic coffee mogul with a ninth-dan black belt."

I wink at him. "I went... how do you say it? Ah yes, *easy on you*."

The look we share is between two men wondering how it would be to give it a go.

"What art do you practice?" I ask.

"Jujitsu," Zaire replies.

We bow at each other, eyes locked—as it should be. Never take your eyes off your opponent.

"Now," Zaire says, straightening, "if you don't have any questions..."

"I have many questions."

Zaire's eyebrow lifts, and the corners of his lips twitch. "Ones I can answer?"

"No."

He opens the door, and I pass through. "Then we're through."

I turn as he shuts the door. I halt the swing of the solid Douglas fir with the slap of my hand.

"I'll see you on Halloween."

"Trick or treat."

Zaire closes the door. It latches softly behind me.

In three more days, the games begin.

CLUB ALPHA

⭐⭐⭐⭐⭐ "It's action-packed and so suspenseful....

ACKNOWLEDGMENTS

I published The *Death* and *Druid* Series in March/July of 2011, with the encouragement of my husband and continued because of you, my Reader. Your faithfulness through comments, suggestions, spreading the word and ultimately purchasing my work with your hard-earned money, gave me the incentive, means and inspiration to continue.
There are no words that are sufficiently adequate to express my thankfulness for your support.
I truly feel connected to my readers. It is obvious to me, but I'll say the words anyway for clarity: the written work is just words on pages if they are not read by my readers. As I write this I get a lump in my throat; your enjoyment of my work affects me that deeply.
You guys are the greatest, each and every one of ya~

Tamara
xoxo

Special thanks:
***You*,** my reader.
***My husband*,** who is my biggest fan.
"*Bird*," without who, there would be no books.

Special mention:
Jackie
Dawn

Susan
Erica
Liz
Cherri-Anne
Theresa
Bev
Phyllis
Eric

ABOUT THE AUTHOR

www.tamararoseblodgett.com

<u>**Tamara Rose Blodgett**</u>: happily married mother of four sons. Dark thriller writer. Reader. Dreamer. Beachcombing slave. Tie dye zealot. Coffee addict. Digs music.

She is also the *New York Times* bestselling author of *A Terrible Love*, written under the pen name, Marata Eros, and 80+ other novels. Other bestseller accolades include her #1 bestselling **TOKEN** (dark romance), **DRUID** (dark PNR erotica), **ROAD KILL MC** (thriller/top 100) **DEATH** (sci-fi dark fantasy) series. Tamara writes a variety of dark fiction in the genres: erotica, fantasy, horror, romance, sci-fi, suspense and thriller. She splits her time between the Pacific NW and

Mazatlán Mexico, spending time with family, friends and a pair of disrespectful dogs.

To be the first to hear about new releases and bargains—from Tamara Rose Blodgett/Marata Eros—sign up below to be on my VIP List. (I swear I won't spam or share your email with anyone!)

SIGN UP TO BE ON THE **TAMARA ROSE BLODGETT** VIP LIST https://tinyurl.com/SubscribeTRB-News

<u>*Connect with Tamara:*</u>

Website: www.tamararoseblodgett.com

TRB for Hire @ Fiverr (*helping other authors become writers!*)

ALSO BY MARATA EROS

💜 **Read more titles from this author** 💜

A Terrible Love (NYT & USA Today bestseller)

The Reflective – REFLECTION

Punished – ALPHA CLAIM

Death Whispers – DEATH

The Pearl Savage - SAVAGE

Blood Singers – BLOOD

Noose – ROAD KILL MC

Provocation – TOKEN

Ember – SIREN

Brolach – DEMON

Reapers - DRUID

Club Alpha – BILLIONAIRE'S GAME TRILOGY

Dara Nichols Volume 1 – DARA NICHOLS (18+)

Her

Through Dark Glass

The Fifth Wife (written with NYT bestseller Emily Goodwin)

A Brutal Tenderness

The Darkest Joy

My Nana is a Vampire

THE TOKEN
ABSOLUTION
BOOK 2

NEW YORK TIMES BESTSELLER
MARATA EROS

ISBN: 9798311542494
COPYRIGHT © 2014 BY MARATA EROS
ALL RIGHTS RESERVED.
NO PART OF THIS BOOK MAY BE REPRODUCED IN ANY FORM OR BY ANY ELECTRONIC OR MECHANICAL MEANS, INCLUDING INFORMATION STORAGE AND RETRIEVAL SYSTEMS, WITHOUT WRITTEN PERMISSION FROM THE AUTHOR, EXCEPT FOR THE USE OF BRIEF QUOTATIONS IN A BOOK REVIEW.

WWW.TAMARAROSEBLODGETT.COM

Printed in Great Britain
by Amazon